WAR OF THE THREE KINGS

WAR OF THE THREE KINGS

Book 2 in the Land of Magadha series

ANNA BUSHI

July Publishing

www.annabushi.com

Library of Congress Control Number: 2021900115
ISBN 978-1-7364103-2-5 (paperback) — ISBN 978-1-7364103-3-2 (hardback)

First Printing, 2021

To my husband: for the countless ways you
support me.

Map of Magadha

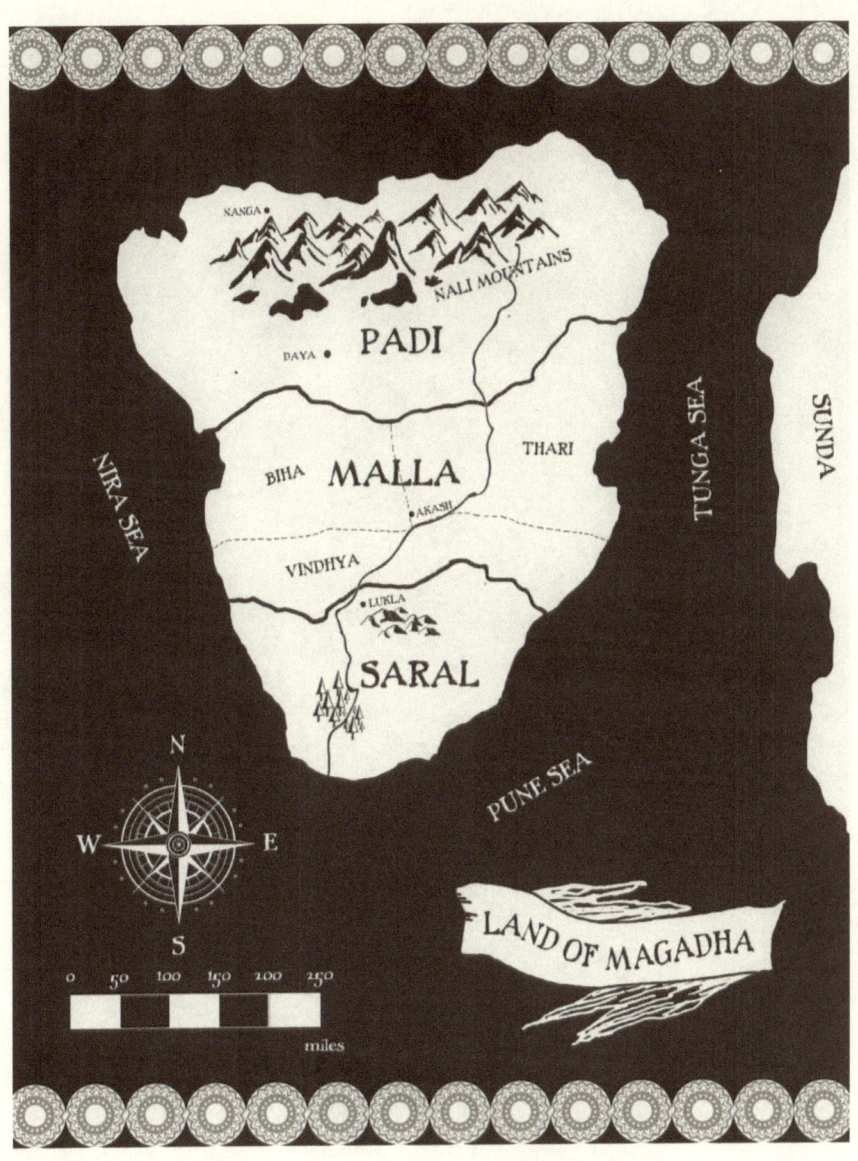

1

Meera

A noise startled me awake, and I reached out to make sure baby Amar was fine. He slept next to me under the woolen blanket. As my eyes got used to the darkness, I observed his chest rising and falling. I gazed at him in tenderness as he stirred in his sleep, then I pulled the blanket up towards his chin.

As my mind cleared of haze, I realized my husband, Atul, no longer lay next to me. I scanned the room in the dim light emanating from the dying embers in the fireplace. Before I discerned him, he saw me.

"Meera," he whispered and stepped closer. "A messenger from my brother, Parth, just arrived. Go back to sleep. I will see you at our morning meal," he said while tying his upper garment. He leaned in to kiss my cheek and left.

We had been waiting for news from Parth. The King of Sunda had requested Magadha's help in fighting off invaders in his land. My brother, Jay, and Parth had set sail across the Tunga sea to aid him. They had been waging a fierce battle in the jungle for many months. I fervently hoped for their safe return.

Amar put his thumb into his mouth and started sucking it. A sign of his hunger. In a few moments, I knew howling would erupt. I gently picked him up to nurse him before this could happen.

The day dawned with the sun hiding behind the clouds. I placed pillows around Amar on my enormous bed of rosewood and approached my window. Snow-clad mountains glistened in the morning rays in the distance. Even after all these years, the view filled me with awe.

Kantha and another maid arrived. While the maid helped me get ready, Kantha gladly took over Amar. She changed his clothes and bounced the now clean baby on her lap, eliciting giggles from him. Kantha had been with me since I was a child myself. Now she helped me raise my three children. Childless herself, she showered her love on us. A decade older than me, she had changed very little in the ensuing years. No lines marred her face, and her hair remained black. She had come to Padi with me and often anchored me when I drifted in loneliness or longed for Akash, my beloved home in Malla.

I draped a sari across my body in the color of the morning sun, eager to greet the world after a night apart. As I slipped on my bangles, my daughter, five-year-old Priya, skipped into my bedroom, dressed in a sunflower color cotton skirt and blouse embroidered with flowers. Giving me a quick hug, she then ran to play with her baby brother.

"Let me hold him," she begged Kantha, and Kantha relented, gently placing the baby on the child's lap while supporting his back. Priya tickled him under his chin while he reached to touch her nose. Her long hair flowed down in waves. Picking up a silver comb, I gently untangled her knots. Her locks felt soft, like finely woven silk.

"Look at his smile, Mother," she implored me with her big brown eyes, and a warmth spread through me as I gazed at them both.

Nala, my eldest son, strode in as I finished braiding his sister's tresses. His hair appeared unruly.

"Nala, watch him hold my fingers," Priya beckoned, and he approached them with mild interest.

I tried to comb his hair, and he stepped back. "Mother!"

Since the birth of his brother, eight-year-old Nala had been resisting my attempts to mother him. I held back the urge to pull him into an embrace. I did not want him to grow up so fast.

I herded the children to the family dining room. A large marble top table that seated ten stood in the center. My hand-picked paintings covered the walls. One side held portraits of our family: Nala riding a horse, Priya on my lap, and Atul on the throne. Another contained scenes from Malla: a temple on the hill, boat races on the Chambal river, and the majestic Akash fort.

As we sat at the dining table, the servants fetched our morning meal. I held Amar on my lap and fed him rice porridge mashed with ripe bananas from a silver bowl. He bounced gleefully, unaware of the connection I had with his uncle of the same name. It had felt strange, at first, having to call this sweet baby the name of a man I'd despised once. I'd named my daughter after my grandmother, a Padi princess. Atul had named the boys, our oldest for a great Padi king and our youngest after his dead brother. While the name Amar would not have been my choice, I could not object. My husband still had no knowledge of my hand in his brother's death, so how could I deny the name for our child?

Rumors floated about what had really happened that night, but without any proof, time dullened any past pain.

Nala attacked his millet porridge sweetened with jaggery and spoke with his mouth full. "Mother, Uncle Rish promised to teach me to fight with a real sword today."

Before I could respond, Priya wondered, "When is Uncle Rish coming? I have a new game to play with Rima." She tore a small piece of bread stuffed with spicy lentils and dipped it into some yogurt before putting it in her mouth.

"Eat slowly, Nala. Uncle Rish is not going to come any faster if you gulp your food. And you have lessons this morning." Rish, my guard, and loyal friend now, had been much more a lifetime ago. We had dreamed of getting married at an age when the future brimmed with possibilities. My duty had required me to abandon that fantasy. Instead, Rish had accompanied a young bride to Padi. In the following years, he had become part of our family.

Atul strode in, and the children yelled at the same time.

"Father, can you come and watch me fight with a real sword?"

"I have a new outfit for my doll," said Priya standing on her chair.

Atul engulfed her in his arms and kissed her cheek. "Finish your food, and then show me your doll."

"I may even pick up my sword and challenge you," he said, tousling his son's hair.

Nala beamed at his father. Atul caught my eyes and smiled conspiratorially about our son. A shared secret between two gratified parents. Since our wedding a decade ago, life with Atul flowed like a snow-melted river. He made no demands I could not keep. The passing years had been good to him. When I had first seen him, I thought his nose was too big for his face. The rest of his body had since caught up. On the rare mornings we stayed in bed, and he leaned on his elbow to talk to me, I even considered him handsome. And the crown of Padi rested very well on his head. He was still the same gentle person with a generous spirit.

Atul sat down and related to me. "Parth wrote that they are in the final leg of the conflict. He expects to return soon."

"Father will be glad to have Jay back," I replied. My brother had been gone for many moon months. Aranya and Sudha, his wives, would be eager for his return as well.

As the servants cleared up our meals, Rish walked in with Rima on his shoulders. "Your Majesty! Queen Meera!" he greeted us and lifted Rima down. His four-year-old daughter ran to join Priya. Rish had spurned matrimony for many years, but his Uncle Kasu wore him down. His wife had turned ill after Rima's birth and passed away two years ago. Rish had refused to remarry and seemed content to spend his days with us. I had taken Rima under my wings and raised her along with my girl.

I acknowledged him with a nod. Having to be in each other's company almost daily, I'd locked my feelings for him in a corner of my mind I seldom visited. I could now greet him as a friend without my heart going into flutters.

Nala ran to him, "Uncle Rish, are we fighting with a real sword to-day?"

He grinned at the boy. "Yes, Prince Nala. You are ready for a real blade."

Nala's eyes lit up at these words. Out of his earshot, Rish whispered to Atul. "Not a sharpened one."

Atul nodded imperceptibly. "Parth and Jay are in their final push," he narrated to Rish.

I turned to my oldest. "Nala, your *guru* is waiting for you. Finish your morning lessons, and then you can head to the training yard." He dragged his feet, reluctant to leave.

Atul glanced at him. "Learning history is as important as learning to fight. More important, some might say, to become a wise king. Go on."

Once Nala left the room, I tried to get up from my chair, but Amar's little fingers were entangled in my hair, and his legs caught in my sari. I attempted to pry his chubby baby fingers as he held onto me tighter.

Rish noticed my struggle and took a step forward. I assumed he would aid me. Instead, he cleared his throat and said, "Your Majesty, the queen needs your help."

Atul glanced up and came to my rescue. Soon, he held the baby in his arms and threw him in the air, eliciting a sound like falling rain-drops. Rish, as my guard, kept his watchful eyes on me. That's why he had discerned my need. *But why did he not assist me?* Feelings that existed for a young girl do not carry over to a woman of almost thirty and mother of three children. Not that I craved such attention. Troubled about the path my musing took, I abandoned it.

I fetched the girls and sat down on the cotton rug made in Malla, with two plates of rice colored with turmeric in front of them. Under my instruction, they drew the alphabet on the rice.

A palace guard stepped in. "Your Majesty, a messenger from Malla."

"Send him in," Atul ordered. He handed Amar to me and headed to the sitting room.

I stopped the lessons and asked Kantha to take the girls to Priya's chamber. Both Nala and Priya's rooms were in the same hallway as mine.

I proceeded to the sitting room, and Rish followed me. I placed Amar on the large woolen rug depicting a wingspread peacock and put a rattle in front of him. He crawled to the rattle and picked it up, and promptly put it in his mouth.

In strode a young man of medium height and noble bearing. Rish raised his eyebrows and exclaimed, "Dayan, what are you doing here?"

Dayan Vindhya, Jay's brother-in-law, scanned the room and greeted us. "Uncle Rish, King Atul, Queen Meera, I bring bad news from Akash."

Atul glanced at me before asking him, "What is it?"

Dayan tightened his grip on his sword handle. "King Vikram is dead. We suspect foul play," he said.

A sob escaped me, and I covered my mouth. This could not be. My father had come to visit me after Amar's birth less than a year ago and had appeared in good spirits. The trees rustling in the wind outside sounded like wolves howling in pain. My heart tightened as I noted the second part of the message. Foul play? What did he mean by it?

Atul stepped towards me and put his arm on my back. His eyebrows furrowed, and he ordered, "Young man, start at the beginning and tell us the tale."

In a low but steady voice, Dayan narrated his story. "Your Majesty, a few days ago, his servants found King Vikram unconscious on his bed. They raised the alarm. The royal physician suspected poisoning and tried several antidotes to no avail. King Vikram passed away the next day."

The faint howling I'd heard earlier strengthened in my head, and I pictured wolves gathered around a dead tiger. My breath caught in my throat. I swayed, and Atul held me by my waist and guided me to a chair.

With his arm around my shoulder, he stared at Dayan. "How did someone get past the guards to poison the king?" he thundered.

Dayan let out his breath and whispered, "We suspect Devan Biha is working with King Nakul of Saral. Nakul wants to free his father from our dungeons. And capture Malla."

My brother, Nakul? Poisoning his own birth father? Except, he did not know the truth about his origins. The howling in my ears reached a crescendo, and I leaned on my elbows with my head in my palms. *What should I do?*

Rish growled, "How convenient that Prince Jay and half of Malla and Padi army are in Sunda."

Atul snarled, "Nakul will pay for this."

They did not know the truth, and because of it, my brothers might destroy each other. *Oh Father, why did you leave me to deal with this?* Hot tears flowed down my cheeks and onto my arms. Feeling me shudder, Atul ordered, "Rish, take Dayan to the small council room and gather the others. I will join you shortly."

2

Jay

The heat oppressed me, and sweat rolled down my back as I rode through the jungle, chasing the last remnants of the invaders. The jungle teemed with insects: big ones, small ones, flying ones, and crawling ones. Any time we paused, they swarmed us, and I swatted them away, cursing my decision to come to Sunda. The smell of wet mud, human waste, scented flowers, and pungent herbs collided and assaulted my nose.

Suddenly an arrow came flying at me, and I pulled the reins to change directions. Within a blink of an eye, my guards surrounded me.

"Prince Jay, this is their last stand. The men are suicidal," cried Kathir Gomti, slowing down. When the King of Sunda had asked for Malla's help, all three Magadha kingdoms joined hands under my command. Nakul had sent my cousin Kathir to lead the Saral army. I'd bonded with him as men fighting alongside do.

"Archers, formation, and fire," I yelled, and our archers formed two rows and nocked their arrows. Just then, a small group of about 50 men rode their horses headlong into us. They sought death and martyrdom, not victory. That made them deadly. Even as our archers showered them with arrows, the fighters still plunged into our midst.

A group of ten men headed my way, and one man threw his spear at me. I sensed the flying weapon in the air and reflexively lifted my shield to block it, but my guard Giri rode his horse in front of me, and the spear sunk into his chest. Slowly he fell off the horse and onto the ground. Before I could go to his aid, an arrow flew in and lodged in my upper arm. Pain seared my mind, and I spun my mare.

Two men came at me with swords drawn. My eyes darted between them. I used the shield to defend blows from the man on my left while my sword danced with the one on my right. What they lacked in skill, they made up in speed. Their weapons weaved in and out rapidly, and my arms grew tired. I did not have the strength to keep them both off for much longer. I focused on the better fighter to my right. I attacked vehemently, and he fell back.

The other man used this moment to get close to me, and his blade nicked my waist. I grunted in pain and swung my shield at him wildly. I heard a thud. Hoping I made contact, I kept my eyes on the man in front of me. Our blades clanged, and he staggered. I swiped at him, and he jumped off his horse to avoid me. My eyes caught a sword coming my way, and I bent backward to avoid the curve of the blade. It made contact with my forehead drawing a thin line of blood. Grasping my sword between my lips, I grabbed my spear and threw it into his chest. Then I kicked him off his horse.

The soldier on the ground yelled and swung his sword at me. It headed towards my stomach, and I stared at the glinting metal in horror. Death bid his time to sink its sharp claw into me.

From nowhere, Kapil rode up, deflected the weapon, and parried with the attacker. Sweat trickled down my neck, and I gulped a breath in. I pulled my spear out of the dead man. I'd thwarted death countless times, but it felt like each time I traveled closer to the rim.

Another arrow hurled through the wind and embedded into my thigh. Anger coursed through me, and I uttered a loud cry and dove in, cutting men left and right. My senses sharpened, and I could see every blade strike, every arrow fly, and every spear land. Nostrils flaring, I threw my spear at an archer trying to bring down my horse, and deflected arrows coming at me with my shield. Blood splattered onto my face, and swords clanged, and it was over as the moans of dying men filled the air.

I viewed the carnage around me with tiredness. Pity arose in me as I surveyed the dead men we fought, in their tattered clothes and starved bodies. I'd exacted a promise from the King of Sunda not to seek vengeance against the family of the fallen. Would he keep it when I headed back? The bloody campaign of the last six moon months had come to an end, and I longed to go home. I smelled of sweat and blood. The stench of dead human bodies and horses mingled with the odor of the living things in the jungle and overpowered me. I remembered the delicate scent of coconut oil that Aranya used to braid her hair and the fragrant jasmine that Sudha wore in hers.

With a sigh, I searched for Kapil and found him a few yards away. I rode to him and jumped off my horse. He stood staring at Giri's body on the jungle floor with a murderous look on his face. If he had held the neck of the perpetrator, he would have strangled him into dust. Maybe he already did. Kapil, on an ordinary day, was a beast on the battlefield. When he had purpose and anger aiding it, he became a war god, impossible to stop.

I knelt beside Giri and placed my finger under his nose. No breath escaped, and a lump formed in my throat. "He is dead," I wailed, closing his eyes. Then anger rolled through me like thunder at the men I lost; my mind illuminated, like a lightning strike brightening the darkness, the memories of the adventures we shared; and pain rained down. I reminisced back to the day Giri joined my guards. He and I were just boys then. He had fought along my side in countless battles since then. His arrows had marked my enemies with precision.

"Let's carry him back," I ordered and mounted my ride.

Back in my tent, Muthu helped scrub the dirt off of me. The reek of death pervaded my skin and wouldn't come out any time soon. Somu, too old to travel with me, had stayed back in Akash. He had helped take care of me since my birth. He would know the right thing to tell me. Muthu kept his thoughts to himself.

A physician came in and applied a turmeric herb mixture on my wounds and wrapped them. No part of my body had escaped unscathed in this war.

As Muthu helped me change into clean clothes, Kapil stepped in.

"Prince Parth, my lord," he announced, and I rolled my eyes. Parth commanded the Padi army. He was a reliable warrior on the battlefield, loyal to his brother and a moron outside of it.

"Send him in," I barked, bracing myself.

"What a victory, Prince Jay," he bragged, striding in. "Enemy routed. No one will dare to raise their heads for a long time. I am headed to celebrate. Your last chance to join me," he smirked.

In a strange woman's arms, no doubt. I had been away from Akash for six moon months. Yearning for home, and the softness of a woman's arms, and the tenderness of her kiss, grew in me. My physical craving burned me, and I wanted to give in. Sorely. I clenched my fist and said, "Not tonight. I have work to do."

He left with a mad grin on his face, and I muttered, "Fool," under my breath. His older brother, King Atul, sat on the Padi throne, and my sister had borne him an heir and a spare. Because of this, Parth had no qualms about sowing his seeds.

Kapil cleared his throat, and I shook my head. "Not today. I am not going to replace Giri today."

Kapil nodded. He stepped closer and whispered, "There is a woman in the village. Word is she is barren."

"Barren? How did you find out?"

He shrugged his shoulders. "Her husband left her for another woman because she did not bear him any children."

I'd no sons. Yet. That stopped me from sleeping with strange women. I did not need one to come, bearing my son, and lay claim to the throne. Imagining a son conceived out of wedlock by a woman with whom I had shared nothing but her bed despised me. It would anger Saral and Vindhya. My wives hailed from these regions. Kapil had found a barren woman. *It would be my luck that her husband turned out to be the problem.* I laughed out at the thought.

Kapil stared at me, and controlling my laughter, I asked, "Has the new wife given him any children yet?"

He chuckled and added, "I found a Buddhist monk in the nearby caves. We can go to him and learn about celibacy."

"I am married to two beautiful women, and my choices come down to a suspected barren woman or a monk."

He snickered, "We could return and stay in Akash for a few years, and you can enjoy the company of your wives." More somberly, he added, "I am sure mine has forgotten my face."

"Time to rekindle our marriages then."

I picked a scroll from my table and glanced at Kapil with a frown on my face. "I received a strange letter from Minister Kripa. He sounds worried about King Surya plotting to escape our dungeons. Who will aid him?"

Kapil growled, "My brother, Puri, sent me a troubling letter as well. My uncle, Devan, has been moving Biha troops."

The news shocked me, and I stared at him with my mouth open. Biha, Vindhya, and Thari were the three territories of Malla. Losing the loyalty of one to Saral would be devastating. Slowly, I recovered my senses. "Chief Devan Biha's daughter, Riya, is Queen of Saral. Is Nakul trying to capture Malla or release his father from the Malla dungeons?"

"Maybe both," worried Kapil, his lips drawn thin.

I rubbed my forehead. "Your father guards Malla's capital. Would he aid Nakul?"

He met my eyes, and my confusion reflected in his. He shook his head slowly. "My father swore an oath to the king. He will keep it."

Suddenly my stomach twisted in a knot of worry. I'd captured Saral in a battle long ago, and King Surya spent his days in a Malla dungeon. My father had wished for his son, Nakul, to rule Saral, and I'd crowned him myself. If Nakul tried to capture Malla with Kapil's uncle's help, I was too far away to stop them. I wished for wings to fly.

"Jay, I understand your desire to wait, but you need to speak to your guards about Giri, and then we must have a council meeting afterward." On rare occasions, he called me by my name to remind me of our lifelong friendship. And his awareness of my feelings. He perceived my reluctance and nudged me towards action.

I took a deep breath and sighed. "Bring them in."

Karan, Dev, and Veer came in, and the five of us formed a circle. We had mourned another one of my personal guards before. Balan. Many years ago. That did not make this easier.

I scanned their faces. My shadows. I spoke softly, "I remember the moment we chased pirates on Tunga sea. I became separated and leaped into the ocean to escape men coming after me. Giri saw and jumped in after to protect me. He forgot one important thing. He did not know how to swim." They smiled. "He put his life at risk for me countless times," I finished. Each then narrated their own tales.

Karan went last. He had shared his quarters with Giri. "He loved his little boy, and when we were in Akash, he would teach him how to string his tiny bow. He..." sobbed Karan, unable to continue.

I hadn't thought about his wife and son. I groaned and patted Karan's back. Taking a deep breath, I said, "We will foster the boy. All of us. Raise him with stories of his father."

With a heavy heart, they dispersed.

All the talk about Giri's son surfaced memories of my girls. I missed my two daughters, singing and dancing. Would Heera even remember me anymore? She was only two when I had left.

Kapil and Dev walked with me to the council meeting.

Prince Kanva of Sunda, Giri Thari, Kathir Gomti, and others were assembled. Seeing Giri, heir of Thari house, my chest constricted for my felled guard of the same name. Taking a breath, I scanned the room. As my gaze fell upon Kathir, it took all my willpower to restrain myself. I wanted to grab his shoulders and shake the truth out of him. Had he known Nakul's plan?

Kanva cleared his throat and marveled, "This victory would not be possible without your men, Prince Jay. My father is grateful for your friendship and Magadha coming to our aid in our hour of need." Just a few years younger than me, Kanva had proved his prowess on the battlefield.

I inclined my head and accepted his gratitude. "My father, King Vikram, values our alliance and is happy we have opened trade routes through the Tunga sea."

I'd many fond memories of my time here. A group of elephants had joined Kapil and me while we bathed in a river. Kathir and I'd found baby tigers in the jungle, and they fit in our palms like cats. Dev and I'd plunged into a waterfall. Giri Thari and I'd talked about his brother, Shiv, under the stars. Kanva had recited poetry he had penned.

We discussed several other matters and finally arrived at our departure. Kanva said, "Prince Jay, your ships will be ready to take you back in a fortnight."

"We have enjoyed your hospitality for many moons, Kanva. Come visit us soon in Malla."

As I strolled back, I decided to talk to my man, who spied among the soldiers. "Kapil, find Champak. I like to train with him."

"The night has fallen, my lord. And you need time to heal."

"I will stick to simple moves," I pacified him.

Champak and I stood facing each other on a secluded field. Insects flocked around us, attempting to carry us away on their tiny wings. My tiredness vanished as I held my spear. Fighting with a spear was almost a graceful dance with your foot while your hand strikes like a cobra. As we spun in a circle, I stabbed at him, and he blocked me.

Taking a pause, I questioned him, "What are the Saral men saying among themselves?"

"Like the rest of us, they are happy to be going back home. I have heard men praise you. For your bravery and kindness."

"Nothing untoward?"

He shook his head.

"Come find me if you hear anything."

Later, I spoke to Giri Thari, the Malla commander. I'd killed his brother, Shiv, for treason years ago, but Giri had served me loyally since then in many battles.

"How many Saral men are traveling with us?"

"Around 200, my lord."

"Keep them spread out among our ships."

He nodded.

Soon the day arrived, cloudy. Sailors thudded on the deck, and the ship vibrated as they hauled the anchor. We set sail for Malla amidst a mild drizzle.

3

Meera

Atul knelt next to me and embraced me. I sobbed into his chest as he stroked my back gently. My father had ascended the throne after the unexpected death of my grandfather and uncle. Despite the rough start, Malla had flourished under his rule. Growing up, he had indulged me and showered me with love after my mother died. I suddenly felt like I'd plunged into a well, drowning in the water. My father had taught me how to swim, but my legs and arms stood paralyzed now. I gasped for breath, and Atul gently cupped my face and wiped my tears. As I gazed into his eyes, my panic subsided.

My father had entrusted me with the secret of Nakul's birth. Now it fell on me to prevent my brothers from attacking each other, or worse, killing one another. I remembered the tale of Mahabharata, where cousins Pandavas and Kauravas fought each other. It had destroyed both families. God Krishna could not prevent that bloodshed. Could I stop this?

Atul stormed, "Whoever did this will face the wrath of the Padi and Malla armies. Once Jay returns to Malla, Vindhya and Thari territories will side with him. If Nakul is behind this, we will hunt him to the end of the world and destroy him."

I dropped into a bottomless pit of worry, and the darkness touched me with it's cold fingers. I struggled to understand Nakul's action. Why would he attack Malla now? Whatever his reasons, I did not want my unacknowledged brother destroyed, even if he had set this in motion. Peering at Atul, I decided to share the secret with him. I needed his help in figuring my way out of this abyss.

"Atul," I whispered, "there is something I need to share with you, away from listening ears."

On catching my voice, Amar crawled to me and stood up, holding my knee.

Atul gazed at me intently, with his eyebrows drawn together. "On any other occasion, I would row you to my favorite spot on our lake. Our bedroom will have to do for now." My lips curled up a tiny grain. He ordered the servants to leave and stood, carrying Amar in his left arm and extending his right hand.

I twined my fingers in his as we walked to the bedroom. Seated side by side, he stroked my wrist while clasping the baby on his thighs. I took a deep breath and revealed the tale my father had told me. He listened quietly, his eyes never leaving my face. His mouth opened slightly when I narrated how my parents had left my older brother, Nakul, with King Surya. He grew up as a Saral prince and now sat on her throne. As I shared my burden with him, a lightness crept into my heart. He squeezed my palm when I got to the end.

He marveled, "Nakul and Jay are brothers. Nakul has a better claim on Malla being the firstborn. Not knowing that, he has launched events that may have killed his birth father. And Jay is ignorant of this relationship."

I stammered, "Atul, my f-father groomed Jay to rule and wanted him to sit on the Malla throne. I agreed with him then. To tell him this now will devastate him."

He mused, "Jay has grown into a legend with all his triumphs. I have overheard my soldiers sing his tale of conquests with reverence. I am sure there are many boys in Magadha named after him. But how do we pacify Nakul if he is sailing to capture Malla? How do we stop Jay from destroying the Saral army when he learns of this?"

I twisted the end of my sari around my index finger. "I think if we talk to Nakul and make him aware that any victory of his will-be fleeting, that you and Jay will fight to reclaim the crown for Malla and Saral, leaving him crownless, he may stop his aggression."

Atul prodded, "If he does not listen to reason?"

I sighed. "I have to tell him the truth then. I can get Jay to listen to me and . . ." my voice shook, thinking about it. Controlling the tremors, I said, "To prevent my brothers from ruining each other, I am open to revealing the truth and crowning Nakul as King of Malla." A sob escaped me at the image, and I clenched my fist. While they were both my brothers, only one of them had grown up with me, and I felt like an elephant pressed my heart at the thought of Jay relinquishing the throne.

Atul, sensing my distress, leaned in and kissed me lightly. "Let us hope it does not come to that."

Then, he tipped back and studied me as if noticing me for the first time. His eyebrows raised, he asked, "Why didn't you tell me this before?"

Guilt crawled all over my skin like spiders, and I gaped at him, intertwining my fingers.

Without waiting for my response, he added, "I can imagine you keeping this from me when we first got married. I'd taken my brother's place after his untimely death, and we were nearly strangers."

Hurt and pain flitted across his face like rain clouds blown by the wind. The imaginary crawling spiders sunk their fangs into my skin. Why did I bring pain to those who loved me?

He whispered, "Ten years of marriage, half of which you ruled Padi by my side, and three children later, and you never found it in you to share this with me?"

I stuttered, "I . . . Atul . . . please forgive me. I should have told you this earlier."

I'd kept other secrets from him, and tears glistened in my eyes.

He touched the bangles on my right arm and moved them. He said softly, "Do you trust me, Meera?"

I felt like a monster that crushed his delicate love. I choked, "Yes, with my life."

His eyes searched my face, and mine implored his. *My heart might not be completely yours, Atul. But my body and spirit are.* He appeared satisfied when the baby on his legs whimpered. "We will get through this, Meera. We will find a way to protect your brothers and Malla."

Handing the child to me, he said, "I will attend the council meeting and plan for a small delegate to meet with Nakul and gather our armies for the worst situation. It is best if you travel to Malla with me. Can you leave Amar behind?"

I nodded, "He is almost one. I will find a wet nurse for him."

He eyed me gently, "Join me when you are ready. I want you to hear the plan before I set it in motion." Guilt rose in me again for the secrets I'd locked away. Secrets about his brother's death and about Rish. I reasoned that I'd done my duties as a wife, a mother, and a queen, happily and faithfully.

With a sigh, I trained my thoughts back to my father. My mother had departed during my childhood. Losing my only remaining parent seemed like I'd lost the direction and the map for my life. Nakul's actions had robbed me of him. Anger rose in me like steam rising off boiling water. He knew his father rotted in Malla dungeons. What would I have done to free my own father? Slowly, the anger subsided, and despair took root.

Kantha arrived to take care of my baby, and I changed into a muted sari in the color of burnt ash. As I headed to the small council, Rish stood at the threshold of my chambers. His eyes met mine, and I bathed in the kindness emanating from him.

He fell in step with me as we walked on the cold stone floors. "My lady, while no words of mine will resurrect King Vikram, I do understand the grief of losing one's father. I am here if you want to talk."

His father had died saving mine. No such men existed to save my father now. How had the killer gotten past my father's guards? A chill spread from the dark corridors. I asked him, "Rish, how could some-one poison the king? Do you think Biha had a hand in this?" Mano Biha guarded the city. Did he and his brother, Devan, side with Nakul against their king? Had Akash fallen to Saral? I pushed my fingernails into my palm as waves of anguish rose in my throat.

Rish growled, "I'm not sure. But whoever did this must have had in-side help."

I remained mired in my thoughts as we reached the council room. A fire burned in the fireplace, radiating a welcome heat. The rich mellow wood furnishings and bright rugs added to the warmth. I scanned the room as I sat beside Atul. The gathered whispered their condolences to me. Atul's uncle, Prince Rudra, stood among the assembled. A lush sil-ver beard covered his face, and rich silk clothes covered his body. Rudra and Chief Devan Biha had married sisters. If Devan sided with Nakul, did his plot extend to Padi? Did he promise the Padi kingship to Rudra and his son, Prince Naren, in exchange for their support? My eyes fell on Naren. The young man stood behind his father, his slender frame half-hidden.

My eyes landed on another cousin of Atul's. No shortage of Padi males to take over the kingdom. I chided myself for such thoughts. Af-ter Atul, the line of succession would go to our sons, Nala and Amar. And then my brother-in-law, Parth, and his son. Naren's place would be behind all of them. I worried needlessly.

Atul's generosity and compassion surely gained him the loyalty of his kin. Yet my father was no less generous, and someone had poisoned him. My turmoil grew once again.

Atul addressed the group, "Minister Drona, now that Queen Meera is here, please share our plan with her. Since this concerns her brother and Malla, I want to gather her view."

Atul had sought my advice openly in matters of governing from the early days of our marriage. He trusted my advice. Guilt gnawed my stomach, in addition to all the other emotions that welled up in me. I steeled myself and focused on the minister.

"My lady, when my mother fell ill, you came to visit her many times, bringing special treats for her from your kitchen. You even sang for her. You made her last days on earth peaceful. Words cannot describe my sadness at your loss, my queen," said Minister Drona. I inclined my head to accept his sympathy.

Then, he stated, "Queen Meera, our actions will be many-fold. We will send a messenger to King Nakul to let him know you seek his audience. A small group of men, along with you and the king, will then meet with him at a pre-arranged place. Prince Rudra and General Gambhir will collect our forces and assemble along our border in case Nakul rejects our peace offering."

Uncle Rudra? My doubts from earlier took root. What if he conspired to usurp the Padi throne? Could General Gambhir, an old friend of Atul's, ensure the men's loyalty to the king?

Another thought bubbled up. I asked, "What about Jay? Are we sending him a message?"

Dayan answered, "My father sent my brother, Darsh, to seek Prince Jay. He set sail on the Tunga sea, hoping to reach him soon."

I swallowed my fear for Jay. He had an army at his command. But, Saral men were part of his contingent, and Kapil Biha commanded his guards. I imagined him being murdered in his sleep by his men. I struggled to banish these dark thoughts swirling in me. Kapil grew up with Jay. Would he betray Jay? If brothers have turned against each other, why wouldn't a childhood friend?

I took a deep breath to calm myself. "Who is going to come with us to Malla?"

Atul responded in a quiet voice, "You, me, our guards, Naren, and a few others. Chief Guard Desh will remain here in Daya."

Naren asked, "How will Nakul land his ships? Wouldn't Malla vessels guard their ports?"

Rish spoke up, "Nakul would not have left Saral if he did not have a place to land along the Malla shores."

Atul and others nodded. Nakul must have a plan to breach our shores with Devan Biha's aid.

I returned to the scheme laid out by Minister Drona. Atul had split up his family and put them with men loyal to him. And he had kept the youngest of them, Naren, in our group. His easy manners hid a sharp mind. He gazed at me, waiting for my reaction. I thought things over and could not find any faults with his plan. I inclined my head in agreement, and we moved to discuss other matters.

Later that evening, I gathered Nala and Priya around me and told them about their grandfather, leaving out the poisoning.

Priya gazed at me with eyes that covered almost half her face and fretted, "Are you going to die too?" I pulled her into a hug and kissed her forehead.

"Not for a long time," I replied gently.

Nala grunted and admonished his sister. "Don't be a baby."

He then added, "Are you and Father going to Malla?" I nodded. He straightened his shoulders and said in a brave voice, "I will watch over Priya and Amar while you are gone."

Atul would share more details with him about the poisoning and some of our plans. To prepare him to rule this land one day. A burden he already carried on his young shoulders.

I asked in a soft voice, "Do you remember your grandfather?"

"He told me stories about Malla when he visited last time and watched me while I trained. He said I fought as well as Uncle Jay," he murmured, gazing at the floor.

A lump gathered in my throat. "I am going to miss him," I stated, and Nala put his arms around my waist and buried his head in my chest. I engulfed both of them in my arms, wishing I could protect them now as I did in my womb.

Troubled about many things, I lay awake that night waiting for Atul. He never came as sleep grudgingly pulled me into a nightmare.

4

Jay

When the sun disappeared, no moon rose to greet us. Countless stars appeared instead like lights being lit one by one on Akash streets. Men on the ship went about their work while I stood at the bow staring at the vanishing sunlight. A few days ago, half of them crawled on their stomach or knees, crowded into the lower deck in pain, and hurling forth their food. I quieted my longing for home and comforted the sick, and rallied the limited crew manning the ships. A diet of clear broth with crushed ginger and calmer seas cured them.

I heard them singing a song now, about a girl pining for her lover, laughing at each other's tone. My yearning grew as they sang, dreaming of the soft touch of my women.

Footsteps approached from behind, and I glanced sideways.

Giri Thari halted a few steps behind me and pointed to the Eastern sky. "A storm is headed our way, my lord." Lightning brightened the night sky briefly, illuminating dark clouds. The air around me smelled of salt, musty wood, and fire.

The biggest danger in a storm at night would be for our ships to run into each other. As soldiers discussed battle formations, my navy captains discussed boat formations. When the wind picked up, they would spread out to avoid a collision.

Thunder pierced through the sound of the ocean to reach us, and a gale blew over, causing the ship to roll on the waves. I walked with Giri to speak to my captain.

He looked up from the scrolls spread on his table as I approached. "My lord, the winds are getting stronger. I want to get our ships out of the eye of the storm. I will ask my men to signal to the other crafts to start the storm procedures."

I asked him a few questions and then left him alone to navigate us.

Giri and I observed two men signal to our neighboring ships using a lantern. Soon, we saw the messages spread across the water, with each boat signaling its neighbors. This reminded me of coming across ox-drawn carts in the middle of the night, with a lantern lighting its path.

The upper deck bustled with activity. Some tied up all the loose items. Others climbed up the mast and furled the sails. Soon, rain streamed down, and I sought shelter in my room.

A honey-colored wooden table stood at the center. Scrolls, parchment papers, and open books topped it. A mess that I did not allow Muthu to clear. A bed stood in the corner, covered with woolen blankets in the color of a dry ripe chili and cushions painted with tiger stripes. Warm rugs covered the dark floors, and I sat at my desk, reading the scrolls from Malla, reflecting what awaited me when I landed.

Kapil entered and shut the door behind him. He came close and whispered, "Saral men appear unaware of any moves by King Nakul or his father, Surya. They are still talking about our battles in Sunda."

"Do we make landfall at a Thari port or a Vindhya port?" I pondered. My father ruled astutely, and I might be worrying needlessly.

"We don't have to decide yet, my lord," Kapil replied. The rainwater running down his face gave him a tearful appearance, and his eyes mirrored some of my concerns. Cut off from land and isolated on the water, no news from Malla reached us. Not even whispers or rumors.

Prince Parth of Padi and Kathir Gomti of Saral traveled on different ships. Once the storms died down, I should bring them to this vessel and seek their counsel. Perhaps just Parth. I still needed to ascertain whether I could trust Kathir. Giri Thari commanded my troops, and I could not keep him in the dark for long, either.

Loud yelling from the stern reached us, and Kapil opened the door. Dev stood guard outside, and Kapil ordered him to find out what caused the commotion.

Dev returned in a few moments and blurted, "Prince Parth fell overboard."

"Drunk fool!"

I rushed outside, muttering, "If the captain had any sense, he would have tied him to a mast." My guards followed close behind.

All my men knew going overboard during a storm meant almost certain death. We'd abandoned a man on our voyage to Sunda. That storm raged during the day. However, I could not abandon Parth though chances of finding him in the dark, turbulent ocean remained slim. And we would risk the lives of good men if we tried to rescue him.

With a grim expression, I reached the stern and found my captain.

"Prince Jay, I assumed you would want to find Prince Parth and ordered the other vessel to lower a boat with two men. One to row and another to rescue." I inclined my head in agreement. He continued as we scanned the sea, "One of his men saw him fall, so we acted immediately."

As my eyes adjusted to the dark, I spotted the boat. The waves tossed it like a cat rolling a ball. In the feeble light from a lamp, I saw a dark shape break through the surface for a moment.

"There," many yelled, pointing their fingers, and several men on both ships trained their lanterns towards the spot. An arm appeared, and the skilled sailor rowed the boat close to him. His companion dived into the water. He approached Parth from behind and swung his double fist at his head, knocking him unconscious. A practice used sometimes to ensure the victim did not drown the rescuer. Soon they pulled Parth onto the raft and bound him to a plank.

I released the breath I held. In the morning, the men would climb the ladder and lift the boat. Tonight, they needed to stay adrift. This storm caused ten feet waves, and I trusted the experienced seaman to keep them safe.

"Have them bring Prince Parth to this ship," I ordered. I wanted Parth and the Padi men on my side to combat the Saral plot if there was one. The additional men would help me thwart any conspiracy.

The next day dawned to clear skies and chirping birds flying overhead. The emerald sea glistened in the sun, deceptively calm and welcoming. The storm turned east and left us safe. Parth rested below with a bulge on his forehead. His man might have used more force than required, but I could not blame him. I would have done the same if I had to risk my life to save that fool.

After getting the captain's report, I headed to the dining hall to break my fast. I stopped and spoke to many men along the way, inquired after the storm, the food served, and listened to what they thought needed my attention. Kapil jokingly called it my long road, though the steps were few.

As I reached my destination, I searched for a spot to sit. I enjoyed sharing a meal with the soldiers and giving heed to their ideas. Rows of men sat on floor mats. Several bowed and hailed me to an empty place next to them, and I chose one near older men. As a servant fetched my plate, I sat cross-legged on the mat and addressed each one by their name or title. Eyes lit up at being recognized. I gained loyalty by simply remembering their names and asking after them. These men might not all know how to read or write, but they kept their eyes and ears open. Some dismissed them as simple to their peril. They trained their senses like a predator and fought like one too.

While I ate the simple millet porridge, I mostly listened. Initially, the conversation was stilted, but they slowly loosened up, and I learned about their problems and gossip swirling around.

Later that day, I summoned the two men who saved Prince Parth. They entered my room nervously, eyes gazing down. I put them at ease by praising their courageous deeds. "You saved Prince Parth's life yesterday by your actions. I want to express my gratitude, and I am sure

Prince Parth will reward you handsomely once he recovers." *I will make sure he does.*

Dismissing them, I went to train with Giri Thari. We utilized every space of this vessel and carved out a small area on the deck to exercise. Two young men practiced with their spears when we arrived, and we halted to watch. Seeing me, they stopped and bowed. I waved at them to continue. As they blocked and attacked in quick succession, I cheered, "Well done, boys. That was some good footwork." I turned to the young man who was almost slashed and said, "Let me show you how to defend against an attack like that." We enacted the same steps, and I showed him how to block. Still recovering from my battle wounds, I exercised care in my movements. He tried it under my guidance, his face beaming. I glowed with delight in helping our young soldiers. Once he mastered the trick, I sent both on their way.

"Ready?" I asked Giri, drawing my sword.

Giri contemplated me with a strange gleam in his eyes. When he caught my eyes, his face flushed, and he mumbled something. The wind and waves drowned his voice, and with my sword in my hand, I raised my eyebrows at him.

He muttered, "I am honored to be your sparring partner." I stared at him for a moment and then understood he was conveying his respect for me.

I grinned and challenged him. "Disarm me, and then you will truly make me happy."

"As you command, Prince Jay," he smirked and circled me. After the battering our bodies endured in the recent battle, our steps resembled those of an aging soldier.

Men gathered around to watch, and we fought evenly, sweat dripping down our chins. I thought I heard my name, and I paused briefly, and Giri lunged at me. I recovered in time and jumped aside.

"Prince Jay," Kapil called again, and I raised my hand to halt our sparring. I clapped Giri's back and approached Kapil. I fell in stride beside him, wiping my sweat with a towel.

Out of earshot of others, he murmured, "Our Patrol boat found a ship hoisting a Malla flag headed our way." With men around, I kept my surprise in check and waited for him to continue.

"Darsh Vindhya was on the ship and requested to see you urgently."

"My brother-in-law?" My eyebrows raised a grain.

He nodded.

"Bring him to my chamber."

I paced the room, my mind racing a thousand miles.

"P-prince . . ." Darsh stammered, entering my room, a mix of emotions washing over his face. Taking a breath, he revealed, "King Vikram is dead, your Majesty."

I don't remember how long I stood staring at him. Time stood still. Slowly the numbness thawed, and I gripped the hilt of my sword tightly. In a voice that sounded strange in my ears, I inquired, "What happened?"

"He was poisoned, my lord . . . Majesty," he stuttered.

"Poisoned?" I echoed in disbelief.

Kapil stepped closer to us.

"You are making no sense," I snarled.

My anger calmed him, and he said clearly, "Your Majesty, his servant had entered his bedroom as the sun rose. The king, usually up by then, still remained on his bed. When the servant tried to wake him, he found the king unconscious. He sent the guard to fetch the physician. Even after trying several remedies, the king didn't recover and passed away the next day."

A strange emotion clouded my mind. One of abandonment. Alone and adrift on an ocean.

Kapil's voice brought me back. "How did the poison reach the king? What happened to his guards?"

"The physician did not find any trace of poison in his water. And the servant and the cook had insisted no one touched his food apart from them. The physician suspected a slow-acting poison, maybe ingested several days prior."

Glaring at Kapil, Darsh whispered to me, "I need to tell you something, alone."

I braced myself for what came next. Devan Biha's daughter, Riya, married Nakul and bore him a son and heir. I suspected Devan had aided Nakul. Despite that, I trusted Kapil Biha.

"Kapil heads my guard. I trust him with my life. Say what you need to in his presence."

With a tiny shake of his head, he muttered, "Minister Kripa and my father suspect Chief Devan Biha."

Kapil flinched on hearing his uncle's name.

I stared at Darsh, and he continued, "King Nakul has set sail for Malla, and we expect him to reach the Biha coast soon. He aspires to free his father, Surya, and capture Malla. Chief Devan Biha covets the Malla throne for his grandson." Darsh's words did not touch my mind filled with grief.

Instead, one image rose in my head. My father had died alone, with neither Meera nor I at his side.

"Did they cremate . . ." I struggled to ask the question.

"We couldn't wait for you," he explained.

As his only son, I'd failed to perform my one duty to my father. Light the fire on his funeral pyre.

"I need to perform his last rites. Kapil, find me a priest or someone who can guide me." As I uttered these words, a river of misery flowed into my heart.

He found an elderly sailor who had outlived many of his family members and was familiar with the rituals. Wearing a ring of sacred grass, I poured the water from an earthen pot into my hands and then allowed it to flow into the ocean. An offering to my departed father and the gods. A silent sob shook me as I remembered my father's arms around Meera and me, comforting us after our mother passed away. Many times, he would come and watch me in the training yard. On occasion, he had picked up a blunt sword to fight with me.

When I sought his blessing before this voyage over six months ago, he had appeared in good health. I'd believed he would be around for many years to come, to rule Malla and to guide me in his wisdom. Panic rose in me, and I tightened my hold on the pot. Emptying its contents into the sea, I then smashed the pot on the deck.

As I walked to the small council meeting, men working on the deck stopped and bowed to me. Some prostrated at my feet, and I scarcely noticed them, my eyes blurred with tears that I could not spill. Kapil came along and steered me in the right direction, and I followed. When I entered the room, the light from all the lamps blinded me, and I paused near the threshold. Giri, my guards, the captain, and a few other trusted men stood watching me.

I stepped into the center of the room, and Giri Thari placed his sword at my feet and bowed with his hands clasped together. "I pledge my life and sword to you, my king."

Others followed, and soon the room rang with, "Glory to our King Jay!!! Victory to King Jay."

5

Meera

The day gave birth to an empty sky. Birds rushed to fill the void, noisily calling out to each other. My aunt, Princess Mohini, came to visit me in my chambers. Draped in a sari the color of saffron, she sat next to me, and I could faintly smell sandalwood emanating from her. She reminisced about my father and his brother. "Vikram's elder brother epitomized the king-in-waiting. Vikram idolized his brother, and he, in turn, indulged him."

Listening to the story of my father calmed my anxiety. I kept my eyes on my aunt as she continued, "Men may have emulated your uncle, but Vikram was the one they shared a meal with. The heir adhered to lofty principles while Vikram played pranks. Vikram, Lata, and I filled our days with leisure and merriment." The sisters, Mohini and Lata, were my father's cousins.

She paused and sniffed. I squeezed her arm, and she peered at me through misty eyes.

"Vikram's world changed when his father and brother drowned. He ascended the throne of Malla. To allies and enemies alike, the new king remained a mystery, and he shed his playfulness and remade himself in the mold of his dead brother. He married his brother's betrothed without revealing that his heart belonged to another."

My heart ached for my father. He had hidden his own son from the world, and Malla might reap what he had sowed.

My aunt sighed and said, "He treated Lata and me as sisters. I attended your father-in-law's wedding here in Padi with your father. He introduced me to the groom's brother. Later that night, he stated that if I wished to marry Prince Rudra of Padi, he could make it happen. Not his command but my wish."

She smiled at the thought, and my mind jumped back to my father, seeking my consent before promising me to Prince Amar. Jay's disappearance had plunged us into despair, and I'd agreed. That wedding never took place after I'd met Amar. I'd seen to that.

She said, "You have never met your uncle, but you remind me of him. Courteous, dutiful, beyond reproach. Men and women revere you. Even Atul has kept you on a pedestal, a paragon of virtue."

I stared at her, no words coming to me. Seeing my shocked expression, she patted my arm. "My old mind wanders. You have your father in you as well. His stubbornness to make things bend to his will. Caring for the land and its people."

Beyond reproach. My shoulders ached from carrying the weight of that burden since my young days. My wrists chafed at the restraint of duty. A hunger to break free swept through me like a flash flood. I remembered my father's words. The primary fealty of a king and queen was to their people. I had to sacrifice my personal feelings to uphold that obligation.

I brought my attention back to the urgent matter I wanted to discuss with her. Searching my aunt's face, I asked, "We heard Nakul had set sail for Malla, and Biha has aligned with him."

"Devan Biha is no fool. He will not make a move unless he has carefully weighed his options. Don't underestimate him," she replied with a frown.

She then answered a question I left unasked. "My sister, Lata, is fond of you and Jay. Whatever Devan and Nakul are cooking, she will want no harm to come to Jay."

What could she do in a battle?

I plowed right ahead, "Aunt Mohini, have you heard from Aunt Lata? Do you know . . ."

She shook her head before I finished. "No, my child. I am in the dark about Nakul's plot or Biha's hand in it. Rudra already asked me, and I am sure Atul has read my letters."

I opened my mouth to protest, and she touched my shoulder lightly. "I know the burden of ruling a kingdom. Atul goes about it with a mild touch, but I don't envy him."

She left my chambers soon after. Her husband, Prince Rudra, and General Gambhir departed the next day to collect Padi troops and assemble them at our border with Malla.

When Kantha came to help me pack, I sought her help with some unfinished charges. I said, "I went to visit Saras after her childbirth, and she told me about her problems nursing her child. I have asked our cook to prepare her some rolled bread stuffed with fenugreek leaves. Take them to her, along with the special balm I use."

Saras, Chief Guard Desh's wife, had just given birth a few days ago. Her mother had fallen ill and could not visit her daughter. Kantha nodded her head as she folded my silk saris.

In the evening, Atul and I sat cross-legged across from each other on the tufted cotton rug in the colors of a meadow blooming with flowers. The light from the lamps hung on the ceiling cast a golden glow around my room. He held Priya on his lap, and Amar slept on mine. Nala sat between us, face turned towards his father, listening intently.

"Your mother and I will meet with King Nakul and make him give up his conquest of Malla. Then we will head to Akash to receive Uncle Jay and crown him King of Malla."

At the mention of the coronation, Nala's eyes widened. He asked eagerly, "Father, can I come to Akash to witness Uncle Jay's crowning?"

Atul glanced at me briefly, and I inclined my head. As our future king, I understood Nala's interest in the ceremony. I wondered if he grasped that only one king ruled at a time. The old king had to die or abdicate for the new king to take his place. I thought about my father's murder. *Who could be the culprit?* What a web for me to unravel.

Atul tousled his son's hair. "If all goes well, I will send Uncle Parth to bring you to Akash." Nala's eyes lit upon hearing this. Atul continued, "In the meantime, I want you to look after your sister and brother. And continue your lessons." He nodded vigorously.

I added, "Listen to Minister Drona and Kantha," tucking his hair behind his ears. He shook his hair and asked, "Is Uncle Rish staying?"

Atul glanced at me and then said, "Uncle Rish is your mother's guard. He goes where she does. Chief Guard Desh will train you." Nala pouted, not happy with the arrangement.

Before I could think about Atul's glance, Priya interjected, "Is Rima staying?"

I pushed the stray thought away and replied, "Yes, she is going to stay with you. Would you like that?"

Her face brightened with a huge smile.

Later that night, I reclined on my bed, going through all the plans in my mind to make sure I hadn't missed anything. I heard footsteps and saw Atul enter the room, illuminated by the light from the fireplace. Undressing, he whispered, "I think everything is in place for our journey."

He slipped under the blankets next to me and leaned on his elbow, facing me. With his right hand, he traced my face. His finger felt warm against my skin. Busy with preparations for our departure, he had slept in his chambers most nights since we received the news of my father's death.

His finger halted on my chin, his eyes searching my face.

"Do you trust Uncle Rudra?" I asked.

"I do," he answered. Lying on his back, he pulled me closer, and I rested my head on his chest. "I trust Gambhir more," he added.

"Are you ready to leave? Did you find a wet nurse for Amar?" he inquired, his fingers combing my hair.

"Hmm," I replied as I drifted off, ensconced in his arms. I found a young girl who had lost her baby. Brimming with milk, she gladly nursed him. She would develop a bond with him that would last till she carried her own.

The next day dawned with the sun hidden behind the fog rolling in from the mountains. Bidding farewell to the children, we set off from Daya. I traveled alone in a horse-drawn carriage. Parting the curtains, I viewed the meadows while my mind raced many miles.

Nakul would have made landfall by now, and I expected our messengers to reach him soon. I fervently hoped he would deter his march to Akash, knowing Padi sided with Jay. He considered Surya his father and would demand his release. A reasonable request to comply with. Another might be for an independent Saral, not under the shadows of Malla. Jay might refuse this, not knowing the story of Nakul's birth. It fell on me to convince my brother to accept it for the good of the three kingdoms.

Nakul had ruled Saral ably for the past decade, but Malla's crown belonged to him by birthright. In my fondness for the brother I raised, was I depriving Nakul and Malla? And Nakul had an heir, while Jay had no sons.

Should I reveal the truth to Jay and let him decide? I imagined telling the story to Jay. He would be ecstatic to learn that Nakul was his brother. And crestfallen about not sitting on the throne. He had sailed the seas and conquered the world. Could he continue his adventures allowing Nakul to rule the land?

What about Malla and her people? While either of them would rule her wisely, Jay had not only the bloodline but had shed his blood for the soil and her people.

I suddenly made a decision. I had to reveal the truth to Jay and let him choose. The burden was too great for me to bear alone. A calmness settled over me, and my eyes glided over a lake sparkling in the sunlight. A deer lifted its head to gaze at us. Spots, matching light filtering through a tree, covered its coat. It galloped away on hearing the clop of the horses. Cold wind crept in through the open curtain, and I spread a blanket over my legs. The wind brought in the smell of distant snowfall.

At night, we set camp, and Atul went to visit the neighboring village elders. Alone in my tent, I missed the liveliness of my children. I longed to hold my baby in my arms and press my face against his. I'd sensed Nala growing away from me. Natural on his side as he learned his place as the heir. My mother's heart ached nevertheless. Priya, my beautiful girl. I wanted to shelter her in my sari, like a caterpillar in a cocoon, and release her as a butterfly, free to fly where she desires. Such foolishness. Better to prepare her for her duty as a queen one day. Putting others before her needs.

The following day, as the men prepared for our departure, I visited a nearby temple with Atul, Rish, and others. The small temple stood in the corner of a wheat field. Its outer brick walls had crumbled from age. Atop this ruin, a peacock welcomed the visitors with his dance. The morning light reflected the blue and green hues of its feathers in brilliance. As I stepped in, I viewed the inner sanctum sculpted out of granite rocks. It had withstood the passage of time. Inside, God Shiva, in his dancer's pose, stood balancing on one leg. A priest lit a lamp and recited some prayers. He then approached me and entreated, "My queen, please bless this temple with a song on Lord Shiva."

I sang mostly for my children now, so I searched my memory for a hymn. One that Madhavi had taught me swam into my mind, about ash-strewn Shiva dancing on snow-clad mountains. I closed my eyes and chanted, picturing snow melting at his feet and flowing like a river.

When I opened my eyes, the priest offered me a flower from God's feet. Pinning it to my hair, I strolled around the courtyard with Atul.

"I haven't heard you sing like that since..." he paused. I hadn't sung since I heard of my father's death a week ago. Our eyes met, and he grasped my hand, encircling his fingers in mine. I cherished the warmth that spread from his hand. The fragrance of the blooming flowers floated in from the temple garden.

The rest of the journey passed uneventfully. I traveled in my carriage with just my thoughts for company. I could glimpse the mountains to the North and fields laden with wheat and millet on either side. The crops planted in the fall would be ready for harvest in early summer. I went riding with Rish once, at the end of the day, after we set camp. When we stayed with a village chief, I met with local women. Otherwise, I stayed alone in my room.

I broke my fast with Atul in the mornings when he shared the day's news with me. Occupied with many matters, he rarely visited me at night.

One day, when we stayed at a small palace, a message from Nakul arrived. He agreed to see us in a village close to the Padi border. General Gambhir amassed our army nearby. Atul invited me to his chamber to join in the discussion and spend the night after. I sat by the fire as he presented the plan to his men.

"What if this is a trap?" inquired Naren.

Atul answered, "It may be, Naren. But if it is, what will Nakul achieve by imprisoning us? Padi will seek revenge, and so will Jay."

Rish mused with a frown on his face. "He will gain hostages in his fight against Prince Jay."

Atul glanced at me. I knew his mind. If Nakul imprisoned me, Atul would want me to reveal his parentage. I preferred to speak to Jay first.

Atul asked, "What is the alternative? We can either face him or stay in Padi waiting for him to make a move."

In the late hours of the night, we decided to meet him. As others left, Rish stayed behind. He cleared his throat. "My Majesty, I suggest Queen Meera ride a horse when we go to encounter King Nakul. Her carriage is too conspicuous."

Atul gazed at him and inclined his head. Then he dismissed him, "Meera will spend the night here."

Alone, he sat beside me and put his arms around my shoulders. "Meera, this secret is yours to reveal or conceal. I will follow your lead."

I leaned against him and whispered, "I hope I choose wisely."

He kissed my head and stood up. "Let us get some rest before the night departs."

The ensuing day, under Rish's guidance, I wore a simple sari in white with gold threads woven in the border. It matched the men's white dhoti. I mounted my horse and stayed at the back. Our scouts came back with the news that Nakul marched towards our meeting spot with fifty men. We traveled with about the same number.

As twilight descended and the sun kissed his earth bride, reluctant to leave her, we heard horses gallop towards us. Rish moved closer and grabbed my reins. We were a day away from our meeting spot. We halted, and the soldiers drew their swords. I scanned the area, my heart beating rapidly.

Kicking dust into the air, horses rode in front of us, and a voice I recognized spoke, "King Atul, you are surrounded, and I advise you to surrender."

General Karan Thari! Malla's Northern commander. Shocked, I glanced at Rish, and he motioned for me to dismount. Confused, I did as he intimated.

He whispered in my ear. "Meera, this was a trap. I need to take you to safety."

Dazed, I mumbled, "I cannot leave Atul."

Rish crouched behind the horses and pulled me down. Undistinguishable voices and noises floated around me. Rish spoke urgently, his lips touching my ear. "We don't have time to waste. I swore to protect you. I need you to trust me."

The pleading in his voice brought me to my senses, and I looked at him. Young Nala's face drifted into my mind. Too young to fight for his father. If Atul was imprisoned, Padi needed her queen. Nothing I could do here to defend Atul. Avoiding capture would allow me to reach Gambhir.

Rish gestured to the soldier next to us, and he signaled back.

As darkness spread around us like a blanket, horses neighed, and men yelled. Rish grasped my hand and crawled away to the sound of metal clanging against metal. I followed with my heart beating like a war drum.

6

Jay

King of Malla.

I stared at the swords at my feet and raised my eyes to the men with clasped hands and bowed heads around me. I knew the throne would pass to me after my father's death. I'd assumed he would die an old man in his bed. Or die on a battlefield shedding his blood for Malla. Instead, someone had poisoned him in Akash and left him to die alone. Someone who served my brother-in-law, Nakul.

A slow fire burned in my stomach. Nakul chose to roll the dice while I fought in Sunda. He must have hatched the scheme before I departed Akash. I signaled to Dev to close the door and addressed my men, "Friends, you fought along my side in Sunda and drove the invaders away. Something far more dangerous awaits in Malla. My father has been murdered, and Nakul is headed to Akash. Pick up your swords and swear to fight with me to bring the murderer to justice. To defeat Nakul and reclaim Malla. To avenge our king."

I raised my sword, and others followed suit, proclaiming, "Justice and Revenge." I looked into the eyes of these men. *Would one of them be the traitor who had betrayed us?*

I beckoned Darsh to come forward. "Recite all you know about what happened in Akash."

He straightened his shoulders and said, "My Majesty, it all started a few weeks ago when someone tried to sneak into our dungeon to pass a message to old King Surya. The man escaped capture, and we immediately strengthened the guards around the cell. Then news reached us that Southern Commander General Satya had mysteriously fallen off his horse and was severely injured."

Giri Thari gasped on hearing the account. He had served as Satya's Lieutenant for many years. I sensed a carefully designed mission by Nakul.

Darsh scanned the room and cleared his throat. Pivoting back to me, he continued, "The king ordered my uncle, Hasan Vindhya, to head to Saral to take command while General Satya recovered. But in the vacuum created by a bedridden Satya, Nakul stealthily left Saral and set sail for Malla."

I gripped my sword hilt tightly. A methodical and careful man like Nakul would not make a bold move like this unless he had allies in Malla. Traitors who had betrayed their oath to their king and kingdom.

My men craned their necks to peer at Darsh. Eyebrows furrowed, he continued in subdued tones, "We received the news about Nakul after King Vikram was poisoned."

Several of them drew in their breath. Their eyes shifted from Darsh to me.

Waves of sadness, anger, and despair crashed into me. Relentlessly. I would not let Nakul get away with murdering my father. I jutted my chin and asked, "Did a messenger go to Meera?"

"Yes, Prin—"

Kapil snapped, "He is our king now."

Darsh drew a breath and answered, "King Jay, my brother, Dayan, headed to Padi at the same time I left Akash."

Meera and Atul would be on my side. If Atul knew about Nakul's movements, he would gather Padi troops. The three regions of Malla: Biha, Thari, and Vindhya, had only a modest standing army under their guard. They used this mainly to protect their families and properties. The king commanded the three military units and the naval ships.

The Malla army by itself was larger than Saral's. Combined with Padi, we could crush the Saral like ants. Under what strength was Nakul acting? A sudden fear gripped my throat. Nakul must have anticipated Padi would come to my aid. I clenched my fist. I needed to find out his next move before I fell into the trap he had set for me.

"What is being done to protect Akash?" I asked.

Darsh glanced at Kapil and replied, "My Majesty, Chief Guard Mano Biha has asked the central command soldiers to return to Akash. He has ordered the city gates to close at sundown, and only trusted men are allowed to enter after. He has also dispatched our patrol units."

Mano trained me in warfare as a young boy. He served my father loyally, and his son, Kapil, had protected my life many times over the years, risking his own. I could not imagine them betraying me.

I moved to the table and opened the Magadha map.

Speaking to Darsh, I observed, "Do we know if Nakul is heading north via Tunga or Nira sea or both?"

Darsh rubbed his chin. "We had no knowledge when I left Akash."

Giri frowned and asked, "Has my uncle, Karan, dispatched men along the Biha ports?"

General Karan Thari commanded our Northern unit.

Darsh answered, "Yes, Minister Kripa sent messages to General Karan to patrol our Nira seaports. Prince Jay, Chief Guard Mano dispatched our navy ships to guard the Vindhya port for our safe passage."

It would take many moons for men to call me king. "Captain, Nakul might attack our ships at sea. Can you communicate with our other captains to prepare?"

He responded sharply, "Yes, my Majesty," then left.

I dismissed everyone but Darsh, Giri, and Kapil. Two of them would rule as chiefs of their territories, and the third one a dear friend.

My stomach growled, and I realized I'd not eaten since that morning. "Have you taken your meal yet?" I asked, and they shook their heads.

"Let's head to my room and continue our talk. Muthu can fetch our food."

Glancing at my table covered with scrolls, I sat cross-legged on the floor, and others followed suit.

Muthu brought in steaming bowls of rice. Instead of handing me a rice bowl, he gave me a bowl of fruit, mumbling, "You are mourning your father, my lord. Simple food is best."

The others stared at me as I swallowed the lump in my throat. I mourned my father with unshed tears. I examined my bowl and picked a fruit piece, neither smelling nor tasting anything. We ate silently as I emptied my mind, letting the rocking vessel soothe me.

Soon, Muthu cleared the food, and all the worries I'd kept at bay rushed in.

"What do we do with Kathir Gomti and the Saral men?" I asked.

"Imprison them," Darsh answered immediately.

Giri and Kapil appeared thoughtful.

Giri said, "King Jay, I knew Kathir in Saral. While loyal to his king, he spoke his mind and based his deeds on what was right. If King Nakul sent him away while plotting this incursion, it might be because he worried Kathir might stop him."

Kapil added, "My Majesty, I watched Kathir save your life in Sunda, in the longest battle we waged. Your mother and his father were siblings, and you are more closely related to Kathir than King Nakul. But, he is sworn to obey his king. Let us bring him on board this ship, and you can talk to him and judge for yourself. Then we can decide whether to throw him in a cell or use his aid in defeating Nakul."

Darsh smirked, "Spoken like a Biha. Your uncle is aiding our enemy, and you want our king to befriend a Saral?"

Kapil's eyes flashed, and I ordered, "Enough. I trust you all. I am not going to tolerate your bickering."

In a calmer tone, I continued, "If Kathir is a friend, I don't want to turn him into a foe. Giri, bring him alone to our boat tomorrow, and I will talk to him."

I moved to the next problem. "Parth Padi?"

Giri wrinkled his nose, and Kapil pressed his lips together. I sniggered at their expressions, and Darsh looked at me, puzzled.

Kapil explained, "We avoid revealing any secrets to Prince Parth because he has a habit of getting drunk and blurting them out to complete strangers."

"I need Padi men on my side," I murmured.

"They are on your side, my lo. . . Majesty. Padi men have been following your command from day one," shared Giri.

I pondered that and agreed, "We will reveal enough to keep Parth aligned with us without making him a danger to our plans."

I intertwined my fingers and placed them around my right knee. Leaning back against a chair, I asked Darsh, "Where are our units placed in Malla?"

"Hasan has half his troops in Saral, and the other half he has moved to Vindhya ports. His ships are patrolling our seas. One of his units and a few ships are guarding our passage to Vindhya. Chief Mano has most of his men in Akash and neighboring cities. General Karan was ordered to move his ships to guard the Thari and Biha ports."

Hasan Vindhya would move the Southern unit where needed.

I mused, "How did we send messengers to Karan Thari? If Devan is siding with Nakul, he will capture any messengers from Akash traveling through Biha. Are they traveling through Thari lands?"

Darsh shook his head. "I don't know, my king."

If Karan remained in the dark about the invasion and acted slowly, that could provide the window for Nakul to land and move his men.

Darsh stayed back as the others left.

"How is Sudha doing?" I asked about my wife and his sister.

He stared at the rug and sighed. "Not very well, my lord. Since she lost the baby, she has shut herself in her room and rarely ventures out."

I winced, thinking about the letters I received from his sister. One long letter told me about the baby on the way, and another short one a few weeks later informed me of the loss. Away on a battlefield, I thought the loss did not touch me the same way it did her. That was not true. When I got her first letter, I'd hoped it would be a son. My heir. And then I'd buried the disappointment deep inside.

The next day, Kathir Gomti was brought to me, stripped of his weapons. Kapil hovered nearby while Kathir spoke, "Cousin Jay, I heard about Uncle Vikram's passing. My condolences."

I spoke sharply, "He was poisoned, Kathir. In a plot instigated by Nakul."

He grimaced, "Jay, I have been by your side for six months. King Nakul did not take me into his confidence."

I stormed, "What do I do with you, Kathir?"

He said, "Arrest me, my lord."

I stared at him, stunned.

7

Meera

I collapsed on the dirt, "I cannot move anymore."

Rish urged me on. "Just a few more feet to that tree, and then we can sit behind it."

Soldiers on the hunt could easily find us by following my breathing. It sounded like a child learning to play the flute. I'd torn my sari, scraped my hands and knees, and crawled through dirt and mud for what seemed like an eternity.

Ants climbed onto my waist, and I brushed them off. I would become ant fodder if I remained here. I dragged my body slowly as if slithering through burning coal. Fresh pain rose through my knees and hands. Rish moved along my side, his breathing even. Did his training include hours crawling through the ground?

We reached the tree, and I flipped onto my back and took long deep breaths with my mouth open. Rish glanced at me and then scanned our surroundings. As my breathing steadied, my eyes observed the night sky lit with countless stars. A crescent moon appeared. The air around burst with the fragrance of flowers, and I could hear wings flapping.

Slowly, I sat up and assumed a more dignified position for a queen. Rish climbed up a nearby tree and disappeared into its branches. I rearranged my sari, and my fear stole in. Nakul had won the allegiance of Devan Biha and Karan Thari. What had he promised them? Had I made a mistake in leaving Atul?

Rish jumped down like a cat and whispered, "I did not see any men tailing us, but it will be easy for them to trace our path."

Gazing at me, he smirked, "They just have to follow the havoc that appears to be caused by a mad elephant."

I responded evenly, "My princess training did not include a mud crawl." While I'd crushed bushes with my stomach, Rish had moved with a light touch, only his fingers and toes touching the ground.

His eyes crinkled in response to my words. We rested for less time than it would take to eat my morning meal.

"We need to put more distance between us and leave them a few false trails to follow. We cannot dither any longer," Rish urged.

I stood up and wobbled on my feet. Rish put his hand on my back to steady me, asking with concern, "Are you hurt, Meera?"

I shook my head slowly, "No, just tired."

He replied thoughtfully, "We can take frequent rests. And I can go alone to create false trails."

"No," I responded, panic swelling in me. "Don't leave me alone," I pleaded.

"We will stay together," he murmured, dropping his hand. "Ready?"

He allowed me to set the pace, and he walked beside me with his hand on his hilt. In the dark, the trees around us loomed like giants, and roots spread like webs waiting to trip us. My parched mouth longed for a drink of water, and my feet felt heavy. With no strength left, I felt the weight of each step.

"W-water," I stammered.

Rish halted. I gazed at him, and darkness shrouded his face. "Let's rest," he said, and I dropped to the floor. After only a few moments, Rish reached out with his hand, "Meera, we cannot stop too long." I grasped his outstretched hand and let him pull me up, and we resumed. I stumbled on a loose rock, and he caught my elbow to steady me. We moved slowly, his hand still on my arm.

After several hundred yards, he stopped and squeezed my arm gently. "Listen."

I heard bats flying around, wind rustling the trees, and then a stream flowing. "Water."

He scanned our surroundings and said, "Meera, you stay here, and I will fetch you some."

Panic rose in me again. "No, I will come with you."

He spoke slowly, as if to a child, "Animals take shelter near water. I don't want to worry about you stepping on a snake."

I faltered, "I don't want to lose you."

He stepped closer and held both my hands. "I will be cautious. Please stay here and don't move." He let go and strode towards the stream.

I shivered in the cold and wrapped my sari around my shoulders. My mind dwelled on what had happened earlier that night. How had Nakul enticed General Karan to abandon his king? The men under his command had sworn an oath to the King of Malla. Not all would forsake their duty. He must be keeping them in the dark about his real intentions. *What happened to Atul and his men?*

I heard soft footsteps and spun around.

"It's me," Rish whispered. He held out a hollow log filled with water. I grabbed it and gulped thirstily, the liquid running down my chin.

The rest of the night passed uneventfully, and slowly the sun rose to greet the world. A beautiful meadow with waist-high grass swayed in the wind, and I headed into it and collapsed. Rish approached me with concern. He kneeled next to me, and I glanced at him. "I cannot take one more step," I gasped. Blisters covered my feet, and scratches from thorns carpeted my arms.

Suddenly we heard horses trot, and I curled up into a ball. Rish crouched like a tiger and peeked through the tall grass. His hand rested on the hilt of his sword, ready to draw it. My heart pounded against my chest, waiting for the sound to halt in front of us. The animals ran past us and then stopped.

"We lost their trail."

Pause. "I see it," shouted another.

My heart nearly stopped. I'd staggered into the grass, leaving a trail behind. It would be easy to follow our path. Running away was a mistake. I should have stayed with Atul. I clenched my hands to keep them shaking.

I heard the horses neigh and the men yell at each other. I'd no weapons. What would I do when they found us?

To my relief, the sound slowly receded. Rish sat up and said words that I never imagined would fill me with dread, "Malla soldiers."

I should not fear them. I was a Malla princess. They would not dream of harming me.

I opened my mouth to state the same, and Rish shook his head, "Devan and Karan have joined forces while Jay is away. We cannot trust the Malla soldiers under Thari command. You are the Queen of Padi, and getting back to General Gambhir is the prudent thing for us."

I snapped, "Prudent? I am on the run with one guard. We have no food or water. I can barely stand after a single night, and you expect us to survive a long trek and reach Gambhir?"

Rish eyed me anxiously, taking in the bruises on my body. Strangely, I blushed under his gaze. My sari torn, hair disheveled, and skin covered with dirt, I wished I could disappear.

He growled, "I am missing something. I don't understand what Nakul is doing. Why ambush us and capture Atul? Padi army is not going to let him kidnap Atul." He pushed his fingers through his hair.

"Rish, it is not your fault. I misjudged Nakul. And possibly put Atul in danger."

He said guiltily, "We have to keep moving, though. The men are looking for us, and I cannot fend off an army by myself. We can rest when the sun is overhead."

With a sigh, I stood. Rish held my elbow again, and I focused on putting one foot in front of the other.

A short time later, Rish nudged me and pointed ahead, and my gaze fell on some wild banana trees. The clusters of red finger-length bananas grew out of one tree with a flower in the middle. Butterflies swarmed the flower. Rish took out his dagger and cut the ripest fruit at the top and passed a heap to me. I slumped onto the floor and peeled the skin and slowly bit into the delicious fruit. Rish popped a whole fruit into his mouth and started peeling another. He reminded me of Nala gobbling his food. I hoped my children were safe in Daya.

"Why don't you eat two at a time?" I teased.

He laughed, "Is that an order, my lady? I did swear to obey you." He proceeded to peel a second fruit and stuffed both in his mouth. I chuckled as I watched him struggle to chew. He licked his lips and said, "The taste does explode in all corners of your mouth."

I averted my gaze as a slow fire spread in my stomach. Like water seeping through a hole in a boat, my old memories of us together bubbled up. An image of a younger Rish laughing while he plucked a ripe mango for me surfaced. Feelings I buried long ago reared their head and threatened to drown me. In my mind's eyes, I drew a sword and cut off the beast's head.

Our hunger quelled Rish cut another cluster and tied it to the sash around his waist. He gathered our peels and hid them in the dirt.

We resumed our slow march, keeping the sun to our right. We stumbled upon a creek, and I greedily drank the snow-melted water and splashed it on my face. Rish refilled our log and gave me a weak smile, "Just a little distance more, and we can rest for the day."

The sun shone overhead, and the warmth induced sleepiness. We came to a clump of trees, and Rish climbed once again. I sat on the ground and observed him. He swung from the lower branches to the higher ones easily and pulled himself up. In another lifetime, I'd dreamed of spending time with him alone. Never even in my nightmare did I imagine I would be on the run from Malla men.

He landed lightly on his feet and said, "We will rest till sundown. I will take first watch."

I urged, "Rish, do wake me up before dusk so you can get some rest too."

He took his cotton shawl and spread it on the ground strewn with fallen leaves. He glanced at me wordlessly and nodded. I rested on his cloth and closed my eyes. Sleep shunned me, and I could hear Rish pacing the floor in measured steps.

I leaned on my elbow and whispered, "Rish?"

He approached me with his sword drawn. I eyed the sword, and he answered my unspoken question, "Practicing some moves."

"What do you think is motivating Nakul?"

He readily answered as if he had considered this. "I would guess guilt. The guilt of a son who failed his father."

I'd let my knowledge of Nakul color my actions. All his life, he had considered himself as the son of Surya. A man held in Malla dungeons for a decade. How long had Nakul planned this incursion? Fear reached its sharp claws and dug into my heart.

Rish added, "When we captured Surya, he swore at his own son and disowned him for treachery. A man like Nakul does not recover from such insults easily. It must have corroded his mind for years."

My heart broke for Nakul. He did not merit being raised by this monster and live under his shadow for more than three decades. *Why had my father abandoned his firstborn?*

Rish said gently, "Get some rest, Meera. We have another long march tonight."

Soon tiredness took over. A voice called out to me, and I mumbled and pulled the sari tighter around me. "Meera," the voice persisted, and I opened my eyes with difficulty.

The setting sun had painted the sky in vibrant colors, and I stifled a yawn. "Rish, you let me sleep the whole time."

He grinned slowly. "You needed it more than me. Look at what I found." He held some mulberries and gooseberries. I lifted my hands to stretch, and his gaze dropped to my exposed waist. He stepped away quickly and turned his back to me. I hurriedly adjusted my sari with color creeping up my neck.

He cleared his throat and said, "Queen Meera, there is a small pond nearby for you to clean up." As he pointed in the direction, I noticed the change in address. *Why did he switch to my formal title? Did he...?* I shook my head. Now was not the time to explore what was best submerged.

Soon, we set out again. "Rish, can you teach me how to wield a sword?"

"A sword," he repeated as if he misheard me. I nodded. "The one I carry might be too heavy for you. Did I lose your trust completely?" he questioned.

Tears stung my eyes as I blinked them away. "I have been useless these past few days and never more so than now."

In a strange voice, he said, "Queen Meera, you have helped King Atul rule Padi wisely. No one who knows you will agree with what you stated."

"Are you able to teach me or not?" I challenged him. He pulled out his dagger and passed it to me. I grasped it tightly. "Loosen your grip," he advised.

I did as he said. "Good. Most men will hesitate to fight you, and that should give you a few moments to attack. If the man is wearing armor, attack his neck or lower down on your knees and hit his thighs."

Rish stood in front of me and said, "Try it on me." Bathed in the soft light, he stood effortlessly capable in front of me. Sudden shyness rushed into me, and I quelled it. The man had seen me crawl on the dirt. I brought the knife to his neck, and he knocked it out of my hand.

I punched his arm and hurt my knuckles. Shaking them, I grumbled, "You asked me to hold it lightly."

He teased me, "That is lesson one, my lady. How to hold your weapon." I raised my arm to punch him again, and he smirked and held his palm up in mock defense, "Does it seem fair to you, my queen? Hitting me when you know I cannot hit you back?"

I colored deeply and mumbled, "Forget this foolish idea."

He picked up the dagger and cajoled, "Let us try it again."

I shook my head. I would not be able to overpower a grown man. "Why? Do you enjoy watching my humiliation?"

He raised his eyebrows. "You asked me to teach you. Did you expect to master it one try?"

Why did he have to make sense? I took the weapon, and he came and stood behind me. With a steady hand, he guided me. I could feel his warm breath on my neck, and for a moment, I longed to lean back on his chest. *What foolishness is this,* I berated myself.

He helped me with my posture and guided my hand. He taught me how to hold the dagger correctly, so a simple swat would not cause me to drop it. And he made me practice it more than a dozen times. My arm grew heavy, and sweat ran down my face. I wiped my forehead and neck with my sari end and heard a sharp intake of his breath.

"W-we can resume the lessons tomorrow," he stammered as he stepped away from me. He appeared caught in the same current of emotions swirling around me. Trepidation set in. I had constructed a fence around my heart with my marriage and children. Palace, crown, and other regalia had strengthened the barricade. Alone with Rish, holes appeared in the barriers I'd erected.

In the dark, we plodded along. As the fragment of a moon rose, flowers burst open around us. Some animals ran overhead in the trees. I inhaled slowly, enjoying the scents and the sounds of the night. I remembered a night an eternity ago when I—why did my mind wander into these futile realms?

Rish seemed immersed in his thoughts.

To get away from my dangerous reflections, I asked, "How long will it take us to reach Gambhir on foot?"

"Too long," he groused. "I have been avoiding villages and sticking to the forest. But once we are further North, we can sneak into a village. I can steal a horse then, and we can reach Gambhir sooner."

Sudden sorrow seeped in at the notion of losing his companionship and shocked me. Despite the many worries festering in my mind, I relished living moment to moment with Rish. I could almost pretend to be a normal woman. But I was not an ordinary person. I vainly tried to brace my heart and cloak it in the armor of duty and tradition.

I avoided mentioning the turmoil raging in me and chose a safe response. "Steal a horse?" I raised my eyebrows.

He laughed weakly, "I will buy it, my queen. I will leave them gold coins from your coffer."

We walked in solitude for some time, and he stretched his arm across to stop me. I stood still as he viewed the tree branches.

"Leopard," he whispered in my ears as I caught sight of two shining diamonds. Rish drew his sword and pushed me behind him.

8

Jay

I sighted land, standing on the deck of my ship. Malla boats guarding our passage blew their horns as we approached. The prince had morphed into a king. Not a king yet. Another man stood in my way. Nakul coveted Malla. Instead of following the warrior tradition, he had stooped to use a coward's weapon. *Poison.* I promised Aranya eons ago to keep her brother safe. That word no longer bound me in this new war. *Nakul, you murdered my father. Be prepared to die at my hands.*

I could see men gathered on the land but could not make out their faces.

"Have you decided what to do with Kathir and the Saral men, my Majesty?" Kapil asked.

I did not answer immediately. What I wanted to do sounded foolish in the broad daylight. And it would be my first act as a king.

Darsh appeared at my side and peered at the land. "My father," he exclaimed, pointing to a man adorned with sparkling jewels.

Trees swayed in the gentle wind as I disembarked. Mani Vindhya, my father-in-law and Chief of Vindhya house, welcomed me gravely. I wanted to touch the soil I ruled now and shed tears for the man who had ruled it before me. Instead, I fell in step with Mani.

"Were there any attacks at sea, my Majesty?" he inquired. I ignored the tightening in my throat at my new title and shook my head. The golden sand crunched under our feet as we headed to the tents pitched several yards away. The familiar smell of the sea mingled with the smell of the land. The fragrance of blooming flowers floated in and mixed with horse dung.

"Will you like a few moments to refresh . . ."

I interrupted him. "No need for that."

We entered a sparsely furnished tent, and I demanded, "What happened to my father?"

Mani fiddled with a long chain around his neck and then regarded me. "He was poisoned. The royal physician suspects a slow-acting venom that he might have consumed several days before his death. A man had tried to sneak into our dungeons to see Surya. The same man might have slipped a poisonous treat into the palace."

"Neither his servants nor his guards would have allowed my father to eat something from an unknown source," I hissed in frustration.

He concurred. "Someone trustworthy must have given this to the king himself."

"And we don't know who the culprit is?" I asked, struggling to stay calm.

He shook his head, and I gripped my hilt tightly. We appeared no closer to identifying the traitor in our midst. I'd expected to learn more when I arrived.

"What else is new?"

"Nakul has alighted, and he is marching an army towards Akash."

Slowly dread filled my chest as I anticipated his next words. "We suspect Karan Thari is siding with him."

Giri gasped at hearing his uncle's name. Karan Thari commanded our Northern troops.

Darsh and Kapil stared at Mani, hanging on to his every word.

"What raised your concern?"

"Several things, my Majesty. We never received a reply to our messages to safeguard the Nira ports. Devan Biha commands very few men.

Nakul cannot move a large army through Biha lands unless Karan aids his passage."

Devan Biha wanted to set his grandson on the Malla throne. What did Karan gain from an alliance with Nakul? He had no sons.

"Are your cousins married?" I queried Giri. He shook his head, unable to speak. A few years back, Karan had sought a royal alliance for his daughter. I'd no inclination to claim another wife and made it plain to my father.

Mani cleared his throat and said, "He was unhappy about your rejection of his daughter's hands."

I glanced at him. "Is he acting on his own or with Bhoj Thari's blessing?"

Mani observed Giri and answered, "Bhoj Thari's health has taken a turn for the worse. I doubt he is in a position to consent."

Giri pulled his hair on hearing this and ranted, "My king, allow me to behead the traitor's head and place it at your feet."

I met Giri's gaze and stated, "Nakul has woven an intricate web. Now is not the time to rush into anything." His lips trembled, but he nodded slowly, and I resumed my questioning.

"What have we heard from Padi?"

Mani replied, "Dayan sent a message that he shared the news of King Vikram's death with Queen Meera and King Atul."

"Did Dayan return to Akash?"

"No, he was accompanying King Atul and Queen Meera to Malla. I have not heard from him since."

Unable to stand still anymore, I paced the tent. Nakul had executed a brilliant plan, anticipating all our moves and neutralizing them. He would foresee my strength as a war commander. Gradually, the cloud in my head parted, and some light shone through.

I came to a halt and scanned the room. Kapil stood alert, Darsh watched me nervously, Giri battled his own demons, and Mani waited patiently.

"What is Minister Kripa's advice?"

Mani replied, "He wants us to free Surya, to avoid bloodshed. He thinks the man is no longer of use to us." He paused and added, "I don't agree with him."

I observed my father-in-law. The man knew nothing about war strategies, but he knew plenty about people. "What is your view, Uncle Mani?"

He took a breath and said, "My king, if all Nakul wanted was to free his father, he need not have set sail for Malla. This is about something more."

I nodded, "Freeing Surya is not going to stop Nakul. What do we know about Karan Thari?"

Giri's brother, Shiv, had turned a traitor to the crown, and Giri now wrestled with the disloyalty of another member of his family.

As our eyes darted towards Giri, Mani said, "His motives, I can only guess. He has two daughters and no sons. The Thari house passes to Giri. Devan Biha has two sons, one of whom will inherit the Biha house. A marriage alliance between them is beneficial to him. But I doubt Karan will come out of his shadows. His men swore an oath to the King of Malla, not to him. They will not fight the Malla army commanded by you. So he will use subterfuge."

Giri took a step towards me and appealed, "My king, allow me to go to my uncle. I will crush him with my bare hands and take command of the northern army."

I patted his shoulder. "You are the best commander I have, and I need you by my side."

He swallowed and inclined his head.

I turned to Darsh. "Are you ready for another voyage?"

He smirked, "The last one was too short, my Majesty."

I smiled, "This one is fleeting as well. Strip Kathir and his men of weapons and take them back to the Saral border on his ship. Disembark inside Malla and let them cross into Saral on foot."

Kapil opened and shut his mouth. Darsh's eyes flew between his father and me. I raised my eyebrows, and he said, "As you command, my Majesty."

"Tell Kathir I want to speak with him before he leaves," I said and dismissed him.

He left the room, and I asked, "Can we trust Mano Biha?"

Kapil stood frozen on hearing his father's name, and Mani grunted, "Yes. He was loyal to King Vikram and will protect Akash with his life."

Kapil relaxed his shoulders imperceptibly.

"What is our plan to reach Akash?"

Mani said, "I have brought horses with me. I have arranged for us to change horses along the way, so we arrive swiftly."

"I don't want to arrive in Akash quickly." I longed to be home and hug my daughters and kiss my wives. But that had to wait.

Kapil, Mani, and Giri studied me as I stood tall. "In each village we pass, I want to greet the people. I am their king, and they deserve to meet me too."

Nakul, while you slithered to Akash, I planned to arrive with a procession of people who wanted to see me crowned.

"Uncle Mani, I will let you make the necessary arrangements. I will head to my tent to wash and join you for my meal."

"Giri, walk with me," I ordered. Kapil and Giri accompanied me quietly. Men going about their day paused and stared at me, uncertainty in their eyes. I called out to a soldier I knew and asked about his health. He was injured in one of our previous adventures and could not join me in Sunda.

"I am well and ready to fight for you again, my lord," he grinned. "My king," he corrected himself. The atmosphere changed instantly. As I strode along, more men approached and greeted me. They pledged to me their life and loyalty.

Dev stood guard at the entrance to my tent. Inside, my table from the ship and a chair were the lone furnishings, along with a basin for water.

Muthu paused rummaging through a trunk. He said, "I will bring your bed if we are staying the night."

"That will not be necessary. Can you fetch me some water to clean up? I will eat with Chief Mani Vindhya."

He stood, and I added, "Have them unload my crown jewels and silk clothes. Time to introduce the new king." He beamed at me and departed.

I regarded Giri, "You have proven your loyalty to me many times. I trust you. I need you to have faith in me and follow my lead." He opened his mouth to speak, and I carried on, "Giri, I am going to send Kapil away, and I will rely on you to protect me." His eyes brightened, and he bowed his head. "Go clean yourself up and wait for my instructions."

Kapil stood like a statue, and the only sign of life was his lip clamped tight in displeasure.

His eyes narrowed when he met my gaze. "Jay, I cannot protect you if you send me away." He had been a near-constant companion of my life.

"You and I spend too much time with each other, and some separation will do us good," I attempted to banter.

He raised his eyebrows. I took a deep breath, "I have hatched a half-mad plot, and I need someone trustworthy to put it into action."

He shrugged his shoulders. "I know several trustworthy men we can use."

"This can only be carried by someone that is widely recognized as my friend," I uttered with a gleam in my eyes. "And can act as my surrogate."

9

Meera

"Hand me the dagger," I demanded.

"That would be unwise, my lady," he grunted. I pictured him attacked by the animal and unable to help him. An image of him dead flickered in my head, and a sharp pain rose in my heart.

"I am weaponless, Rish," I protested.

He spun suddenly and faced me. His flared nostrils shocked me. "This is not a game, my queen," he hissed. He turned back and yelled at the animal, his sword raised over his head, "Jump, you beast. I will tear you limb to limb with my bare hands."

Rish stood menacing, and the leopard slinked away into the trees. In the stillness, I could hear my heart beating and his breathing. He took a few steps forward and then stood still, waiting for me to join him. Anger erupted in my stomach, and the reason confounded me. I'd a sudden urge to shake him.

I plodded slowly. Though I could feel his breath on me, a chasm had opened between us.

Gradually light chased away the darkness, and I saw a shimmering lake through the trees. Rish led us towards it, and I dropped to my knees at the sandy shore. I drank the cold water deeply and then washed my face and hands. Dirt clung to my body, along with sweat, and I longed for a soak in the lake. Rish dunked his head into the water and stood to shake his hair. The droplets in them glinted in the sun.

"My lady, would you like to bathe? I can keep watch," he offered. The thought of undressing even partially unsettled me. I trusted him, but I did not trust myself. I shook my head.

"I like to take a dip then," he said.

I nodded absently. "I will wait behind those trees."

"Do you need the dagger, my lady?" he teased, his eyes crinkling in a smile.

"I have no need for it, now that I know you can chase a leopard away by shouting at it," I replied.

He laughed and said, "I won't be long," as I sauntered away.

I found a peepal tree and leaned against its trunk. I picked one of its heart-shaped leaves fallen on the ground and twirled it around. My loved ones flitted in my mind. My heart plunged to the depth of my dread. I imagined my brothers, Nakul and Jay, swords drawn, fighting each other, maiming and killing one another; Atul languishing in a dungeon or worse; Malla torn apart with Biha and Thari fighting Vindhya. Wave after wave of worry drowned me. Among all these troubles, Rish's crinkled eyes and wet hair wafted into my head, and I banished that image. I could not let this weakness prey on me.

Atul excelled in finesse and subtlety. He would find a way to diffuse the situation. I needed to help him by mobilizing the Padi army and be ready to act.

Jay was another matter. He would have heard about our father's death. As any rightful son and king, he would see it as his duty to seek revenge. My first charge when I reached Gambhir should be to send Jay a message about Nakul.

I heard a cry and was roused from my thoughts.

"Meera," Rish called out. Hearing the urgency in his voice, I ran towards the lake.

I stopped a few feet from the water. "What is wrong?"

He choked with emotion, "A snake is coiled around my legs. Can you pass me the dagger?"

He stood in chest-deep water, and his clothes were on the shore, along with his weapons.

I picked up the smaller blade and waded in.

"What kind?"

"A python," he grumbled. "Not poisonous."

As I approached him, I held the dagger to him.

He appeared troubled and muttered, "The snake has bound my arms. I need you to cut its head."

"Why didn't you call me earlier?" I said in a panic.

"I was a fool. I didn't see the creature until too late. I had drifted off to sleep," Rish said abashedly. I saw the shadow under his eyes. How long had it been since he had gotten any rest?

I held the dagger as he taught me to and plunged underwater, keeping my eyes open in the murkiness. A snake, the size of my thigh, crept up his hip. Controlling my tremors, I jabbed the snake. Blood squirted from the cut I made, and my stomach retched. I poked the beast again, but I missed and sliced Rish instead. Blood oozed out of his waist, and I came up gasping.

Rish said something to me, but it failed to penetrate my daze. I looked at the dagger and my blood-stained hands, and a piercing cry escaped me. Fear clawed up my throat at the thought of losing him. *I could not let him die. Someone help me.* I couldn't move or think. I stood rooted in fear.

Suddenly, he leaned in and kissed me. Gently at first and then with fire. My body awakened, and I grasped his hair in my fingers. Before my mind came to its senses, he pulled away and gazed at me. "I am not going to die," he said.

I took big gulps of breath and stared at him. The fog in my head cleared. I could do this. To save him. With that, I dove in. I pierced the snake over and over again. Finally, the python unraveled, and Rish reached and grabbed the dagger and chopped its head off in one swift motion.

My hair spread around me like a feather fan, and pieces of the python floated alongside. I emerged from the water slowly. As my mind whirled in emotions, I swayed on my feet. Rish caught and cradled me in his arms. I held his neck and buried my face in his chest. My body shook from fear, panic, dread, and something more powerful.

He whispered in my ear, "I'm sorry I kissed you. You were panicking, and I had no other way to snap you out of your fear."

"Do not be sorry," I said back, fire in my voice. "It saved your life."

Rish carried me out of the water and laid me on the ground gently.

As he tried to move away, alarm rose in me again, and I clung to him desperately. My breath rasped in my throat. Rish cursed. Then he sat down on the sand and leaned my back on his chest and held me around my waist.

"Are you in pain?" I quavered, nestling in his arms.

"No," he faltered, breathing hard.

In a haze, I scanned his face, "You are, aren't you?"

"N-no," he stammered. I sat up and looked at his waist. The gash was only skin deep.

"So much for a clean bath," he mumbled as I regarded the rest of his body covered in snake parts. He wore only a loincloth, and color rose in my cheeks as I eyed his chiseled frame. Tissue and blood covered my damp sari. It revealed more than it concealed, and sudden embarrassment filled my heart at the sight of my sagging breasts and stomach marred with scars and marks. *Not the young girl he had loved ages ago.*

"My lady, it is time to move," he mumbled, and I looked up. His lips were wet, and I remembered them on mine. A violent yearning shook my body, and I pulled his head down to kiss him. He smelled of rain, and I never wanted to let go.

"My lady—Meera, you are in shock," he agonized, pulling apart.

"Do you think about the past?" I asked, gazing into his eyes. They flashed with untold emotions.

His brows furrowed, and he fretted, "My control is hanging by a thread, Meera. This is not a conversation we should be having now."

What I'd shunned became clear to me now. My love for him never disappeared. Hidden poorly over the years, it now spilled into the open. As an ache filled me, anger surged as well. From birth, I'd sacrificed my feelings and needs. For duty, for kingdom, for father, brother, husband, and now my children. I almost lost Rish to a snake. Did I even know what desire tasted like?

"I don't want to lose you," I worried, rubbing his cheek.

"Meera, I am not going anywhere," he groaned.

"I never stopped loving you," I murmured against his throat. My fingers dug into his chest. *He could have perished today without hearing me state it.* Tears glistened in my eyes.

"My love," he moaned and kissed my tears. "You drove me mad every day," he added, his fingers tracing my chin.

Then his lips found mine, and he kissed me angrily. I responded with equal rage, at the world, at him. Then slowly, the fury gave way to fervor. His kisses traced the base of my neck, and our bodies melded together as a male koel bird sang its mating song. No vows had to be said to make us one. We gave ourselves completely to the other, our hearts beating in unison.

10

Jay

I entered the village seated on an elephant, with thronging crowds throwing flowers at its feet. My father-in-law took my idea to meet the people as a king and embellished it with dancers, flame throwers, elephants, and feasts. Still, it had achieved my objectives. I met the village elders along my meandering path to Akash and won their support. I recruited young men to join my army, and Giri had started training them already.

The animal stopped in front of a mansion, and I slid down its back. The brick building entrances were strung with mango leaves to ward off malevolent spirits. I mingled with some of the villagers waiting outside, flanked by my guards, Karan and Dev. My father and his peaceful rule were a constant topic. Some wanted to ask me about our victory in Sunda. Very few brought up Nakul and the Saral invasion.

"My Majesty, welcome to my humble abode," the wealthy merchant who lived in this mansion greeted me.

I made my way into the mansion with him. We reached a courtyard decorated with local tapestries depicting everyday village scenes.

Pointing to the beaded hangings, I said, "My grandmother had fallen in love with these works and collected several pieces by the local artists." After her death, I'd sent many of her priced rugs and tapestries to Meera in Padi.

"If you desire, I can take you tomorrow to some of the local households that have been doing this craft for generations," he beamed.

I accepted, and he took me to a spacious room.

"This is our most desirable room, King Jay. Not what you are used to."

I smiled. "I have been sleeping in tents, and this room will serve me well."

After he departed, Muthu helped me change into fresh clothes. For months, blood and mud had coated me. Now I covered myself with silk and jewels. I picked a plain gold crown to wear today. The Malla crown, while mine now, was beyond my reach in Akash.

I joined the family that lived here and other local merchants for our midday meal. As I ate the food served on a banana leaf, I listened to their concerns. Saral invasion did not bode well for trade, and these merchants sold their tapestries and rugs near and far.

"King Jay, our livelihoods are at stake. We use the finest dyes and materials. Those come to us via ships. We send our finished rugs and tapestries to far-flung lands."

I scanned the men in the room. Once I'd their attention, I stated, "I fought pirates off our coast to keep the seas safe. I fought off invaders in Sunda and opened new trade routes for your goods. Now, support me in this campaign against Nakul. You prospered under my father's rule. Once we squash this attack, I promise you years of prosperity under my reign."

Afterward, I spoke to them individually or in small groups. They pledged their support to me. I went to my chamber to catch up on my messages.

Parth stormed in, "My brother needs me. I am going to Daya."

"Don't be a fool. You will be captured or killed," I scolded him. With no word from Meera, I did not want him in Daya commanding the Padi army. I wanted him close by where I could keep an eye on him.

He stared at me, lips pressed together.

"You think you are beating Nakul. You are wrong," he raged.

I signaled to Dev to shut the door. He did and came to stand between us, his hands on his sword hilt.

I looked at Parth's bloody eyes. He had started drinking early today. Who supplied his habit? I'd tried vainly to put an end to it.

"What do you know?" I inquired.

"I know that you are a fool," he spat. I waited stoically, not letting his barbs taunt me.

"While Nakul is marching an army to your doorsteps, you are feasting and riding on elephants. I cannot waste any more time with you. I don't know what you are afraid of. But my loyalty lies with King Atul, and I am going to him."

I feared the crown snatched from my hands. I feared the taunts of my ancestors if I let Malla fall into Saral hands. I'd no intention of sharing my fears with him.

"I am no coward, and I have battle scars to prove it," I said, not answering his question.

He smirked in response.

"You are safer under my protection. I won't stop you from leaving, but don't expect me to come to your aid if you are ambushed," I declared and dismissed Parth.

I paced the room, deep in thought. Veer entered and stood patiently.

I glanced at him. He whispered, "Messenger from Commander Kapil, my Majesty."

"Is there a place for me to train?" I asked in return. In an unknown house, I would have to imagine even the rugs had ears.

"Yes, King Jay," he answered loudly this time.

"Get Giri," I ordered to a servant and strode with Veer. Karan joined our march.

Outside, three horses stood at the ready, and we mounted them. We rode at a steady pace, and soon, I heard sounds of hooves behind us, and I glimpsed back at Giri.

We moved past a clearing just outside the village where my soldiers had set up tents. We came to a small hill, and Karan led us up a single horse path. We dismounted at the flat top. I followed him and tied the reins around a tree trunk. Then I walked to the edge to observe the surroundings. The tents and the village beyond it rose in front of me like weaving on a tapestry. A gentle breeze wafted in, and I could see the smoke rising out of the cook fire at the camp.

I spun around and faced Giri, "What are you waiting for?" I asked, unsheathing my sword.

"For you to recover from the ride, my king," he mocked me, drawing his sword.

"You forget you are older than me." I attacked him. He parried it and stuck a blow to my shoulders. The sun shone in my eyes, and I slowly rotated, so he faced it. He laughed and moved around. We were evenly matched, and it reminded me of training with Rish Vindhya in Saral. No word of him, Meera, or Atul yet, and that worried me.

In a quick step, he pushed forward. Distracted, I stumbled and stepped back. His sword cut through my clothing, and Karan blocked him and threw him back.

"My king," Giri howled.

"No harm done," I dismissed the damage. As we paused the practice, I said, "Parth is impatient to leave."

"Do you want me to stop him?"

I shook my head. "No. Let him go but slow him down. Have someone track his movements and report back to me."

Giri looked at me with hesitation, and I nodded encouragingly, "What is on your mind?"

He said, "After my initial outburst about my uncle, I have had time to think. When my brother betrayed you, and you punished him, I raged against you." He glanced at me apologetically and continued, "My uncle argued for you. He told me he would have done the same if a soldier under his command turned traitor."

He eyed me beseechingly, and I said gently, "The truth will come out."

Giri left shortly after, and I waited till his hooves receded.

"Bring him in," I ordered. Veer brought the man from Kapil.

I recognized the soldier who had fought with me before. He approached me and bowed. Dirt settled on his cloth, but his eyes were alert.

"Did you speak to anyone on the way?"

"No, my lord. Commander Kapil sent me with strict instructions to only talk to you."

"Go on, give me the message," I ordered.

"My lord, the commander asked me to tell you the operation is going well. He is ready for the next phase."

I smiled, "You did well. Get some rest today. I will send you back with a message for Kapil."

I hoped I'd judged Nakul correctly. Last time I faced him on a battlefield, a necklace of his mother's protected me. Nothing to stop him from plunging his sword into my chest now.

That evening, I sat in the temple courtyard, watching a play about my Saral conquest. They depicted me as a young warrior, winning battles with just a thrust of my sword. The all-female dance troupe wore bright saris and fought with wooden swords. I watched their footwork mesmerized. Maybe, I should learn some of these steps. They might come in handy in a battle. The musicians, all men, performed standing on the right corner of the stage. Drums made of animal skins and clay pots produced sounds that matched the clang of metal and trot of a horse. Smoke from the flaming torches cast an eerie atmosphere. Melodious music from the bamboo flutes filled my mind with vivid images.

Giri leaned in and whispered, "Prince Parth just left with his men."

Without turning my head, I asked, "Do we . . ."

"Yes, my king."

As the dancers shouted, "Victory to Prince Jay," I remembered the terrified young boy fighting his first battle in Maram.

Back in our mansion, I gazed at the stars from my room. "Veer, I need to send a word to my father-in-law."

I sat at my desk and wrote on a dried palm leaf with a feather tip. "I am coming to the Vindhya Palace."

I added a blank leaf to the front of my message to cover it, tied and sealed the letter.

He fetched one of the Vindhya men to my room, and I gave the letter to him. "Hand it to Chief Vindhya."

Time for my sword to speak.

11

Meera

Everything had changed. And nothing had changed. Eerie quietness surrounded us in the darkest hour before dawn. The nocturnal animals rested in their nests, and the morning birds awaited the sun to rise.

Rish cleared his throat and said, "My lady, we will come upon a village soon. I will sneak in and get us a horse."

I listened to him absently while I dwelled on what happened yesterday. Queen of Padi, wife of Atul, and mother of three children, I'd let my heart rule over my mind. While a part of me did not regret what had happened, the other part scorned me for giving in to my human weakness.

"Rish," I whispered.

"Hmm," he responded, deep in his own thoughts.

"I'd no liberty to proclaim . . ." I paused, unable to utter the word love. I'd a greater claim on me.

"Meera," he said my name as if tasting snow for the first time. I could not make out his face in the darkness. "I don't expect anything to change between us."

"Rish, why are you not mad at me?" I despaired. I'd played with his emotions and still counted on him to keep me safe. I'd treated him poorly.

"How do you know I am not mad at you?" he teased.

He halted and took both my hands in his. "I have dreamt of holding you in my arms and claiming you, body and mind. Never believing it would come true." His thumb traced the lines on my palm, and my skin came alive at his touch. "I will savor the memories from yesterday for this lifetime. And it will remain our secret to be burnt with us. I watched you help Atul rule. He knows, as well as I do, that he has to thank you for the prosperity of the past few years. Magadha needs you more than ever, and don't let me distract you. I am the soldier you send to die in the front lines of the battle."

"Rish!" I tried to admonish him.

He squeezed my hands, and the warmth from his fingers spread into my heart. "Meera, I am the second son of a second son and will never be worthy of you. I knew it then and now. I will die happily for you, with a sword in my hands and your lips in my mind. We have bigger things to worry about."

He let go of me, and I sighed, "I have made a mess of things."

"You are allowed to make mistakes," he stated. "Atul, Jay, even I exalt you, but you are human." He resumed walking, and I fell in step. "The greatest kings in Magadha history made many mistakes, Meera. What counts is that they made fewer blunders than their enemies."

My life would be simpler if I could find a foe in this. Instead, the three kings at war were related to me by blood and marriage.

"I don't deserve you," I murmured.

He laughed heartily.

"What is funny?"

"You are, my queen," he sang. The sky lightened, and he gazed at me with smoldering eyes. My insides melted, and I longed to touch him. I turned away.

At the edge of the forest, he handed me his dagger. "I will have one made, especially for you," he whispered.

I held the weapon and said, "I will dread the day I have to use one again."

"It gets easier the next time," he said and marched into the village.

There cannot be a next time. Not for what happened yesterday. While the fate of Atul, my king and husband, remained a mystery, I indulged in my passion. Rish was right, though. I needed my wits about me, and I did not have time to wallow in my guilt.

Jay must have landed by now and marched towards Akash. I must let him know about Karan Thari's treason. What if Kapil Biha or Giri Thari had betrayed my brother, and I lost him at sea? I'd believed I lost him once many years ago as a young boy. Instead, he had escaped captivity and defeated the Saral. He had fought in many battles since then and vanquished his enemies. No, he would be alive and would seek revenge for our father's death. I had to talk to him before he faced Nakul. I'd read histories of other kingdoms where sons murdered their fathers. Brothers had plotted the death of each other to claim the throne. Nakul had slain his kin unknowingly. I could not let either one of my brothers descend further into this.

A cool breeze wafted in, and I found a rock to lean on. Tiredness overtook me, and I drifted off.

"Is she dead?" asked a voice. I curled up into a ball and went back to sleep.

"She is alive," exclaimed another.

"Seems like a stranger."

"A poor stranger from the looks of it."

The words reached my sleep-addled brain. I realized I'd fallen asleep, and two villagers on the way to the forest found me. I kept my eyes closed while frantically trying to think of a way out of this. Since they did not recognize me, they would consider me mad if I announced I was Queen of Padi.

Before an idea came to me, I heard Rish. "Kantha, I was gone only for a few minutes. Did you fall asleep already, you lazy woman?" he said in a Padi dialect.

I opened my eyes and saw Rish standing with two other men. Rish had tied a turban around his head and stood with a slouch.

"We were lost traveling at night. I went to the village to find out where we are," he told them.

"Get up. We have another ten miles to walk to your sister's village," he yelled at me.

I stood up meekly and covered my head with my sari end. He marched off without waiting for me, and I followed him. I heard the two men walk further into the forest, muttering something.

A crumbling building stood at the edge of some fields, and Rish went into it and beckoned me. Dirt on the floor had no footprints other than ours, and cobwebs hung from the walls.

"I hope you never spoke to your wife like that," I muttered.

He raised his eyebrows. His wife had died young. Why did I bring her up now?

"Please stay here, my lady. I left the horse in the forest. I will fetch her."

Within moments, he arrived on the animal. He lifted me to sit in front of him, and we trotted off.

What I wished to forget came flooding back with Rish's arms around me. Riding on a single horse left me with no room, and my back leaned on his chest.

Anger flared in my stomach at my weakness, and I stormed, "I could have ridden my own horse."

He said in icy tones, "This is not easy on me either, my lady. And I found only one horse."

Ashamed at my outburst, I stayed quiet.

After some time, I said, "You know me better than I do."

"That knowledge is not very helpful at the moment." What did he mean? Did he know how his proximity tormented me? He hid his unease better than me.

I wanted to thank him for many things, but no words formed in my head.

As the sun rose overhead, I could no longer keep my eyes open.

Strange dreams filled my fitful sleep. Elephants ran wild on a battle-field, Priya searched for me, Nala fought with a wooden sword, and two men reached for me at the same time. I heard a voice calling to me, and I opened my eyes slowly.

Rish said, "My lady, we are a few miles from the Padi army camp."

He cradled me with one arm while the other held the reins. For a moment, I imagined a life where I belonged in his arms. I only made things harder for him. And impossible for me.

Reluctantly, I sat up straight. He released me and added urgently, "Scouts will be around. It is best if I walk beside the horse."

He dismounted, handing me the reins. "You may want to fix your hair, my lady."

Color spread on my cheeks as I tidied up. I doubt even my children would recognize me in this state.

Then, slowly a coldness spread in me. The fate of a queen commit-ting infidelity might be uncertain, but her companion's fate was certain. Death, not in the glorious manner a warrior longed for, but a disgrace-ful one. My actions caused this, and I needed to fix it. I knew then what I had to do. *Did I have the courage to do it?*

As he predicted, two scouts rode towards us soon. Rish signaled me to halt and stood in front of the horse, his sword drawn. Even in his di-sheveled state, he made an imposing figure, hard to miss. The soldiers halted a few yards away and peered at us.

"Commander Rish!" one exclaimed.

"Yes, and Queen Meera is with me."

They jumped from their horses and bowed to me.

"My queen, we were worried about you," said the older of the two.

"I want to reach General Gambhir quickly. You can tell me the latest news on the way," I said.

"Yes, my lady. Commander, you can ride with me," said the younger man.

Rish mounted his horse, and we rode forward.

The older man answered. "My lady, yesterday, one of the men with

King Atul reached us. He said Malla men captured them all, and he alone escaped."

My heart stood still. I prayed no harm had come to Atul.

He continued, "General sent a search party and increased patrol in the area."

By twilight, we arrived at the campsite. Tents stretched as far as the eyes could see. As I rode past them, soldiers gathered and whispered to one another.

I dismounted in front of a large tent, and General Gambhir and Prince Rudra strode out. As I approached them, they stared at me.

Recognition flashed in Gambhir's face, and he cried, "Queen Meera!"

Bowing to me, he guided me inside. Rish and Rudra followed.

"What happened to my nephew, King Atul?" asked Prince Rudra.

I ignored the reproach in his tone and decided not to speak of my suspicions of Karan Thari. "The message from Nakul was a trap. Instead of meeting us at the assigned place, a large group of men charged us. Rish took me to safety while the attack started."

I glanced at Rish, and he continued, "For a day, I found men on our tail. So we traveled through the forest and avoided going back to our camp."

"Any idea who the men were?"

"They sounded like Malla men," he answered.

Prince Rudra glared at him and asked in an accusing tone, "Why did you abandon the king?"

That seemed directed at me, and with great difficulty, I kept my emotions under control.

"Prince Rudra, I am the queen's guard. I swore to protect her," Rish answered in a chilling voice. "Both the king and queen of Padi being captured would have been worse."

"I heard one of our soldiers escaped. What new information do you have?" I questioned the general.

General Gambhir, a man of medium height, said, "My lady, one of the king's men arrived yesterday. He said Malla soldiers ambushed them. Padi warriors put up a fight, and he was hurt and lost his senses.

When he came to, in the dark, he looked for other survivors. He found none and crawled away to safety. He is in our physician's care now." My stomach tightened. Still no report of Atul.

"Any news about Jay?" I asked Gambhir.

"Yes, my lady. We received news that Prince Jay has arrived in Vindhya. He appears to be traveling by elephant, stopping at every village."

The news puzzled me. Why didn't Jay head to Akash immediately?

"And Nakul?"

"He is in Biha territory. Our scouts reported only a small army with him."

I stifled a yawn, and Rish reminded them, "General Gambhir, the queen has traveled for days with little food and rest."

Next to Prince Rudra's rich silk dhoti and shawl with gold threading, I appeared like a tramp.

"My lady, this tent is yours. I will have someone fetch you water to clean. Your maid and others from the king's camp are on their way here. I will send her to you as soon as she arrives."

As both men headed out, Rish said, "General, I would like a word with you."

Prince Rudra left us with a frown on his face.

Rish continued, "The queen's other guards were at the camp. I would like to pick a couple of men to guard her till they arrive."

General glanced at me and answered, "I want no harm to come to the queen under my command. Yes, pick as many men as you need."

They both left soon after, and a young man brought me a bowl of water, and another brought a simple cot.

As I dipped a clean cotton cloth into the water and wiped the dirt off my face, Rish called me from outside the tent, "My lady."

"Come in," I responded.

He walked in with yards of silk in his hands. "In a camp full of men, this is the best I could find, my queen," he said and handed the bundle to me.

I stared at the cloth in the color of the peacock feather and asked, "Is this tent material?"

He smiled, "Flag material."

I took the cloth from him. "Perfect ending to my day to be draped in a flag."

He stepped closer and whispered, "My lady, I found two trusted men to guard you while I get some sleep. I suggest you get some rest too. A lot is happening that I don't understand, and I want us to be on guard."

I nodded, and he departed.

I removed my torn sari and draped the material Rish found. One of my guards brought me a plate with thinly rolled wheat bread, bottle gourd stew with chilies, and a rice pudding sweetened with coconut milk. I ate hungrily, tearing the bread to scoop the stew. The lightly sweetened pudding reminded me of the red bananas Rish and I ate in the wild.

Though I was tired, sleep eluded me that night. The sounds of the camp: horses neighing, men talking, guards on patrol drifted in. I woke up the next day, sore and fatigued.

My maid arrived at night and lifted me from despair. I soaked in the tub she set up, letting the bael flower-scented warm water remove the grime and guilt.

I dressed in a sari in the color of purple heart glory and wore earrings and a necklace shaped like the same flower.

"My lady, Commander Rish is waiting to see you," said my maid.

"Send him in. And let General Gambhir know I would like to break my fast with him."

In walked Rish, traces of the journey gone from his face.

"Did you get some rest?" I asked.

"After I left you, I went and trained with some men. Then I ate and collapsed on a straw mat and woke up with the sun this morning."

His face beamed as he added, "A plunge into the cold lake this morning, and I am ready to face the world."

At his mention of the lake, my mind wandered to our last encounter on the lake shores. I reined it in with difficulty.

"I am headed to General Gambhir's tent to get the latest news," I informed him, and he accompanied me.

Gambhir greeted me, "My lady, there is a message from King Nakul for you."

Prince Rudra stood beside him, and I acknowledged both men and took the palm scroll the general handed.

Opening the sealed letter, I read the short note inside, "As long as Padi stays out of the conflict, no harm will come to King Atul."

"What does it say?" inquired Rudra, and I handed the scroll to him.

After reading it, he said, "I agree. Let Jay and Nakul fight this out. No need for Padi to get involved."

He handed the scroll to the general. Gambhir read it slowly and regarded me, "My lady, this is a threat against Padi."

I nodded. "Saral does not dictate to us."

Prince Rudra stormed, "Queen Meera! This is an affair of war. Let men who fight decide what is best."

Gambhir said sternly, "Prince Rudra, King Atul has consulted with Queen Meera in all matters."

Rudra pressed his lips together. "My son, Naren, is held captive along with our king. Prince Parth has returned victorious after the Sunda battle. We should wait for him before we decide on any course of action."

Was Parth still with Jay or on his way to Padi?

Gambhir ignored him, "My lady, before King Atul left, he instructed Minister Drona, Chief Guard Desh, and I to seek your advice in his absence."

My heart pounded. Dear Atul. He had been good and kind and loving to me. And I betrayed him in return. I would face the consequences later. I needed to save him first.

"General Gambhir, Padi will not remain neutral in this conflict. It is tied by blood and marriage to Malla. I want to avoid bloodshed, though. I need to send a message to my brother, Jay."

"My lady, I can find a trustworthy soldier."

"Not necessary. This needs to be someone who knows Jay well. I would like to send the message with Rish."

Shock flitted through Rish's face, but he remained silent. My body betrayed me, and I could not let that happen again.

When I returned to my tent, Rish stood in front of me.

"My lady, I swore to protect you. I cannot do that if I am sent away."

Emotions welled in my heart.

"Rish, I need someone trustworthy to carry the message."

His eyes pierced my heart, and I held his gaze. He sighed with understanding. I wanted to send him far away, where he could not tempt me. One misstep, one look we might share that someone would see, could mean his beheading. I wished I could banish him as easily from my thoughts.

I moved closer to him and whispered, "This is only for Jay's ears. Tell him all we saw on the way. Also, tell him I want Nakul to live. Even if it means Jay gives up the throne."

He opened his mouth in shock. "My lady, are you asking . . ."

"It may not come to that, but Jay needs to know what I am willing to give up. What I am asking him to relinquish."

He contemplated this and stared at me intently, "Do I return to Padi or stay and help Prince Jay?"

Now that my heart had opened, I knew I could not hide my true feelings anymore. Someone would notice one day. I would not be the reason for Rish's death. "H-help Jay," I stammered.

His eyes devoured my face like a blind man sensing light momentarily and storing the vision for eternity. The ripples of intensity emanating from him swept me off, and I struggled to land on my feet. He'd sworn to protect me, and I wanted to protect him too.

He departed soon after, leaving me standing alone. I watched him go, and I let him go, and in the coming days, I persuaded myself that my heart had let him go as well.

12

Jay

The sun vanished many hours ago. In the darkness, we left our horses behind and marched towards the secret entrance to the palace.

"It is just a few yards from here," I said, observing the signs etched into the trees in the moonlight. Almost all of the trees in the forest adjoining the palace had carvings on them. Only a few knew how to interpret them.

"Here," I pointed to the ground underneath an ordinary-looking peepal tree. Dev dropped to his knees and cleared the leaves. Giri Thari and two of my guards, Dev and Karan, had accompanied me on this expedition.

"Remove the jute cloth," I directed, and he slowly pulled the fabric in the color of the ground to reveal a trapdoor.

He opened the door and jumped in first.

"Clear," he said from below, and Giri followed him. I lowered myself into the hole, and Karan brought up the rear.

We stepped carefully on the uneven tunnel floor and made our way forward in complete darkness. I ran my fingers along the walls, waiting for the branch in the path.

"Take the trail on the left," I instructed at the junction.

Rats scattered on hearing our footsteps, and we progressed towards our destination.

Presently, the mud floor of the forest gave way to the granite floors of the palace. I quickened my steps, and others matched my stride.

A light appeared in the distance, and soon two guards patrolling the tunnels approached us, holding a torch.

"Halt," one called, and they both drew their swords.

Giri Thari answered, "Careful. We are accompanying King Jay to his chambers."

The man holding the torch lifted it, and I stood tall as the light illuminated my face.

"My lord, blessed to see you," he mumbled.

"My visit needs to stay a secret. Don't repeat that you saw me here to anyone."

They both agreed, and one of them remarked, "We will escort you." The men who patrolled the tunnels were part of the elite king's guards, so I relied on them to stay silent.

With the light from their torch showing our way, we moved faster.

"The door should be above us," a guard said, halting. The tunnel had three secret entrances: the king's and my chambers and the throne room.

As I glanced up, he continued, "My lord, there are guards in your chambers. Let me go up first."

With that, he climbed on top of the other man's shoulder and opened the door.

Voices questioned him from inside.

"Prince Jay is here," he said as he grabbed the edge and lifted himself. We waited, hearing feeble sounds from the room.

A light appeared from above, and he dropped a ladder.

I climbed up into my bedroom after Dev and scanned the room. The four-poster bed made of satinwood and covered with luxurious silk sheets stood in the center. Swords and shields presented to me by kings and noblemen for defeating their enemies decorated the walls.

In the middle of the room, four guards stood on a tiger skin rug, watching me. I regarded them and said, "I cannot stay long. My visit today needs to remain under the sack. Fetch Somu for me."

Karan climbed through the door last and closed it behind him.

I wandered to my dining room. A faint light from a floor lamp illuminated portraits of Malla kings on the wall. I glanced at the portrait of my father on the Malla throne and my younger self standing next to him.

I tightened my grip on the hilt of my sword. Nakul would pay for killing him using a coward's weapon.

I heard footsteps and spun around.

"Prince Jay," Somu exclaimed, coming closer. His familiar face cheered my mind. He came to Akash with my mother, Kayal. After her death, he'd remained to take care of me.

I hugged him tightly, almost imagining I hugged my father. When we pulled apart, his eyes glistened.

"What do I do, my lord?"

I said, "Bring Mano Biha to me. I don't want anyone else to know I am here, not even Aranya and Sudha."

Shortly, he brought back Chief Guard Mano Biha. Mano stepped into my chambers, and Somu closed the door behind him.

Eyebrows raised, Mano approached me. "Prince Jay, I thought you were headed to the Vindhya Palace."

"That was a decoy, Uncle Mano. When you seat a man with a crown on an elephant, no one looks closely at the head wearing the crown."

He viewed the men with me. I answered his unasked question about his son. "I sent Kapil away on a mission."

He smiled, "Must have been an important one for him to agree to leave your side."

My lips curled up as I remembered all the times he had caught the two of us causing trouble.

Giri Thari cleared his throat, bringing me back to the present.

I stated coldly, "A hundred men to protect the king, and yet he was killed in this palace."

I looked at each man, and they stared at the ground.

Mano's shoulders slumped, and he stammered, "I failed the k-king and the kingdom."

He gazed at me in agony, and I stated softly, "I am giving you another chance. Fight for me and this land."

Suddenly, he fell at my feet. "My king, I pledge my life and loyalty to you."

I stood frozen at seeing the man who taught me how to fight prostrated on the floor.

The other guards imitated his action and laid their swords at my feet, repeating his words.

Recovering quickly, I replied, "I will strive to be worthy of this honor."

As they rose, I asked, "Any news from Padi?"

"We heard Nakul had captured Atul."

I raged, "With what army?"

His lips drew into a thin line as he said, "With Malla army."

Giri gasped as he pulled his hair. "Uncle Thari!"

I clenched my fist and demanded, "And Meera?"

Mano rubbed his chin, "Queen Meera and Rish Vindhya are not among the captured."

I released the breath I held. With Rish by her side, she would head back to Padi. *If any harm comes to her, I will shower a hundred arrows into Nakul and let him die a slow, painful death.*

I paced the room, aware of the others watching me. Did it affect the plan I'd set in motion?

I stopped and asked, "What does Nakul want from Padi?"

Mano regarded me and said, "I will venture he will ask Padi to stay out of the conflict."

I agreed and resumed my pacing. A rooster crowed, signaling the arrival of a new day.

"Where is Parth?"

Mano answered, "The Padi Prince is still south of us. A mysterious ailment has affected his men."

I glanced at Giri, and he tilted his head. He'd followed my earlier directive to slow Parth down. "Keep him there. Cause chaos in his camp," I ordered. With Atul missing, I could not have him questioning Meera's authority.

"I want to send a message to Queen Meera. In her absence, General Gambhir can receive it as well."

I told him what I wanted to convey to her, and Mano viewed me with his eyes narrowed.

"Can we provide the Padi men safe passage through Thari?" I inquired.

Giri spoke, "Yes, my Majesty. I can make arrangements for that."

"I want it done discreetly."

As Giri and Mano worked out the details, I observed the sun looming on the horizon through my window. Birds chirped as they took to the sky in delight.

Mano affirmed, "I will find a trustworthy man to send this message to Padi."

I combed my hair back with my fingers. "Uncle Mano, here is what I would like you to arrange here in Akash."

His eyes widened as I explained parts of the plan to him.

"My Majesty, you are putting your life at risk."

"It will not be if all goes according to plan," I argued.

He gazed at me and then said, "My king, allow me to submit some adjustments to the plan, to keep you safe."

I listened carefully, and then Giri, Mano, and I deliberated and settled on it.

Afterward, I asked, "My guard perished in Sunda. Did you take care of his family?"

Mano replied, "Princess Aranya visited the widow and her son several times, my Majesty."

I remembered writing to her about his death. She would be the queen of this land and would dispatch her duties well. A coldness swept my heart when I imagined telling her about Nakul's death at my hands.

He'd murdered my father and was invading my land. I'd no choice but to fight him.

Having accomplished what I set out to do, I said, "We will leave now . . ."

Somu interrupted me and said, "It is time for our morning meal. Allow me to fetch you some food before you go."

I gazed at his lined face and kind eyes and nodded.

Two of the guards accompanied him. They brought back steaming rice cakes, spicy lentil stew with eggplant, broken wheat cooked with jaggery, long ripe plantain bananas, and slices of guava.

"Eat with me," I said, and we sat at the dining table, sharing stories as we ate.

Before I departed, Somu applied a tilak to my forehead. "Victory to Malla," he said, and others echoed it quietly. I longed to see Sudha and Aranya and my daughters, but instead, I dropped into the tunnel and walked out.

That night, I entered the Vindhya Palace through a secret entrance.

The next day, Mani Vindhya approached me.

"My Majesty, my astrologer suggested postponing any conflict in the next month." The diamonds and gold adorning him glittered in the light.

"Uncle, I doubt Nakul is listening to your astrologer. He is not going to sit by idly while I wait a month," I sounded exasperated. *Absolute madness.*

"Please talk to him yourself before you decide," he pleaded.

I exhaled slowly and agreed.

A man with a shaved head and well-fed stomach sat in front of me later that day. His gaze darted between a stack of scrolls in his hands and my face for a few moments. An incense of sandalwood burned near us.

"Horoscopes like yours are rare, my lord. You are destined to be king," he said gleefully.

I had been the crown prince for a decade. I did not need an astrologer to tell me my destiny. I stared at him in disbelief. How much gold did my father-in-law pay for this?

Then his face darkened. "These are terrible times for the Malla kingdom," he said.

"Kingdoms have horoscopes?" I asked innocently.

"No, my lord. But I checked your father's. It is a dangerous time for his offspring."

It was always dangerous times when you were the crown prince.

"Can you be more specific?" I inquired, my patience at an end.

"My lord, horoscopes and star alignments only provide a glimmer of what is going to happen. King Vikram's horoscope . . ." he paused and took out a sheaf and stared at it.

After waiting for a few breaths, I cleared my throat.

"Your father's horoscope predicts tough times for him and his children." Unknown men murdered my father. I did not need an astrologer to tell me times were tough.

"Thanks for your advice," I said, trying hard to keep my impatience out of my voice. I hauled myself up to leave.

"One more thing, my lord. Your sons cause you hardships." My eyebrows lodged at my hairline. Sons? I'd no son. *Sheer madness.*

In a few days, I marched north. With a hundred men on horses, we rode swiftly. Word reached me that Nakul traveled towards the capital as well.

When we reached a meadow surrounded by hills north of Akash, I commanded, "Let us camp here."

Tents rose under the twilight sky, and birds returned to their nests in the surrounding forests. The scent of the flowers floated in the air, and I stooped to pluck a daisy. My oldest daughter, Kayal, named after my mother, loved gathering flowers from the palace gardens.

Under the rising full moon, I joined my men in training with a spear in my hand. Swords, spears, and shields clanged against one another, and the din mingled with the sound of hammers and pots.

After a meal of rice and lentils, we gathered around a wood fire to watch men wrestle. The stars twinkled overhead, and we cheered on as friendly fights ensued. This is what drew me out of the palace to go on long voyages across seas and march through forests and deserts. Spending time with my men.

Karan whispered in my ears, "You have a visitor, my king."

I retreated to my tent with Karan and Veer. The barren tent only had straw mats spread on the floor.

Dev entered with Rish Vindhya.

I gaped at him in shock. He placed his sword at my feet and proclaimed his life and loyalty to me.

Recovering, I observed, "Rish, you are sworn to protect Meera. Why are you here and not with her? How is she? What happened to Atul? Tell me everything."

He pushed his long hair away from his forehead and began his tale, "My Majesty, Queen Meera is safe and is with General Gambhir. Dayan Vindhya, my nephew, came to Padi more than a fortnight ago. He brought the news of King Vikram's death and Nakul's invasion. King Atul then sent a message to King Nakul.

"We were on our way to meet with King Nakul when Malla soldiers ambushed us."

He paused, and I drew in a sharp breath.

"I thought I heard General Karan Thari's voice in the scuffle, and so did Queen Meera. But I cannot be sure. I took her to safety and never came in contact with the men who attacked us. Some were still on our tail the next day, so we stayed in the forests till we were safely in the Padi region. Once there, I took a horse from a village and reached General Gambhir's encampment."

I clenched my fist. Thari, Biha, and Vindhya, the three regions of Malla, had pledged their fealty to the Malla king. General Karan Thari and General Devan Biha seemed to have betrayed their oaths. Retribution for such a deed needed to be severe enough to deter these acts in the future. The repercussions from this treason would reverberate for many months to come.

"There is more," Rish continued. "King Nakul sent a message to Queen Meera. He warned Padi to stay out of the conflict. He holds King

Atul hostage, along with Prince Naren. The queen sent me with a message only for your ears."

I signaled to Karan, Veer, and Dev. Karan and Veer stepped out, and Dev moved out of range.

Rish whispered in my ear, "My Majesty, Queen Meera wants King Nakul to live. Even if it means relinquishing your throne."

I stared at him with my eyebrows raised. The man murdered our father, and Meera wanted no harm to come to him. I'd been thinking of all the ways I could kill him since I heard the news. It made no sense. And she wanted me to give up the Malla throne? To a Saral? What madness!

"Repeat it," I ordered, and he obeyed. I thought about her words. I could imprison Nakul and throw him in the dungeon. That would keep him alive. Still, why would she send this strange message? She'd nourished my dreams to rule this land and championed it.

I'd another question for Rish, "How did you find me?"

"It wasn't easy, my king. Till yesterday, I heard rumors about your whereabouts, and I went to the wrong place. But today, both my contacts told me I could find you here. It almost appeared like you wanted to be found."

He eyed me, and I let no emotion show on my face. "It is late, and I know you have traveled far in the last few days. But you cannot halt here tonight. Leave immediately and return to protecting my sister," I commanded.

He stared at the ground and mumbled, "Queen Meera wanted me to stay with you."

"What? Are you crazy? We cannot leave her alone in Padi. Go back to her."

He gazed at me with a haunted look. *What demons was he fighting?* "My Majesty, Queen Meera's orders were clear. She requested I remain with you."

I asked him gently, "Should I overrule her? And send you back?"

He shook his head with a sigh. "No, King Jay."

I did not have time tonight to worry about this. "Go find Giri Thari and tell him about his uncle. And get some food and rest." He bowed and left.

Karan and Veer came in and claimed two mats. I sat on the remaining one, my mind playing through the various scenarios.

Dev urged me, "Get some rest, my Majesty."

I laid on the mat and closed my eyes. Warm hands raked through my hair, and soft lips caressed mine.

Rough hands shook my shoulder, and a voice whispered, "King Jay."

I opened my eyes and noticed my guards stood with drawn swords. I jumped up and tied my sash around my waist, and picked up my weapon.

As my mind awakened, I heard the sound of horses drawing near. I stepped outside and joined my men as a small dust cloud floated into view.

Nakul appeared at the head with General Devan Biha.

"Prince Jay, we can avoid bloodshed if you surrender," he crowed.

I stared at his sunken eyes and thin drawn face in shock.

13

Meera

Surrounded by a camp full of soldiers, loneliness swamped my heart. I visited a Goddess Parvati temple yesterday to pray for the men in my life: my brothers, my husband, and the man I needed to forget.

A messenger from Minister Drona had arrived yesterday. He brought a scroll from Nala. My son described his brother, Amar, walking a few steps holding his sister's hand, Priya and Rima running off with his sword, and his lessons with Chief Guard Desh. Reading his words intensified my longing to return to Daya and my children.

This morning dawned to a clear sky, mocking my trepidations and fears. My maid put my hair up in a bun and clasped it with a pearl hairpin. Atul liked pearls in my hair. He once described it as many moons shining in my dark tresses.

A guard announced himself outside my tent, and my maid let him in.

"Queen Meera, a messenger from Prince Parth has arrived, and General Gambhir requests your presence."

I accompanied him to the council tent. Raised voices greeted me as I entered. General Gambhir and Uncle Rudra stood across from each other with a round mango wood table in the middle. Seeing me, they grew quiet, and the general bowed. My eyes darted between the two men.

"General, I heard a message arrived from Prince Parth."

"Yes, my lady," he said and handed me a scroll.

I read the words noting the handwriting was my brother-in-law's.

"After our long and victorious campaign in Sunda, our men and I were looking forward to returning home. Then, news of King Atul reached me. Since hearing of his father's death, Prince Jay appears unwell of body and mind. Instead of aiding the search for my brother, he has been wasting time on feasts and festivals. I will advise Padi to stay out of this struggle for the Malla throne and focus on getting our king back. We have shed enough blood to protect Magadha."

With a grim expression, I handed it back to the general.

"General Gambhir, what do you suggest we do?"

"My lady, Prince Jay's actions remain a mystery to me. But he has led several victorious offenses over the years, and I don't doubt his acumen. King Atul wanted to side with Malla and his brother-in-law. I suggest —"

Uncle Rudra interrupted angrily, leaning his palms on the table. "My nephew, Atul, is held captive by King Nakul. I cannot condone any action that is a threat to Atul's life."

He glared at me, and I replied calmly, "Uncle Rudra, keeping Atul safe is my priority as well."

And keeping my brothers safe. Fear twisted my stomach. Had Rish reached Jay? Would Jay listen to him?

Turning to the general, I asked, "Any word from Commander Rish?"

"None yet, my lady," he answered. He continued, "My lady, word of King Atul's capture will have reached Prince Jay. I suggest we wait for a message from him or Commander Rish before moving the troops."

Prince Rudra grunted his disapproval. Ignoring him, General Gambhir added, "I am taking the necessary steps to leave swiftly. My lady, a battlefield is no place for a queen. It will be safer for you to return to Daya."

Before he could continue, I asserted, "No, General. I am not leaving till I can ascertain King Atul's safety." He regarded me and did not contest my statement.

We did not have to wait long to hear from Jay. In a few days, a messenger arrived from him. General Gambhir brought the young man to my tent as night descended upon us. A five-wick brass lamp cast a dim light about us. The frangipani scented oil spread a sweet earthy aroma around the chamber.

He scanned the room, and approached me, and bowed.

"My lady, King Jay instructed me to deliver this to you privately." *King Jay!* On hearing it, my heart stood still. I'd sent a message through Rish to ask him to give up the throne. Jay had been raised since birth to assume the crown. How could I have sent a dispatch like that without thinking through what it meant for him?

"Go ahead. General Gambhir can hear it as well," I answered, controlling my tremors.

The man started narrating what Jay required us to do, and the general and I gaped at each other.

After he left, the general stayed to discuss it with me.

"This requires stealth, my lady." I nodded. "I will send a large contingent back to Daya with Prince Rudra. Please consider traveling with them. Then I can arrange for smaller groups to travel to Malla as Prince Jay instructed."

I shook my head. "General, here is what I would like to do," I stated my plan.

He listened closely and protested, "My lady, you and King Atul welcomed a nobody like me into the royal world and treated me as an equal. I will do everything in my power to bring King Atul back. But I cannot jeopardize your safety, and I cannot guarantee it in Malla."

I persisted and won him over after a lengthy discussion. Images of Nakul and Jay, with their swords held at each other's throats, erupted in my mind, along with Atul in chains.

The next day, General Gambhir dismantled the tents. Word traveled fast through the camp that we were heading back to Daya. All my supplies were loaded onto carts, and my maid traveled with them. I stepped into my horse-drawn carriage as before, and a long procession set off, along with Prince Rudra and others.

As we stopped to water the horses, my maid switched places with me in the carriage. Dressed in my silk saree and jewels, she appeared to be the queen through the curtains. I changed into a man's clothes and turban and hid behind some trees.

As the procession left for Daya, my guards and I rode our horses south to Thari.

14

Jay

Once I'd idolized Nakul as the paragon of royalty. The man in front of me seemed a husk of his former self. Unkempt hair and an overgrown beard could be excused on a battleground. Muck and dirt had covered me for days in Sunda as I fought wars deep in the jungle. His thin body and wasted muscles told a different story. One of neglect. Maybe Meera was right. I might not need to kill this man. He seemed partially dead already.

"I don't want to kill you, Jay," he rasped. "Drop your weapons and surrender."

I scanned the crowd in front of me. Devan Biha avoided my eyes. *Traitor!* But I found my object. Hidden behind a grey mustache and beard, a pair of eyes peeped at me for a brief moment.

I thundered at Nakul, "I spared your life for Aranya once. I won't make that blunder twice. I am not going down without a fight."

He sneered, "You are still wearing my mother's chain. If not for that and Aranya, you would be dead by now. Don't provoke me."

I lifted my sword above my shoulders and taunted, "My sword is thirsty for blood. Come and quench it."

We stared at each other across the distance, our men watching us.

He raised his spear in his left hand and pointed at me. "Attack," he yelled.

Momentary panic stabbed me. Was I foolish to gamble the lives of my soldiers on my insane plan? I took a deep breath to calm the storm raging in my head. With a gesture, I motioned my men to hold their ground, and they followed my command.

Confusion erupted on the other side. A few men rode forward and were stuck by spears thrown at them. Cries reached us as we watched men collapse. Alive a few moments ago and now fallen on the ground and trampled by the horses.

I leaned forward to peer across and tightened my grip on my hilt. Swords cut through bodies, and blood rained on the ground. A storm swirled around Nakul as he fought like a man possessed. I scanned the field, and I found the man I sought surrounded by Saral men. In terror, I realized I'd waited too long to enter the fray. I stepped a few paces forward and turned to face my army. "Soldiers, let us avenge the death of King Vikram and restore Malla glory." I raised my sword in the air, and it glinted like molten gold. I glanced at Giri and tilted my head. With a shout, he guided our force on foot to join the fight. Dust rose into the air as we entered the fray.

Donning the memory of my father as my armor, I fought in a trance. I sliced a man's neck in one sweep and plunged my weapon into another. An arrow stabbed into my right waist, and I staggered in pain. Clamping my lips, I snapped its tail.

A battle-ax came swinging at me, and I blocked it with my shield. Gritting my teeth, I switched my sword to my left hand, and I chopped my way forward. Crimson blood splattered on my clothes.

Karan and Dev flanked me, watching my back and deflecting blades. A spear headed for Dev's back. *Only a coward attacked a soldier's back.* I uttered a curse and pushed Dev aside, and the spear landed on the ground with a thud. With a side glance, I saw Dev getting to his feet.

I scanned the field. Rish and Giri advanced steadily towards Nakul, leaving a trail of bodies on the grass.

It ended as rapidly as it began. We had slaughtered the remaining Saral army.

Nakul and Devan sat alone on their horses surrounded by Malla men, the Saral forces decimated. I wanted to order my men to shower them with hundreds of arrows and spears. Punish them for slaying my father. I suppressed the rage coursing through my blood and marched forward to meet them.

Devan stared at the ground, and Nakul stared at me, dazed. Slowly, understanding sprung, and anger crept into his eyes. Along with a mad gleam.

He screamed, "Devan, you betrayed me!"

Devan choked, "No, my king. I would never . . ."

I offered, "Never betray your oath?"

He glanced at me in fear. "Malla men under you remembered their oath to the King of Malla."

I searched among the soldiers and found my friend. He came forward with his drawn sword coated in blood.

When he arrived alongside Nakul, he took off his disguise.

Devan blurted, "Kapil!"

He hissed, "Uncle Devan."

Devan faltered, "You turned my men against me."

He shook his head. "I reminded them of their vow."

Nakul's eyes flew between them, and he exploded, "You fool. You let your nephew ruin our plans."

I commanded, "Put them in chains and take them away."

My men dragged Nakul away while he shouted curses.

Devan trembled, "My lord. I made a mistake because of my love for my daughter and grandson."

I ignored him and turned to the men of the Northern command who had butchered the Saral men.

"Soldiers, you shed your blood today to defend Malla. Your valor will not be forgotten. Victory to Malla."

Chorus echoed, "Victory to Malla. Victory to King Jay."

I walked back to my tent with Kapil and waved at Giri and Rish to join us.

A physician arrived to treat our wounds. I waited for him to clean and wrap our injuries.

Once alone, I asked, "Where is Atul? Is he safe?"

Kapil said, "He is safe. I replaced his guards with men faithful to us." Then, he mentioned the location Devan kept him.

"Dayan?" I asked about Sudha's brother.

"He is held with King Atul," Kapil stated.

I said, "Rish, start immediately to free them and bring them to Akash. Take enough men with you." He hesitated and opened his mouth to say something. As I raised my eyebrows, he whispered in my ears, "Please remember Queen Meera's words about King Nakul, my Majesty." He bowed and departed.

"Giri, send a message to Meera."

They left me alone with Kapil.

"Kapil, tell me all that happened since you left me."

He narrated, "My Majesty, after I left you, I made contact with my brother, Puri. He told me many Biha family members opposed Nakul's invasion. They worried about Biha's place in Malla. Using his help, I met with many of them in secret. My uncle, Devan, had spread rumors that you were hurt in Sunda. I told them the truth about our Sunda campaign and that you are back in Malla to claim your throne. Your ask was simple. Don't lift the sword against a Malla king. That made it easy for me to win over my family's support."

I snorted, "My ask? I have seen an entire army cower under your glare. If you walked in with your swords drawn, I am sure they fell at your feet, begging for mercy."

He laughed, and that erased the weariness from his face. "Your prowess on a battlefield is better known than mine."

"Where is Karan Thari? Why is he not here? How did Devan get the Northern troops to follow him?"

Kapil shrugged his shoulders. "I never saw General Karan, my Majesty. One of the men who served under him told me he went to stop an attack from the North. His men came back with King Atul. He never did. Devan had spread the same lies among the Northern troops that you were wounded and that King Atul wanted to capture Malla. And the falsehood that King Nakul was fighting on your side to defend Malla."

They were both my brothers-in-law. It would not be difficult to twist who allied with me.

"With the help of Puri, I took a Northern commander into confidence, and he helped me infiltrate the camp. I talked to the men and found who were loyal to you."

He paused and looked at me with a strange glint.

"What?" I asked.

He answered, "I have not left your side in years. Talking to regular soldiers, without being known as your friend and guard, I learned many things. The fighters in the Northern command had fought beside you in many wars. At campfires, these men regale each other with stories about you. They have all been on at least one of your expeditions. You had shared a meal with them, or trained with them, or led them in battles. You are a living legend to them."

"Tales grow in the telling, Kapil."

He eyed me intently. "I know you better than most, my Majesty. While I doubt you killed anyone with a scowl, the rest of the accounts sounded close to the truth. These men believe in you. They derive a great sense of pride in following you. With their honor at stake, they are true to you and willing to die for you."

They also entrusted me to keep this land and its people safe. I straightened my shoulders.

Kapil continued, "Slowly, I planted seeds among Nakul's trusted men, knowing it would reach his ears. He erupted when he heard about your procession atop an elephant. Even Devan feared his temper. My cautious uncle would not have moved hastily to come and capture you here. I'd spread the word among the Saral commanders that you had become complacent, and it would be easy to seize you. Nakul raged like a chained dog, howling at everyone, and my uncle relented to come here.

He did not know I'd turned the northern unit commanders against him. Devan wanted to keep it under the sack about your presence. The ordinary soldiers did not realize they were being led to fight against you. On the way here, I let it slip, and they were ready to behead Devan immediately. I cajoled them to wait until I gave my signal."

I clapped him on his shoulder. "I am not one for prayers. But I must have committed many good deeds in my past lives to deserve a friend like you."

"The honor is mine," he said solemnly.

"My father? Did you find out how they poisoned him?" I whispered.

He shook his head. "It is a closely kept secret. Probably only known to Nakul."

I rubbed my forehead. "Devan Biha committed treason," I muttered.

He agreed, "Knowing fully well the punishment. Serve him the king's justice, my Majesty."

I paced the room. Nakul's actions bothered me. Why invade Malla? Why capture Atul?

"What happened to Nakul?"

Kapil mused, "He hates you. I don't know why, but he hates you. That hate has driven him mad. My uncle tried his best to keep Nakul isolated, but Puri had seen and heard enough."

Why would Nakul despise me? Why did Meera want me to keep him alive? I'd been away from Malla, sailing the seas for many years. Away from the royal games. I rubbed the bridge of my nose.

Giri returned. "King Jay, I dispatched a messenger to Queen Meera."

I nodded. "Giri, your uncle is missing. Find out what happened to him."

"Missing?" he asked, his eyes darting between us.

Kapil replied, "I never saw Karan Thari, and I'd been busy with other matters to pursue it."

I added, "Devan was spreading rumors about King Atul and me. He convinced some of the northern troops that I was injured, and King Atul rode south to seize Malla."

Hope grew in Giri's eyes. He mumbled, "My uncle may have been misled."

I dismissed him to get to the bottom of this.

Dev entered. "Some of the Northern commanders want to speak to you, my Majesty. They want to affirm their loyalties to you and Malla."

"Send them in."

A group strode in anxiously and bowed to me. "Our king, General Devan had assured us we were heading to Akash to defend it. If we knew he brought us to fight you, we would have killed him as a traitor."

I regarded them and said, "Kapil informed me about what happened. You fulfilled your oath faithfully."

They relaxed visibly on hearing my words.

"Would you like to join me for my meal?" I asked, and they agreed readily.

We headed to a large tent, and I sat down with them to eat boiled rice and lentils seasoned with salt and black pepper. The men shared their stories, and I listened and asked questions.

Afterward, I headed to see Nakul with Kapil. His hands and legs were in chains, and his sunken eyes glared at us.

"Remove his hand chains," I ordered, and a guard untied it.

He rubbed his hands as I approached. "Nakul," I started, and he spat at me. It landed near my feet, and I glanced at it. Kapil pulled out his dagger, and I shook my head. I regarded the man in front of me coldly.

I stormed, "You poisoned my father and brought your men to invade my land."

He snarled, "My father has been rotting in your dungeons."

I replied quietly, "I captured him in war. I did not send an assassin to kill him."

He sneered, "I helped you then, like a fool."

I snapped, "You chose peace and prosperity, which is what you have had the past decade."

His face grew dark. "Peace? I have never had peace." Hatred brought his face to life.

My hands itched to draw my sword and cut him down. I remembered Meera's strange request to protect his life. I clenched my fist. "Why attack now?"

"Why? Because the time was ripe," he crowed.

15

Meera

We left our horses in Padi and crossed into Malla on half a dozen bullock carts. Two bulls pulled each of the four-wheeled carriages. The soldiers loaded rolls of carpet into the cloth-covered wagons while singing a song about playing in the snowfall. Bells adorned the horns of the bulls, and they chimed as the animals shook their heads. When they rang, the soldiers sang the chorus.

"Join us, my lady," urged a young man.

I chanted a couple of lines of the melody while they hummed. I relished the simple music.

We appeared like normal merchants bringing woolen rugs to sell in Malla. Colorful embroidery embellished the plain cloth tops of our carts, evoking the intricate patterns in the Padi rugs. They reminded me of my grandmother's collection, some of which adorned my floor now.

Our colorful procession made slow progress. The animals only traveled a few miles from sunrise to sunset. We then slept in the wagons at night after watering and feeding the beasts and ourselves. While other men shared their carriages, I'd one to myself, and I unrolled the carpets and slept on top of them.

I sat in a different vehicle each day and talked to the soldier driving it. I learned about where they came from and their families back home. Some of them were young men who cherished departing Padi for the first time, while others were veterans who had served their king for many years.

"My lady, the last few years, we got good rains, and farmers are happy, and food is plenty. These young men itch for a fight, but I prefer to be fat and home," said one of the older men with children and a wife in Daya.

"I want to be home with my kids, too," I remarked.

"My lady, kings send their daughters away as brides to prevent kingdoms fighting. Why is King Nakul fighting his own brother-in-law?"

Worse. He is fighting his own brother. I did not know what had fueled Nakul's enmity. I prayed that my brothers would live for many years and rule their lands peacefully.

"I don't know why. I do know it is not good for our kingdom to be fighting with each other."

"I fought alongside Prince Jay, my lady, when he destroyed the pirates raiding our seas. He took good care of us, and I have never seen a better swordsman. He will be a good king for Malla."

Without Atul by me, I'd developed a kinship with my travel companions while we slept under the stars. These men were almost like my brothers after traveling together for just a few days. Men who had fought together shared a deeper bond that I could only imagine. Most men who had served Jay revered him. They had elevated him to a war legend, and that adulation was good for a new king. He also needed reliable men who would tell him if he was wrong. He had that in Kapil.

One night, as we sat under a half-moon sky and ate a simple meal of roasted yams, we heard the sound of a barnyard owl hoot. The men touched their daggers and knives hidden in their clothes.

"That is our signal," one young man whispered.

"It is. Go and find out," ordered another.

He left and quickly brought along a messenger from General Gambhir. The man walked with a limp, and a scar ran from his eyebrow to his chin.

He joined us around the fire and accepted some food.

"My lady, King Atul is safe," he said, and my hands shook as I set my food down. Tears gathered in my eyes, and I took a deep breath.

Slowly finding my voice, I took a gold coin from my pouch and offered it to him. "You have the gratitude of a queen and the entire kingdom."

He accepted it and continued, "My lady, King Jay sent a messenger. He has captured King Nakul and sent Commander Rish to free King Atul. Some of General Gambhir's men are headed that way, too."

Jay and Nakul are safe. The tears threatened to spill down my cheeks. I wiped my eyes discreetly with my finger.

"General Gambhir asked me to guide you to King Atul."

I lost interest in the food and said, "I want us to leave before dawn. Let us get some rest."

The air remained still, and insects hummed around the lantern hung under the wagon. Sleep eluded me as the knots in my stomach unwound. With Atul safe and my brothers alive, the worries I held slowly dissipated. A prolonged war between the three kings would have ruined Magadha.

I had decided to reveal the story of Nakul's birth to Jay. My father had groomed Jay to rule. Jay would not make any hasty decisions about relinquishing the throne to his older brother. He deserved to hear the truth before he sat on the throne.

Moments later, I changed my mind. With Nakul imprisoned, why burden Jay with the truth now? What if he decided to abdicate the throne? Wouldn't Malla deserve Jay as their ruler?

Amongst all of this, a tiny part of me fretted about meeting Rish again. With my weakness known to me, the only option would be to avoid any temptation. Images flooded my mind of our time alone, leaving me mourning what I had lost. I reached for my sari and realized I wore a man's clothes. Letting out a breath, I forced myself to think of my children and Atul and the Padi people. A calmness settled in me as the sky lightened.

We departed soon after. In the next village, one of the men went to barter carpets for horses.

"Get me a sari, too," I said. I did not want to meet Atul dressed as a soldier. The man returned with the horses and a young girl.

She could not have been more than ten, barely older than Nala. She bowed to me and said, "Queen Meera, my mother has her wedding sari that she is happy to give you. My house is just around the corner, and you can change there."

I thanked her profusely and accompanied her to her house. The single-story whitewashed brick house glimmered in the sun. Flowering shrubs planted as a fence in the front yard greeted the visitors. A pleasing fragrance floated in the air along with the buzz of bees. On the entryway, someone had drawn a beautiful lotus flower on the ground with rice flour. Ants swarmed the artwork, scurrying away with rice particles.

As I admired it, I asked. "Did you draw this? It is lovely."

She beamed and said, "I got up at dawn to do it."

Her mother greeted me at the door and welcomed me in. She had pulled her hair into a bun and a few gray hairs shined near her ears.

"Queen Meera, my sari is not fit for a queen, but I will be honored if you wore it."

She handed me a cotton sari in the color of a blooming sunflower. Tiny leaves were weaved in throughout the fabric.

"It is beautiful," I smiled at the mother and daughter. Their kindness warmed my heart. I'd not merited it through my actions. My father's benevolent rule did.

I stood in a large room that served as the main living quarter. A carved wooden chest stood on one side, and some sculptures of Lord Ganesh hung on the wall. A door in the back opened to the backyard. I could see a shed with a couple of cows and a calf. One tiny room to the right appeared to be the kitchen. At night, the family would sleep in rolled-out mats in this room.

The mother led me behind a rosewood screen panel. "My husband and son are working in the fields, my lady."

I stood behind the six-foot screen and changed into my sari. Emerging outside, I handed her a gold coin. She shook her head and refused. "Your father ruled these lands wisely, my lady. We wish King Jay's rule will continue our prosperity."

I thanked her again for the sari. As I left to join my men, I pressed the coin in her daughter's hand.

No crown sat on his head, but many saw Jay as king already. About sharing the truth with Jay, my mind oscillated like a cradle rocked side to side. I decided to wait after the crowning ceremony to reveal the truth to him.

By noon the next day, we rode on the king's road to Akash. Suddenly, a dust cloud rose in front of us, and magnificent beasts emerged from the cloud and approached us. A peacock flag fluttered in the wind, and one lone brown mare left the pack and galloped towards us. My heart skipped a beat as I peered at the rider.

Atul pulled his reins and halted in front of us. He scanned the group, and they bowed to him. Then he gazed at me, and his eyes lit up. I nudged my horse forward to be beside him, my heart thudding loudly, and he reached out to hold my hand.

"I spent many a sleepless night fretting about you. Rish assured me you were safe, but my mind remained in a fog of agony until now," he said gently.

My breath caught in my throat as I regarded him. No sign of any injury. In my mind, I'd despaired that he would be hurt as a punishment for my deeds. Seeing him whole, I felt like I'd been given a second chance. For my life with him. I squeezed his hand, and he brought my knuckles to his lips and kissed them lightly.

"Jay and Nakul are safe," he whispered as we moved forward. "War averted without much carnage."

"Were you treated . . ."

"Yes," he interrupted me and answered. "No harm done."

"What now, Meera?" he asked as his eyes scanned my face.

"I am tormented, Atul," I admitted about Jay and Nakul.

We joined the other group of Padi soldiers, and I spotted Prince Naren in the crowd. He appeared unharmed.

We came upon a field with banyan trees, and Atul signaled with his hands. A couple of the guards inspected the fields and waved to him. He dismounted and held my waist and helped me down. We strode to the trees with his hand on my back, and he guided me to a swing made out of the tree roots. A family of monkeys sitting under the tree glanced at us and then swung up in the trees, a mother holding her baby tightly to her chest.

Out of earshot, he leaned on one side of the roots and stared at my face.

"All I want to do is kiss you and not worry about the propriety of it."

"Is that why you brought me here?" I teased him with a smile spreading on my face.

"I'd other things on my mind, but I cannot remember what," he said playfully.

"You are the king. Order your men to close their eyes," I played along, the tension of the last few weeks dissolving in my stomach, replaced by a pleasant tingling.

He straightened and shouted, "Guards, avert your eyes. I am going to kiss my queen."

His eyes twinkled as he held my elbows and helped me up.

Cupping my chin, he moaned, "Meera, I went mad worrying about you."

His lips touched mine gently, and then the kiss deepened with hunger and passion. Tears rolled down my cheeks as I kissed him back fervently, my fingers on his chest.

He pulled back and gazed at me. Seeing my tears, he kissed my eyes, first one eyelid and then the other. Then he embraced me tightly and whispered in my ears, "Your brothers are safe. You are safe. If the tears were for me, I am safe as well." I laughed weakly, wiping my eyes, and sat on the swing.

He continued seriously, "After I was captured, I realized you and Rish were missing. Nobody knew what happened to you. While part of me trusted Rish to keep you safe, the other part was torn in agony. I raged like a bull, ready to strangle Nakul with my bare hands."

I gaped at him in shock, trying to imagine my mild Atul mad with rage.

"Don't look shocked, Meera. Love can make you do crazy things," he said, moving a strand of my hair away from my face.

My heart tightened. I knew all about love causing one to abandon reason. I'd loved two men, but I stood pledged to only one. Any lingering threads of confusion cleared in my head as I looked into his eyes.

"Did you hear from Nala?" he asked about our son.

I nodded. "He wrote to me. Amar is walking," I told him the news from Padi, and he listened intently.

"Meera, here is what I wanted to mention earlier. I met Nakul a few times. He is a changed man. He tried to mask it, but I sensed his contempt for you and Jay. This is beyond his father Surya's imprisonment. He is nourishing a grudge, and till we learn the nature of it, I will advise you to refrain from telling Jay the truth."

I listened carefully and said, "All along the way, I talked to ordinary folks. They prospered under my father. Hearing their hopes for their future, I realized this isn't a family matter for us to resolve. This is about the welfare of the kingdom."

He inclined his head in agreement. "We can observe Nakul and then decide what to do."

I'd made the right decision to share this secret with him. The only mistake was keeping it from him for so long.

We traveled in silence for some time. Then I inquired, "Where is Rish?"

Atul answered, "After he freed me, he went back to Jay. He said something about his order, and I assumed Jay asked him to return."

I'd sent Rish away to avoid any temptations. And to protect him from my poor choices. He had honored my wishes. A lump formed in my throat at his loyalty.

Atul's guard commander drew up near us and said, "My Majesty, there is a mansion in a mile. We can rest there and head to Akash in the morning."

"Meera, I prefer to reach Akash tonight. Are you up for traveling in the dark?"

I nodded, and Atul said to him, "We will halt at the mansion to eat and exchange our horses and then travel to Akash."

The mansion belonged to a Thari cousin. My mind jumped to hearing Karan Thari's voice on the night of our capture. I needed to ask Atul about the men who captured him.

I sat down with the women of the house for my meal. Banana played a conspicuous role in our food. Rice and lentils stewed with banana flower stalks in a peppery sauce, was served on banana leaves, along with banana flower fritters. Listening to them, I learned Jay might arrive in Akash that night. Nakul would be with him. As Atul advised, it would be wise to observe Nakul and learn what ailed his mind.

Shortly, we continued our journey to Akash. A mile from the city, at a crossroads, I saw a large group of travelers on the road going east to west. A tiger flag fluttered in the moonlight. Several yards from us, they halted. A man blew his horn and heralded Jay. A Padi man followed him and proclaimed Atul's greatness.

Three horses galloped forward, one holding a lantern. As they approached, I spotted Jay in the middle. Unruly beard on his face and his hair almost to shoulder length, he stopped a few yards from us and alighted.

Atul and I got off our horses and walked towards him. As Jay bent to touch my feet, I pulled him into a hug. He enveloped me tightly in his arms.

As he released me, I uttered, "King Jay!"

His eyes glistened as he choked, "I have not had any time to mourn our father."

My dear brother. He must have found out about our father on his voyage to Malla and then immediately dropped into this fight to defend the kingdom. I'd many things to share with him.

He touched Atul's feet to seek his blessing. As he rose, he said graciously, "Thanks for coming to my rescue, King Atul."

Atul grinned and squeezed his shoulder. "It was you who rescued me."

"Nakul?" I asked, and Jay nodded towards his men. "He is here."

Just then, a small army arrived from the road west of us, flying another peacock flag.

Kapil, who stood with Jay, muttered, "Prince Parth!"

As I glanced towards the newcomers, I noticed Kapil gesturing out of the corner of my eye. Dev, another of Jay's guards, joined us as Parth rode to us and jumped off his horse.

He strode to Jay and barked, "Where is King Nakul?"

Atul cleared his throat, and Parth, remembering the custom, touched his older brother's feet. Atul pulled him into a quick embrace and asked, "Parth, what are you doing here? I thought you would be with General Gambhir."

He glared at Jay and slurred, "Sabotage, Atul. I have been thwarted from reaching you."

Jay replied easily, "Prince Parth, I am surprised you are still near Akash. You left me a fortnight ago."

Parth sneered, "More than a fortnight. And..."

Before he could finish, Atul interrupted him. "Queen Meera is with me."

Flushing slightly, he approached me and sought my blessings. I touched his head lightly as he stood up unsteadily. A faint smell of something sour assaulted my nostrils. I considered the hostility between Jay and Parth. They had fought together for many moons in Sunda. What soured their friendship?

Parth yelled, "Where is the man who detained my king?"

Jay said calmly, "I have captured him and am taking him to Akash."

Parth spun, "Is he here?"

Before anyone could stop him, he ran to his horse and mounted and waved at his men to follow.

The moon disappeared behind some clouds, and darkness descended around us. Before I sensed what happened, Jay and his guards followed him, yelling at him to halt.

In the chaos that ensued, I heard cries and laughter, and then something hissed past me.

Atul groaned and clutched his stomach. In the feeble lantern light, his body flickered between light and shadow. I glanced at him and saw an arrow embedded in his gut. I screamed and ran to hold him as he crumpled to the ground. Blood spread slowly, tainting his clothes.

16

Jay

After the battle, we packed up immediately and journeyed to Akash. General Devan Biha and King Nakul were in chains and rode with the rest of us. Devan seemed subdued and downcast. I'd served under him in my first battle in Saral. Now I had to serve him judgment as a king. I rubbed my forehead, wondering what sentence he merited. Nakul cursed vehemently for the first few miles of our journey, and I'd men gag him. If his eyes had the ability, I would have been burnt to ashes by now. They bored into my back, and I tried to ignore it.

The men with me were elated to be going home, and I shared their joy. A young man sang a ballad about a lover waiting at home. Some joined him while others snickered. An old warrior sang of men we lost on the battlefield, and a chorus echoed in praise.

I would meet with the families of the fallen in Akash and write to the ones in distant lands. When I sat on the throne, the decision to fight and the death of my soldiers would rest on me solely. My father had taught me to avoid bloodshed when I could. At six and twenty, I hoped I was ready for the crown. While younger than me, my father had unexpectedly stepped into the role when his father and brother had perished at sea. I wished I'd talked to him one last time, about his early years as a king, and heard his voice once more. Nakul had gloated when I asked about his death. Only Meera's words prevented me from cutting his head off. Why did Meera want to protect my enemy? I'd ways to get him to talk in Akash. Unpleasant ways.

Rish joined us a few miles from Akash.

"Is King Atul safe?" I asked.

"Yes, my king. He is headed to join Queen Meera and will accompany her to Akash."

"Meera is here in Malla?" I asked.

"Yes, my Majesty."

I stared at him, wondering why he had chosen to join me instead of her.

Just outside Akash, at the crossroads, I encountered the Padi contingent. I hurried to greet Meera and Atul.

She wore an old worn-out sari and almost no jewels. Her face lit upon seeing me. I clung to her tightly, remembering her comforting me in the days after we lost our mother. Now with our father gone, I wanted to hold on to her, fearful of losing her and my one connection to my parents.

Before we could exchange any words beyond our initial greeting, Parth arrived. I'd forgotten about him in recent days.

He barely acknowledged his king and queen and stomped like a mad elephant. He questioned me about King Nakul, and before I uttered much of an answer, he jumped on his horse and raced off towards Nakul.

Kapil and I followed him.

"What is he trying to do?"

"Nothing good, my king."

He ranted for Nakul to show his face, and Nakul cackled. A flaming torch threw the king's face in sharp relief.

Parth cried, "You held my brother prisoner."

I watched in horror as Parth threw his spear at Nakul's chest and the force unhorsed him. Nakul shouted something inarticulate and collapsed.

"Restrain Parth and his men," I commanded. Kapil left to get the Padi men under control.

Suddenly, Karan yelled, and I saw an arrow glide towards my chest. In the blink of an eye, I crouched low on my mare, and it grazed my hair, flying into the night. My heart raced as I drew my sword out and scanned the darkness for the archer. My guards scrambled around me, trying to protect me from an unknown assailant.

Piercing other sounds a heart-splitting wail arose, and I recognized the voice. Meera! Was she hurt? I spun and dashed towards her. Another caught up with me, and I noticed Rish's horse burst next to mine.

She sat dazed on the ground with Atul held against her body. In the dim light, I spotted an arrow stuck to his stomach, and blood pooled around it. My heart leaped into my throat at the sight.

I jumped off my moving horse and ran to her. I discerned Atul's chest rising and falling slowly. He is alive! Relief flooded my mind, and I sprang into action.

"Meera, let us take him to the royal physician," I urged and lifted him. She let go and stood. His guards aided me, and I handed him to Rish to carry on his steed.

I helped Meera onto my horse and climbed behind her.

Rish and I hastened to the palace. Atul's periodic moans kept my hopes alive. Meera stayed eerily quiet with her eyes closed and her head resting on my shoulder. Our animals raced to the city fort at breakneck speed. The fort doors were shut, and men with arrows notched stood in the towers. Karan, who rode with us, shouted, "Open up. It is King Jay!"

Several of the guards shined a light on us, and cries went up. "It is Prince Jay!"

The ramp lowered, and the fort doors opened, and several voices greeted us.

I'd imagined arriving in the city as the triumphant son, the citizens showering me with flowers. Not in the middle of the night in this unceremonial manner.

"Find the royal physician and bring him to my palace," I commanded one. "Get Chief Guard Mano Biha. I have prisoners outside that need to be put in the dungeons," I told another.

Rish found men to carry Atul gently to a room in the king's palace set aside for visiting royalty.

"Meera," Atul whispered as the men deposited him on the bed.

"I am here," she said, and she sat beside him, stroking his forehead.

The physician came soon with his assistants. He dispatched the servants to fetch several oil lamps to give him light. Then he gave Atul a liquid to drink. I took Meera aside while two of his men held Atul. Using sharp knives, he made a few incisions, and then he pulled the arrow out cleanly. Atul uttered a grunt, and Meera dug her fingers into my arm. I squeezed her hand and watched as the physician cleaned the wound and wrapped it up in some hot herb mixture.

Wiping his hands, he said, "The arrow missed his vital organs. He should make a complete recovery. One of my students will stay with him tonight."

A gasp escaped Meera, and she moved towards Atul. Dipping a cloth in clean water, she set to washing his face. I unclenched my fist.

I called a palace guard and instructed, "Find Princess Aranya and bring her to Queen Meera."

Rish waited for me at the palace stairs. He must have left before the physician arrived.

"How is he?" he inquired.

"He will live," I answered, and he covered his face with his hand and let a deep breath out.

Without waiting for him, I ran down the steps with Karan on my heels. I met a grim Kapil near the gate.

"Nakul is dead," he said without any preamble. Dread pummeled my chest, and he continued, "I have sent my uncle, Devan, and others to the dungeons with my father and his city guards."

When I thought I'd been clever with my plans to capture Nakul, I'd not foreseen Parth ruining everything. I'd not seen Aranya in six months. On my lonely nights, I had imagined a warm welcome after our time apart. Instead, I brought news of her brother's death.

"Keep the news about Nakul under the sack. I need time to tell Aranya." He agreed.

"Who shot the arrow at Atul and me?"

"We are looking for him, my Majesty. Our men did not notice anyone in the dark." He added, "What do we do with Prince Parth?"

I rubbed my forehead. Nakul had captured Atul, so Parth had reason to attack him. I wished he hadn't because many questions may go unanswered now. But I could not hold him for that. With Atul hurt, I did not want to trouble him with these petty concerns.

"Find him a room in the palace and have guards restrain his movement discreetly."

Kapil tilted his head, and I ordered, "Send men to get Minister Kripa and Chief Guard Mano. Have them come to my chamber."

Somu waited for me there. "I sent Muthu to get some rest, my Majesty."

I acknowledged him. "Minister and Chief Guard will be here soon. I will take my bath afterward."

Minister Kripa entered the room shortly after. His lined face viewed me kindly. "Prince Jay, I am glad to see you whole."

"Uncle Kripa, I hope I can benefit from your wisdom like my father."

He smiled and touched my shoulder.

Kapil came in with his father.

"Are the prisoners settled?" I inquired.

Mano stammered, "Y-yes, my Majesty. I have Devan in a separate cell." Facing his older brother must not have been easy on him.

"King Nakul?"

Kapil replied, "One of the healers confirmed his death and is cleaning up his body."

I clenched and unclenched my fist. Meera's message disturbed me, but I did not want to bother her about Nakul now. I took a deep breath.

"I will talk to Aranya and decide what to do about him."

Mano cleared his throat and hesitated, "Prince Parth wants to see his brother. He is raising a storm."

I snapped, "Not now. Thwart Parth. Or better yet, put something in his toddy to knock him out."

I wanted to wring that idiot's neck.

Kripa spoke slowly, "Prince Jay, the first thing to do will be to crown you King of Malla. I can talk to the royal astrologer and find the earliest auspicious day."

I inclined my head in agreement. "Please send messengers to Chief Mani Vindhya and Chief Bhoj Thari to invite them to the capital for that occasion."

Mano mused, "Chief Bhoj Thari is too ill to travel, my Majesty."

"Any word on Giri Thari?"

He shook his head.

"Uncle Mano, please find out who fired the arrow at King Atul and put his life in danger."

He regarded me and asked, "Do I have permission to question the Padi men?"

"Do it quietly."

We discussed a few other matters, and I dismissed them.

After washing the travel dirt, I put on clean clothes and went in search of Aranya. I found her with Meera. I peeked at Atul and found him sleeping.

"How is he?" I asked.

Meera suppressed a yawn and said, "He drank some milk with herbs and is resting."

"Did you eat, Meera? Join me . . ."

She interrupted me. "I am not hungry, Jay. I simply need some sleep. Aranya has been eyeing the door every few moments, anticipating your arrival. You have not seen each other in many moons. Take her and go," she dismissed us.

Aranya glanced at me with her eyes piercing my heart. I took her hand and strolled to her chambers in silence. Panic stole my voice as I thought about her dead brother. On the way, she led me to our daughters' room. They slept on a large four-poster bed. The silk curtains depicting scenes from a forest hung from the posts.

I sat down on one corner and gazed at them. My youngest Heera slept near me, sucking her thumb. I barely recognized her. Would she even know me? My older one slept on the other end, her hair in a braid. I'd been gone too long. I leaned in and kissed their heads while Aranya adjusted their quilts.

In her chambers, I sat down on a bench and pulled her next to me. Her long lashes framing her eyes, she leaned in and kissed me. I kissed her back fervently, my hands unraveling her bun. I wanted to forget Nakul and our battles. Forget about my father and the crown. I pulled her onto my lap and traced her throat with my lips.

"Jay, I am sorry about your father," she murmured against my chest.

I exhaled slowly and sat up. With one arm around her waist, I intertwined my fingers in hers.

"I bear terrible news," I said softly. Aranya straightened and held my gaze.

"Outside our city fort, Prince Parth plunged a spear into Nakul. He was wounded fatally and passed away on the battlefield," I said, rubbing her back. She bolted out of my lap and stood facing me, her lips trembling.

"That cannot be true," she pleaded. I rose and held her elbows.

"I am sorry, Aranya," I whispered, her grief affecting me. I'd just days ago thought coldly of murdering him myself. What would I have told her if he had died on my sword tip?

"Please take me to him, Jay," she urged.

"Now?"

She nodded. I took a deep breath and called my guards.

When Dev entered, I whispered, "Aranya and I are going to visit King Nakul." He glanced at me and inclined his head. Aranya had shown remarkable courage on many occasions, but battle wounds left a mark. Nakul fell off a horse with a spear to his heart. Many men had soiled themselves in the face of imminent death. I did not want her to remember her brother as a broken man. Dev went off to alert the physician.

We ambled along slowly after him, both drowning in our thoughts.

We descended several stairs and entered a narrow hall. The mounted flaming torch cast the dark stones in shadows. At the door, I halted and gazed at Aranya.

"Let me go and see him first. I will bring you in after."

She nodded and interlaced her fingers, staring at the ground.

Dev held the door open for me, and I went in. The door shut behind me, and I let my eyes get used to the darkness. A feeble lantern illuminated a long wooden bench. Two men moved aside, and the light fell on a dead man covered with a cloth.

I stepped forward and uncovered one end. Nakul's thin face seemed serene, and all his rage wiped out. I lifted the blanket further and observed the gaping hole on his chest and broken bones in his ribs. The smell of blood and rot pervaded the room. In the end, death reduced us all. No difference between a monarch and a tramp. I covered him up, leaving only his face exposed.

"Leave us," I ordered and fetched Aranya.

She entered slowly, her eyes drawn to the bench. A sob escaped her as she touched Nakul's head. She fell on his chest and wrapped her arms around him. Her shoulders arched as her tears wet the cloth covering. I stood beside her helplessly, not wanting to intrude upon her grief. Slowly, her movements subsided, and she rose and faced me.

"I started all this, Jay. I killed him," she grieved, and I stared at her stunned.

17

Meera

I woke with a throbbing head. I'd fallen asleep sitting on a chair by Atul's side, and my body ached all over. My neck creaked as I stood up slowly with my eyes closed. I massaged my temple as I opened my eyes. The sun rose reluctantly at the horizon, and I welcomed the dim light spreading in the room.

As I turned to Atul, I found him staring at me.

"You are awake," I said. I went to Atul's side and pushed his hair out of his face. His forehead burned my fingers.

Panic growing, I blurted, "Are you hurting? Let me get..."

"Meera," he interrupted me.

He reached for my hand and continued, "I called out to you earlier when I saw you asleep on the chair."

That was what aroused me.

"You are hot. Let me get the doctor," I pleaded, worried about him.

Ignoring me, he remarked, "You are still wearing the sari from yesterday."

"I did not want to leave you," I said, adjusting his cushions.

"The physician should be here soon. My servant can take care of me this morning. Go take a bath. Find some new clothes to wear. You can join me for my morning meal after," he said, squeezing my hand softly.

"I don't think you can eat yet. The doctor was going to bring you some broth," I mumbled, lifting his blanket to look at his bandage.

He murmured, "I will watch you eat then."

Blood soaked the cloth, turning it a deep red. My stomach twisted into a painful knot. I struggled to keep the fear and worry from coloring my face. He knew me, though.

Before either of us spoke, the royal physician entered with two of his assistants.

"He is hot to touch," I stuttered.

He touched Atul's forehead and said, "This is normal, my lady." He moved on to unwrap the cloth on Atul's stomach, and Atul halted him.

Looking at me, Atul said, "I am in good hands. Leave now. Consider it an order from your king if you are not inclined to listen to your husband." My dear Atul. I did not want to lose him. I bent to kiss his forehead and went to find Aranya.

Guilt rose in my heart as I walked the still dark halls. Did I cause this by my infidelity? I wanted to go to the temple and fall at God's feet and pray for Atul's health.

Aranya's maid admitted me into her chambers, and I found her sprawled on her bed. Alone, with no Jay in sight. Seeing me, she stood and approached.

Observing her tear-streaked face, I asked, "What happened, Aranya? Is Jay okay?"

"I made a mistake, my lady. I don't know if he can ever forgive me," she sobbed.

I gathered her into an embrace and held her for a few moments. Then, I guided her to a seat and sat beside her.

"It cannot be that bad. Tell me what happened," I said softly.

She wiped her eyes and straightened her shoulders.

Slowly, she narrated her tale, "My brother, Nakul, sent me a messenger a few months ago. He said our father had languished in the dungeons long enough, and he wanted to free him. I agreed with him. Jay was away in Sunda, and I should have reached out to him, but I was torn between helping my father and staying loyal to my husband."

She sighed, and her hand twisted her long braid. Her eyes reflected a pool of emotions. I reached out and patted the back of her hand. I knew how being torn by love felt.

She continued, "I became the conduit for Nakul and my father and took messages between them. During my visits, I thought my father had changed. He rued his past mistakes. It broke my heart to see him spend his twilight years in a cell. The notes I took all seemed innocuous to me, and I never thought Nakul would harm King Vikram or Jay. Then, Nakul asked me to allow two men entry into the palace."

Her hands trembled, and she clutched her fingers together.

My heart thudded. *What did you do, Aranya?*

Gazing at me with guilt, she said, "I allowed them into the palace through the tunnel in Jay's room. He was not in Akash, and his room was locked and not guarded like the king's. I thought they were going to help my father, King Surya, escape. Instead, one of them may have poisoned the honey in King Vikram's chambers. He died because of me. And now Nakul is dead. All because I'd forgotten my duty as a future queen."

My heart stopped. What did she say about Nakul? That could not be. Jay had captured Nakul alive.

I stammered, "Nakul? What h-happened to him?"

She sobbed into her hands, and tears trickled down her fingers. I pulled her hand urgently.

"Where is Nakul?" I demanded.

She peered at me through hazy eyes. "My brother is dead. Prince Parth killed him just outside the city."

I stared at her with my mouth open. Nakul was gone. My father had entrusted me with a secret to keep my brothers safe. I'd failed. Wave after wave of sorrow pounded my heart.

She mistook my grief as compassion for her and continued, "Jay and I went to view Nakul last night, and I told him what happened. He accused me of killing his father and left angrily. My lady, King Vikram treated me like a daughter. I never intended him any harm. But now Jay will never forgive me."

Her words reached me, but I did not comprehend them.

I struggled to form words. "Aranya, I need to check on Atul," I faltered and left the room as she gaped at me, confused.

Somehow, I reached Atul's room and staggered in. Dressed in fresh clothes, he glanced at me.

"Meera, what is wrong?" he asked.

Before I could answer, his servant fetched a bowl of clear broth. I took it and dismissed him.

I sat on Atul's bed and dipped the spoon into the bowl.

"Meera?"

"Nakul is dead," I cried.

Wordlessly, he put the bowl aside and pulled me into a hug. I adjusted myself, so I did not touch his wound and buried my face in his chest. He rubbed my back while I wet his skin. He still felt warm, and I lifted my head.

"Are you in pain, Atul?"

He wiped under my eyes with his thumb.

"No more than you," he whispered.

I sat up, and picked up the bowl again, and started feeding him. His eyes, full of love and understanding, tangled my insides. *I did not deserve him.*

"Do I tell Jay?" I asked.

"Yes," he answered. "He is going to be crowned king. Better to tell him before. No more secrets."

At his words, a heavyweight crushed my heart. I'd kept secrets from him. One, in particular, prickled my skin.

He shut his eyes, appearing worn out. I helped him into a better position and stood. Drowsy, he muttered, "Find Jay and tell him."

I wanted to see Nakul first, so I made my way down. Even in daylight, the corridors remained dark, and torches lit the path.

Two guards stood outside the door, but they recognized me and let me in with a bow.

He rested on a bench, covered with a cloth, lifeless. With effort, I made my way towards him.

My heart stood still as I uncovered his face. My dear brother. What hopes and dreams had perished with him? I wished I'd a chance to tell him the truth.

I bent down to kiss his forehead, and I heard footsteps behind me.

"Meera," Jay exclaimed.

I rose slowly and turned to look at him. A tightness appeared around his eyes.

He came closer and grumbled, "Why did you ask me to spare Nakul?"

18

Jay

Aranya stood there and hesitated, "I let Nakul's men into the castle."

A deep shudder of horror passed through me as I stared at her. "Are these the men who sneaked into the dungeon to see Surya? Did they poison my father?" I hissed with barely suppressed rage.

She stammered, "I-I don't think so." Her eyes grew wide.

"You don't think so? Why do you think Nakul wanted access to the palace? To kill my father and me," I said harshly.

Her hands flew to her mouth, and she mumbled, "Jay, I just wanted to free my father."

"Are you mad? We had a decade of peace and prosperity because Surya sat in the dungeons instead of on the throne. What part of being on the run do you miss?"

Her eyes glinted. "My father has paid for his mistakes."

"We will all pay for yours." I stomped out of there.

With no purpose, I marched through the palace. For weeks, I'd worried about a spy in my midst. The one who had poisoned my father. I'd never considered Aranya would be responsible. Anger coursed through my mind, and I wanted to head to the training yard and try to spend it. Better to wait until dawn. It would be unseemly for me to be down there at midnight.

I ended up on the stairs leading down to the dungeons. I descended rapidly and strode to the entrance. I imagined crushing Surya's skull and shattering his bones. The heavy wooden doors to the dungeons remained closed, and two guards stood outside. They recognized me and bowed. One approached me, "Do you want to see the men who arrived tonight, my lord?"

"No, not tonight. I will come back later," I stated and headed back to my chambers. Nakul was gone, and no good could come out of visiting Surya. Not while anger flooded my body.

Dev followed me like a shadow. He remained quiet, sensing my mood.

I woke before the sun and headed to the training yard. Rish had reached there before me.

I noticed his rumpled clothes. "What are you doing here this early?"

"Sleep eluded me, and I decided to come here instead of wasting my time lying in bed."

"That makes two of us. I have not fought you in years. Have you kept up?"

"Let us find out, my Majesty," he smirked and unsheathed his sword. We danced around the yard, our swords clanging, our feet pivoting, our hands flying, and our eyes following each other. He fought better than most men.

A crowd gathered around us, watching and cheering. Sweat dripping down our chins, we halted, neither prevailing. Wiping my face, I said, "I missed this, Rish."

"Prince Nala will love to train with you, my Majesty."

Young Nala. My nephew had played with a toy sword last time I visited Padi.

"If you are training him, he is in good hands."

His brows furrowed, and he opened his mouth to say something. Abruptly, he changed his mind and walked away with a dip of his head.

My feet took me to the room where the physician kept Nakul's body.

Anger still burned inside me at Aranya's action. And at Nakul for driving my wife to betray me. When I arrived, I'd no desire to see him. Nakul was dead and beyond my corrosive rage. I turned to leave when the guard said, "Queen Meera is visiting, my lord. Do you want to go in?"

Meera? What is she doing here?

I signaled them to open the door and entered. She stood in front of Nakul, his face uncovered. She smoothed his hair fondly, and I stood shocked. Did Meera have feelings for Nakul? It could not be.

She kissed his forehead, and I exclaimed, "Meera!"

She spun around to regard me, her face pale.

I approached them and asked, "Why did you ask me to spare Nakul?"

She twisted the end of her sari and said, "I have committed a terrible mistake."

I clenched my fist and snapped, "This day is turning out dreadful. First Aranya, and now you have talked about blunders."

"I heard Aranya's tale," said Meera dismissively.

I gaped at her, startled. What did she mean? What could be worse than Aranya's deed? Fear clutched my throat.

She continued, "I need fresh air. Do you want to go to the garden?"

I regarded her carefully. She still wore the clothes from yesterday.

"Meera, I came here from the training yard. Let us clean up. Then we can go to the palace pond and take a boat."

She laughed with no joy, and faint worry lines traced her forehead. "This tale started in the pond. It will be fitting to share it with you there."

I viewed her, puzzled. She covered Nakul's face and left the room with me.

"How is Atul?"

"The physician said his wounds would heal in a month. He is resting now."

"I can send men to fetch Nala, Priya, and Amar."

Her face brightened, and she said, "Nala wanted to attend your crowning ceremony."

I smiled, "I will make the arrangements."

We parted in a hallway, and I marched to my room.

Chief Guard Mano waited for me there.

"My Majesty, Prince Parth wants to see his brother."

"Tell him King Atul was shot by an arrow yesterday, and he is resting. I will go visit Parth later today." I inquired, "Any news of Giri?"

"None, my king. I have sent a small contingent to fetch him."

After discussing other matters, he left.

"Kapil, can you fetch Rish?" I asked.

I donned the clothes laid out by Muthu when a guard announced Rish.

"Send him in."

"My Majesty," he greeted me.

"Rish, I want you to head to Daya and bring my nephews and niece to Akash. King Atul's recovery will take time, and he and Meera might remain here for a few months. Is Rima in Daya?"

He dipped his head.

"Bring your daughter back too."

His lips curled up.

"Take as many trustworthy men as you need. Talk to Meera before you leave. She may have additional instructions about the baby."

His eyes clouded briefly, and he stammered, "My king, I don't want to bother Queen Meera now. Can you—"

I asked, "What is going on, Rish? I ordered you to protect her, and you have been avoiding her."

He mumbled, gazing at the floor, "I swore to obey her as well."

I must be the least informed person on this land. *How will I govern when everyone appeared intent on keeping secrets from me?*

I rubbed my forehead. "I am going to see Meera now. I will ask her myself. Make the necessary arrangements and come see me before you leave."

As I strode to the garden, leaves on the ground swirled in the wind. The fragrance of ripe fruits floated in the air. I saw Meera standing by the pond and went to her. She wore a silk saree in the color of new leaves that grow in spring on barren tree branches.

I helped her onto a boat and climbed in. The water rippled golden in the morning sun. Grabbing the oars, I rowed, passing blooming lotus flowers. Their heady scent permeated the air around us.

When we got to the middle of the large pond, I rested the oars on my lap and observed Meera. She sat like a statue, her eyes glazed.

"Meera," I called, and her face emerged from a trance into that of a mother protecting her child. I tightened my grip on the oar and waited.

Her eyes resting on mine, she said, "When you went missing in Saral, a turmoil brewed in Akash. Father's recovery from his injuries in the Lukla war was slow. He worried about leaving the kingdom heirless. Vultures from Padi and Malla circled us, pecking at our wounds."

My boyish adventures led to that nightmare. I let out a breath as I watched my sister intently.

She wound the sari end around her finger and continued, "One day, Father took me on a boat ride and narrated a tale about how he met our mother and won her over. They said simple wedding vows and got married in secret. Before he could publicly claim her as his wife, news of our uncle and grandfather's death reached him. He came back to Akash alone and assumed the throne and married his brother's betrothed, our stepmother Queen Charu."

My heart thudded loudly while my mind raced to where the story headed.

Meera regarded me keenly and took a deep breath. "One day, Somu arrived with a message from our mother. She was carrying a child."

I gasped, and she plodded on. "When our father arrived in Saral, our mother had already given birth to a boy. With her marriage remaining a secret, her family would have shunned her. Her cousin Queen Lata had wedded King Surya and given birth to a stillborn. The two women schemed to shield themselves. Lata claimed Nakul as her own, protecting both women from ill chatter. King Surya believed Prince Nakul to be his son and raised him as his heir."

I spluttered, "Nakul was our brother?"

Tears glistened in her eyes. "Yes."

A lump formed in my throat, and I murmured, "The man I fought and who lies dead on a cold bench is the rightful heir to the Malla throne?"

Her eyes appeared haunted.

"He died hating me, Meera. Why did you conceal the truth from me all these years?" I groaned.

"When Father was alive, I should have urged him to reveal the family ties. That is my terrible mistake," she mumbled.

"This is no mistake. It is disloyalty to the crown," I said, aggravated. The crown never belonged to me. It belonged to Nakul, and I stole it from him.

"Jay, you were groomed to rule Malla. He never was. Father never wanted him to sit on the throne."

I erupted, "What about Nakul and I? Did it ever occur to either of you to ask us? Before deciding the fate of the kingdom and ours?"

Shock and then anger flitted across her face. "Father thought about the welfare of the kingdom first. I agreed with his decision, then and now."

I growled, "You trusted me to rule Malla wisely, but you could not trust me with this secret? Nakul poisoned his own father. He wanted to murder me as well. I came close to killing him. What would you have done if we had murdered each other?"

She said gently, "Jay, I never thought he would attack Malla. I'd struggled with this since I heard of our father's death."

I fumed. "Our brother is dead, Meera. Never acknowledged by his father. I could have been sailing the seas. And traveling to distant lands. Instead, I will have to sit on the throne I stole from my older brother."

"You don't think I mourn his death? I have known our relationship for years. And I could not tell him the truth even when he expressed an interest in marrying me. You are not stealing anything from anyone. You are the rightful heir. And others have given up more than you for this land," she upbraided me coldly.

I looked at her tired face and sensed she had made her own sacri-fices. *When did Nakul seek her hands?*

Something else bothered me. "Why would Father leave his firstborn behind in Saral?"

Meera sighed. "He made a mistake. He thought he could claim Nakul and Saral as his when the time was right."

"Mistakes," I grumbled. "Who else knows about this?"

"Somu and his sister, Thangam, knew from the beginning. I told Atul after our father's death."

Somu, my faithful servant, concealed this secret from me all these years.

Pain contorted my mind. "Why tell me now, Meera? Nakul is gone."

She gazed at me, "Jay, you don't have a son. Nakul does."

I stared at her. I failed at my one solemn duty to preserve the Malla bloodline. "How old is that boy? You want me to abdicate for him?"

"No," she shook her head. "We don't know anything about him. Bring him to Malla and foster him. In time, make him your heir."

My thoughts twisted like a boat caught in a storm. I'd many men imprisoned for wanting to seat Nakul on the throne. When I'd thought their efforts were treasonous. Apparently, mine was the treasonous act. We sat quietly for a while.

"Jay," she said softly.

I looked at her.

"I raised you as a child. You have all the qualities to be a great king."

"Are you trying to convince yourself or me? I have been living a false-hood all my life, Meera."

"Punish me all you want. You cannot shrink from your duty."

I picked up the oars and rowed back to the shore. Nakul's son should rightfully sit on the throne. A sudden urge to disappear took hold of me, and I pushed it away. I pulled the boat in and helped Meera out.

"Jay, I am sorry," she squeezed my hand.

"Not as sorry as I am," I said and left her alone.

19

Meera

I watched Jay leave with sorrow. I suppressed the urge to comfort him as I used to when we were younger. Destined to the throne, he needed to figure this one on his own. What I just divulged called into question his identity. I remembered how long it took me to come to terms with my father's revelation. Jay needed time. With his impending coronation, it was time he did not have. A cool breeze blew from the lake, and I wrapped my sari around me.

I'd another important matter to attend to. I strode to my step-mother's chambers. Among the deities on her wall stood a painting of goddess Durga depicted riding a lion with each of her ten arms holding a weapon. A demon had received a boon that no man or animal could kill him. Gods combined their powers to create the Goddess to defeat him. In a kingdom that worshipped warrior goddesses, why did we stop training princesses in the art of warfare? *I should ask Rish to train Priya along with Rima.* As the thought appeared in my mind, I remembered I'd banished Rish from Padi. I had seen him, briefly, on the night Atul got hurt, but he had kept his distance since. A fierce longing spread in my heart.

Before it could take root, my stepmother called me.

She entered her sitting-room wearing a sari the color of a half-moon. Devoid of the red *Kumkum* on her forehead and stripped of all her jewels, I stared at her widow's attire. My grandmother, a widow all my life, shunned the traditional practice of wearing colorless saris and no jewelry. The lack of the red dot on her forehead provided the only sign of her widowhood. My devout stepmother had chosen differently.

I touched Queen Charu's feet, and she offered me a blessing, "I pray for a long life for the man you love." I swallowed on hearing it.

"Mother, I am still shocked by my father's untimely death. Please tell me about his last days."

She sighed and guided me to a chair. As she sat beside me, I observed the shadows under her eyes.

"He had his mid-day meal with me the day before and appeared healthy. Then the next morning, his servant came running to my room. Your father was found unconscious and never gained consciousness again. The royal physician tried several remedies to no avail," she said, wiping her eyes with her sari. I reached across and held her wrist. My dear father had died alone. A sudden gaping sense of loss overwhelmed me.

"With your brother away, my brother, Mani, lit the pyre."

My heart went to Jay. Too far away to save our father or even perform his last rites as a son. Bringing my attention back to my stepmother, I said, "I am sorry Jay or I were not present to offer you comfort."

Tears glistened in both our eyes. "Your father was very fond of both of you. If he did not reach the almighty's feet, he might be reborn as one of your sons." My father had not led a spotless life to escape the cycle of life. Did we seek familiar places and people to be reborn? The answer seemed beyond my grasp. It unsettled me, thinking of my father reborn as my son or nephew. Do we retain our gender in the next birth? He could be born as a girl. Or a horse.

"I heard Atul was injured in a scuffle. How is he?"

I shared the details of what happened outside the city.

"Two kings dead and a third one injured. I pray Atul survives his injuries," she stated.

My insides contorted in fear. We did lose two kings. My father and my brother. I did not want to lose another.

"Why hasn't Jay come to see me yet, Meera? Has he forgotten me?"

"No, Mother. He has not had a moment's rest since he arrived last night. I am sure he will come soon to pay his respects."

What an inopportune time for him to learn about Nakul.

She gazed at me sharply and said, "Meera, I don't want Jay to rush into deciding who occupies the queen's throne beside him. With her brother dead and her father in prison, Aranya has no allies. Mani has been a loyal supporter of the crown. My niece Sudha is heartbroken after losing another pregnancy."

What she described paralleled my mother and her tale. The childless woman sat on the throne then. Who would be the better queen for Malla? Aranya or Sudha? Jay seemed angry about Aranya's betrayal. But that happened before he learned about Nakul. I needed to appease my stepmother now and find time to talk to Jay soon.

"Mother, Jay will consult his elders before deciding something as momentous as this."

She glanced around the room at the portraits of other Vindhya queens and said, "Many Vindhya women have served this kingdom. Why crown a woman whose brother waged a war against us?"

With the Biha house openly betraying the crown, Vindhya and Thari ties became vital for the new ruler. She wanted me to side with her and influence Jay. I'd been away from the Malla court for a decade, and I did not know where the allegiances lay.

"Mother, I am sure Jay will like to hear your thoughts on this," I said noncommittally. I left her soon and made my way back to Atul.

Parth stood in front of his brother, wailing. "Why did nobody tell me you were hurt?"

Parth had murdered my brother. I took a deep breath to control my tremors. He did not know the truth about Nakul's birth, so I could not blame him for fighting Atul's capturer. Glancing at Atul, I entered the room and greeted them both.

Atul asked me with brows furrowed, "Meera, Parth tells me Jay detained him in a room last night. What is going on? Where is Jay? I need to talk to him."

Parth grumbled, "My righthand man Sarp has gone missing. If any harm comes to him—"

Atul interrupted him, "Parth!"

Atul appeared pale and tired. I sat next to him and stroked his forehead.

Without looking at Parth, I said, "I am sure there is a simple answer to this. I will find out from Jay."

Parth raged, "Atul, I will find out who hurt you, and I will not rest till I bring them to justice."

Atul eyed him and said, "Work with Jay."

Parth grunted and left us.

I whispered to Atul, "I told Jay."

"How did he take it?"

"N-not very well," I stammered.

He patted my hand. "He will come around."

"Jay is making arrangements to bring the children to Akash."

His eyes brightened. "Is Amar old enough to travel?"

I nodded. "I will send special instructions for him. I miss them all. I have been away from them for too long."

I administered to his needs, hiding my concern for his well-being. The physician came midday to check on him and give him some medicine.

As Atul rested, Jay entered the room. His eyes softened as he looked at me and whispered, "How is he?"

Before I could respond, Atul opened his eyes and answered, "I am not in pain, Jay. Nothing more I could ask for at present. Parth was here earlier. Did you confine him?"

Jay straightened his shoulders, "Yes, King Atul. He killed Nakul, my brother——," he paused and added, "my brother-in-law in a rage. I thought it best to isolate him, so he had a chance to calm down."

Atul inclined his head in understanding. "I am sorry for his death. Any idea who shot me?"

Jay shook his head. "It was dark and chaotic last night."

Lowering his voice, he added, "There are too many threads here. I want us to be cautious."

Atul agreed.

"King Atul, do I have your permission to question Parth's men?" Jay asked.

"He is my brother and has been loyal to me. Why do you want to question them?"

They stared at each other. Jay did not need Atul's permission to question them, but I hoped he would drop this for now. With all else going on, I did not want them to clash about Parth.

Jay said easily, "Just gathering information about last night."

Atul muttered, "Leave him alone, Jay. I don't need any trouble now."

Jay acquiesced.

"I want you to take your sister away and feed her. She has been toiling at my side since last night. While worrying about you and me and all of Magadha. And forgetting to take care of herself."

I adjusted his pillows. "How do you know I am not eating when you are asleep?"

He smirked as he lifted my hand and kissed my knuckles.

"After I rest, I am going to have my men help me move around the room, so no need for you to rush back."

"Is that wise?" I asked in a panic.

Jay and Atul said in unison, "Yes."

Jay added, "When I got hurt in Saral, instead of staying stationary, I moved around slowly. It helped me heal faster."

Soon, Jay and I strolled to his chambers, and he murmured, "I apologize for leaving you alone by the lake. I was not thinking clearly."

"I gave you a lot to think about," I said, glancing at his face.

As we sat at his table, Somu set our plates in front of us.

I eyed Somu and mumbled, "He knows, Somu."

"He told me, my lady," he said softly.

He left us alone, and Jay said, "I am thinking of performing Nakul's last rites. His son is too far to arrive in time and—"

He paused and gazed at me.

"You did not perform Father's," I said as I covered his palm with mine. He exhaled and nodded.

"Nakul deserved better. His life was cut short too early. A proper send-off is the least we can do for him."

"He hated me, Meera. I don't know why. When I last spoke to him, he spilled venom. And I gagged him and put him in chains."

He rubbed his eyes, and my stomach plunged to the ground. *What cruelty to both.*

He gazed at me, and the hurt and agony in his eyes caused tears in mine. I wished again I could make his pain go away. But it was beyond me. Only time could heal this wound.

As I stared at the plate of rice and assorted lentils and vegetables, he said, "I am spoiling your appetite."

I ate a few morsels, not tasting the food.

"You look thin, Meera. Atul is right. You are not taking care of yourself," he added with concern.

I changed the subject. "How are my nieces?"

"Have you seen them yet? They both have grown up so much since I left for Sunda," he said with his lips curling up.

"I have never seen Heera," I answered.

"She looks like you, Meera. She did not recognize me initially. We sat on the floor and played, and in the end, she put her tiny arms around my neck and kissed me." The warmth in his face transformed him. I smiled at his delight.

His brows furrowed, he continued, "I met our stepmother. She wishes for Sudha to occupy the queen's throne."

Before I could respond, Kapil entered the room.

"My Majesty, we found Sarp with his throat slit."

"Parth's man?" Jay groaned.

Kapil dipped his head.

20

Jay

After I left my sister at the lake, I wandered the palace garden aimlessly. For years, my father had groomed me to rule Malla. In his elaborate lie, I'd lived as the crown prince. All the while, the real heir had grown up as my rival. For days, I'd plotted his downfall. Anger flared in my chest at my father. He had been kind to me but turned his back on his firstborn. His reluctance to destroy Surya, for the fear of hurting Nakul, made sense now.

Meera had kept the secret from me for more than a decade. She had claimed that I would rule wisely. If she could wish those words into existence, she would. Many wise men had turned out to be poor kings. An overwhelming desire to hide ran through my body.

One of my guards approached me. "My Majesty, Minister Kripa seeks your audience."

With my mind in turmoil, I made my way to my chambers.

Minister Kripa greeted me. "I have a few coronation dates from the royal astrologer," he said.

I laughed at the cruelty of fate, and he regarded me with concern.

"Prince Jay," he said tentatively.

I held the hilt of my sword tightly and brought my emotions under control. I could not change the past, and it would be imprudent to waste my time dwelling on it. I needed to keep my mind focused on the future. I asked, "What are the dates, minister?"

He recited a few dates, allowing me to come to my senses. My father and brother were dead. I'd a solemn duty to protect Malla. No amount of wishing would change that.

"Minister, my nephews, and niece are coming from Padi to attend the ceremony. Please consult with others and pick a date that allows them time to arrive."

He agreed. I never set much faith in astrology. Royal astrologer and his disciples would want me to consult with them for every step I took. Their vague predictions for the future were all based on stargazing. In my view, any day was a splendid day to do good deeds. I needed no horoscope for that prediction.

He brought several other matters to my attention, and we discussed them. After he left, I sat at my desk. I studied some correspondences, engrossed in them, and a voice pulled me out of it.

"My lord," said Sudha as she strolled in with Kayal and Heera.

"Sudha," I said and stood up. Approaching her, I grasped her hand.

Her lips trembling, she whispered, "I lost the baby."

I squeezed her hand. "There will be others." I did not know if I believed it.

"I might be doomed to be childless like my aunt," she murmured. She twined her fingers, her knuckles turning white. Her aunt. My stepmother. I'd almost forgotten her in all that happened since yesterday. I had to pay my respects to her soon and consult her about my coronation.

I put my stepmother out of my mind and turned my attention to my wife. I lifted her chin. "We are both young," I said to reassure myself as much as her.

Heera hid behind her legs and peeked at me.

I went on my knees to look at my daughters.

Kayal regarded me for a few moments and then took a step forward tentatively.

"Do you remember me?" I asked, holding my arm out.

"Father," she said shyly and took another step, and I drew her into my arms. She buried her face in my chest, and I embraced her tightly. All thoughts of hiding or running away disappeared. Instead, a sense of purpose filled me.

I sat on the floor and pulled Kayal onto my lap. Sudha imitated me and sat beside me with Heera on her lap.

"What did I miss while I was gone?" I asked.

Kayal spun around to glance at me and said, "Grandpa is gone."

I swallowed and kissed the top of her head.

Sudha said, "He would play with them. Did my brother, Darsh, reach you?"

I inclined my head.

"My father performed the last rites," she mumbled. My throat tightened, and she reached out to interlace her fingers with mine.

"What did you see in Sunda, Father?" Kayal asked.

Banishing the images swirling in my head, I said, "Your uncle, Kathir, and I found these tiny baby tigers in a jungle. They were smaller than our cats, and I held them in my hands. They loved it when I tickled their bellies." I stretched my fingers and tickled Heera's belly. She giggled, sounding like tiny bells ringing. Soon, Kayal and I rolled on the floor, acting like the wild animals I saw on my travels. Roaring and trumpeting, we enacted the sounds, and Heera squealed in delight.

Slowly, she left Sudha's lap and joined our antics. When Kapil found us, I was on all fours with Heera seated on my back, pretending to be an elephant.

"Uncle Kapil," shouted Kayal, and he joined us on the floor.

Kapil signaled he had some important matters to discuss.

Before I replied, Sudha stood up. "My lord, it is time for Kayal's lessons. I will take the girls with me and leave you two alone. Welcome home, Cousin Kapil."

My daughters hugged me without hesitation now, and I promised to tell them more stories. Sudha eyed me and whispered, "Come join me for your night meal, my lord."

My body desired more than a meal, and I agreed.

"Did you see your family yet?" I asked Kapil.

"I did," he grinned at me.

"From that smile, I assume your wife took you back after the long absence."

"I got quite the welcome home," he smirked.

More seriously, he whispered, "Dev mentioned you barely slept last night." He regarded me with concern. "Anything I should worry about?"

Plenty. I'd found out my wife worked with her brother to murder my father. Only he happened to be my brother and heir to the throne.

I rubbed my forehead. "I took Aranya to see her dead brother," I said as a way of explaining things.

Kapil knew me better and searched my face.

"We fought afterward," I added. He nodded sympathetically.

"What is the important matter you wanted to discuss with me?"

"Prince Parth declared his man Sarp has gone missing."

"Missing?" I asked stupidly.

Kapil replied, "He was with Prince Parth last night, but no one has seen him since."

"What do you think?" I asked.

Kapil shrugged his shoulders. "Sarp accompanied Prince Parth on his quest to get drunk in Sunda. He could have found a stash here and gotten sloshed."

"Nevertheless, I don't want this to get out of hand. Help Parth search for him," I said.

Kapil agreed.

He said, "My Majesty, after the coronation, you will be under the protection of the king's guards. The guards have an able commander today."

I looked at him. I could not remember a time when he was not beside me, fighting for me or protecting me. He proved himself as a commander and warrior many times. Should I appoint him as a Commander for the Southern unit?

"Kapil, staying as my guard seems like a waste of your talent. Our

Southern commander is hurt. With King Nakul dead, I need a loyal man
to command the unit."

Without any hesitation, he answered, "I would rather be on your
guard, my king. There are many able men to lead armies. Not many that
understand you as well as I do."

I patted his shoulder. "I will talk to Chief Guard Mano and see if we
can promote the current commander of the kings' guards and put you
in his place."

I made my way to my stepmother's chambers. Seeing her devoid of
her jewels and the dot on her forehead, I stood perturbed. It brought
the loss of my father to the forefront. My chest contracted in agony.

"Jay, I have been waiting for you," she called.

"Mother," I stammered and sought her blessings.

Soon, we sat across from each other, and I gazed at her.

"Meera came to see me earlier. I heard King Nakul is dead, and King
Atul is hurt. It has not been a good time for kings. We should consult
the royal astrologer and pick an auspicious day for your coronation."

"Minister Kripa has already talked to the astrologer, Mother. He has
chosen a few dates. I asked him to select one that allows all guests to
arrive in Akash. I am sure he will come to consult with you as well."

"Son," she said, and I regarded her.

My stepmother hesitated. Our relationship had always been distant.
During my youth, Meera fiercely protected me from the palace machinations. She had acted as my surrogate mother. Reflecting on it, I regretted my anger directed towards my sister earlier. Meera was a victim
of my father's ploy, and blaming her for what ensued seemed stupid. I
dragged my mind back to the present.

"What is it, Mother?" I prompted. Royal children addressed all the
queens as mothers by tradition.

"Have you given any thought to who will sit next to you as your
queen?" she asked, observing me.

"No, Mother. I have had no time to think about it," I said, surprised.
A few days ago, I would have responded with certainty that Aranya

would occupy the queen's throne. Now, doubts plagued me. I'd no desire to share those with my stepmother.

"My brother and your father-in-law, Mani, has been a loyal supporter of the crown. We need Vindhya support to rule Malla. Sudha, my niece, is a wonderful girl. She is devoted to you and your daughters. She understands Malla customs and will make a fine queen."

What she stated about Sudha had its merits. Unlike her, Sudha seemed to care for her stepdaughters. And Aranya had let me down.

"Mother, I will carefully consider what you said," I stated.

"Jay, if you make the arrangements, I will move to the queen mother's palace," she said with a sigh.

I frowned, "Mother, there is no rush——"

"Son, the king, and the queen traditionally occupy the largest quarters. I don't have the heart to go through your father's belongings. I will let you and Meera take care of it. But I am ready to move."

I dreaded entering my father's rooms. My skin crawled, considering sleeping in his bedroom.

Later that day, I sat down to eat my mid-day meal with Meera. I'd many things to discuss with her. I needed to send a messenger to Saral. I wanted to discuss Nakul's son. And my doubts about Aranya.

I decided to tackle the matter of my coronation first. I said, "I met our stepmother. She wishes for Sudha to occupy the queen's throne."

Before I could continue, Kapil burst upon us suddenly.

"My Majesty, we found Sarp with his throat slit."

"Parth's man?"

Kapil nodded. Parth suspected I sabotaged his trip up north. I could not afford to antagonize him further. Not while Atul laid on his sickbed.

"Tell me all you know," I ordered.

Kapil said, "My Majesty, this morning Prince Parth lamented that we had arrested his man Sarp. He last saw him yesterday night, but then in the chaos afterward, did not miss him till this morning. My father made arrangements for Prince Parth to visit the dungeons, and he confirmed Sarp was not among the men we captured. We mounted a search for him and found him with his throat slit in the fields outside the fort. In our search, we also found a quiver of arrows abandoned."

"Does anyone remember seeing him?" asked Meera.

Kapil shook his head. "None of our men do. My father is questioning the Biha and Saral men."

"Has Parth been informed?" I inquired.

"Not yet. I wanted to share the news with you first."

"I will go see him," I said, and Kapil took leave.

"What is going on between you and Parth?" Meera asked, studying my face.

"Parth is a great warrior on the battlefield. Off it, he indulges in women and liquor. He tended to blurt our plans in the local brothels. I had to be careful what battle strategy to reveal to him," I said with disdain.

"Jay, with Atul sick, you cannot continue this spat with Parth," Meera advised.

I agreed. "When you were missing, I tried to prevent him from reaching Daya. I will go smooth things with him."

Meera regarded me and said, "Jay, on the subject of queens, Aranya was trying to save her father. She made a blunder in placing her trust in people she should not have. But she will learn from it. Sudha is a wonderful girl, but she is not going to stand up to you. You are going to make mistakes, and you need a queen to tell you when you are wrong."

My nostrils flared, and I growled, "Aranya went behind my back. How do you expect me to trust her?"

Meera dismissed my concern with a wave. "You were at war, and she did not want to burden you with this. I agree she showed poor judgment by trying to free a prisoner of war without your consent. But, she shared the details readily with you when she saw you. She lost her brother, and her father is in the dungeons. She needs you as much as you need her."

I remained unconvinced. "Meera, I need to be able to trust my queen without a shadow of a doubt. There will be many around me, plotting and conspiring for their benefit. I want to surround myself with friends and family I can trust completely."

Meera's face dropped. With her eyes downcast, she twisted her sari around her finger, a sign of her nervousness. "Love can make you do something you may regret, Jay. Even if one's loyalty is above reproach."

Words caught in my throat. I gazed at her with dread.

She looked haunted. *Love? What act did she rue?* I recollected the strange way she and Rish avoided each other. Was this about him? I knew he had feelings for her, and that was one of the reasons I sent him to guard her. *Were the feelings mutual? How did I never see it? Did she act on her feelings?* A queen's behavior needed to be immaculate. Any hint of scandal would be detrimental to her and Nala.

"Meera, I need Rish with me here. I can send Dayan Vindhya to head your guard in his place," I said. I could not utter some words out loud.

She nodded slowly. Wordless understanding sprung between us. She had talked about sacrifices before, and now I'd a window into hers. Fear gripped my throat. Did anyone else know about them? Not from her. She most likely buried her feelings.

Tentatively, I asked, "Meera, does anyone else know?"

Her eyes widened. She stuttered, "Jay . . ." and reached out and grasped my hand.

Her concern worried me. Our food went cold.

"Meera, I need to go take care of this situation with Parth. I will come to find you later."

I needed to discuss this further with her, away from the eyes and ears that littered the palace.

I went to find Parth, and he accosted me on the way.

He poked my chest and yelled, "You killed Sarp, and you probably ordered your men to shoot Atul. I am not going to stand by while you destroy Padi."

"Don't be a fool. Do you think I want to see my sister as a widow?" I said and swatted his hand away.

"I don't know what games you are playing. Maybe you don't care about your sister. You prevented me from going to her aid," he snarled.

"While Atul rotted in a cell and Meera ran from her captors, you feasted your way through Malla," he added with scorn.

My nostrils flared, and I resisted the urge to squeeze his throat.

Turning away, he continued, "I am going to see my brother and seek his consent to head back to Daya. If any harm befalls him in Akash, I will search you through earth's ends and destroy you."

With that, he strode away, leaving me fuming.

Soon after, Parth left Akash with Rish and my men in tow. I gave up placating him and talked to Atul instead.

"Jay, he warned me to be careful of you. He means well. And, I don't think you had anything to do with my injury. You love your sister too much to cause me harm," he said and smiled weakly.

Suddenly, I worried about Meera. If folks suspected her and Rish, that would be treasonous behavior that would get him killed and her banished. Nala did look like his father, so questions may not arise about his birth. But kings needed loyal subjects to rule, and a mother accused of treason would not be a way to gain it.

As long as Atul recovered, all will be well.

I made my way to Sudha's chamber later than I'd planned. Brass and earthen lamps were lit and cast her room in a golden light. Herb-infused oil spread an aromatic fragrance around the room. Sudha stood upon seeing me.

"I will ask the servants to fetch our food," she said.

"Later," I muttered, and I put my arm around her slender waist and pulled her closer. Jasmine flowers on her hair greeted me with a heady scent, and I lowered my head to kiss her lips. Like a man dying of thirst finding water, my body acted of its own accord. I lifted her off her feet and carried her to her bed while she moaned my name. As I lowered her gently, she rolled away and sat up.

"Jay," she added breathlessly.

I removed the sash around my waist and dropped it on the floor.

"Jay," she said more urgently, and a blush spread across her cheeks.

I stopped and gazed at her. She looked beautiful in the lamplight, with her hair disheveled and her chest rising and falling.

"Hmm," I answered, my mind distracted by my body's need.

"The physician," she started, and my mind snapped to attention. She had recently lost her pregnancy.

"We have to wait?" I asked, saving her the trouble, and she nodded. "One more moon cycle."

I sat on the bed and tucked her hair behind her ears. I'd waited for what seemed like an eternity. What was one more month? My body disagreed with me, and I ignored the acute ache.

She sat beside me and leaned her head on my shoulder, and I put my arm around her.

"I am drinking saffron milk," she said.

"Anything I should be drinking?" I teased, and she pushed my chest to chide me.

"Jay, we need an heir."

Not anymore. I had an heir. Nakul's son.

21

Meera

Atul moaned in pain, and I held his hand. His skin was still warm to the touch. The physician I sent for arrived shortly. He replaced Atul's herb wrap and gave him a potion to drink. Atul gradually slipped into sleep. After adjusting his blankets, I followed the physician into the sitting room.

"Is he getting better?" I asked, wiping the sweat dotting my forehead.

"His wound is not healing, my lady. Not to worry. I am expecting fresh herbs soon, and I will prepare a new mixture to try on him."

Easy for him to ask me not to worry. My worries had become my constant companion. Atul's health was my primary concern. By now, his wound should have started healing. But his health remained precarious.

After the physician left, I curled up on a corner of the bed and fell into a fitful sleep. When my maid came to wake me up, my limbs protested.

"Prince Jay is here, my queen," she said.

I rubbed my eyes and glanced outside. The sun had climbed to the level of treetops. I washed my face and put my hair up in a bun, and went to the sitting room.

Jay stood with his back to me, staring outside the window. On hearing my steps, he turned around.

"Did you——?" I asked, unable to complete my sentence.

He nodded. "I lit the pyre, releasing Nakul's soul from his body."

He gazed at me with red-rimmed eyes and added, "I thought of our father as I set fire to the sandalwood."

"They will move on to their next lives," I added.

"Hmm," he said absently. "Aranya gave me this chain years ago," he said, pointing to a gold chain around his neck. "She claimed it belonged to Nakul's mother," he said and glanced at me. His meaning sunk in slowly. Did this chain belong to Kayal, our mother?

"This chain protected me from death many times, Meera. Call it fate or destiny. Maybe, it is my destiny to be crowned," he stated.

"May it protect you during your reign," I whispered. We had settled on a day for Jay's coronation. He had overcome his doubts in time. While many troubles festered my mind, it appeared this wound had healed.

"How is Atul? Any improvements in his health?"

"None, Jay. I am worried about him," I said, my heart plunging to the floor.

Jay furrowed his brows. "What did the physician say?"

"He is getting some new herbs that he wants to try. I get the sense he is not sharing all the details with me."

"I will talk to him," he said and squeezed my arm.

"Take me with you. I want to hear it firsthand from the physician," I stated. He agreed and left.

After I took care of Atul's needs that morning, I headed to see Aranya.

"Queen Meera," she greeted me. Her hair was let down, and her eyes were puffy.

Without a word, I pulled her into an embrace. She had lost her brother, and so had I. She sobbed into my shoulders, and tears flowed down my face.

As her anguish subsided, she took a step back. "My lady, I want to go see my father. Can you accompany me?"

I stared at her, registering her request. "King Surya?" I asked idiotically.

She affirmed. The rift between Jay and Aranya had not closed yet, then. Still, I could not come between them.

"Aranya, that would not be appropriate. Talk to Jay," I urged.

"Talk to me about what?" asked Jay, entering the room.

Aranya eyed him like a frightened deer ready to bolt. I'd enough of their squabble.

"Jay," I began sternly.

He interrupted me and said, "You are right. Foolish of me to let this row continue."

He stepped towards her and clasped her hands. I started to leave, and Jay said, "Stay, Meera. We can go talk to the physician afterward."

"Aranya, keeping your father imprisoned for this long was a mistake. I will rectify it soon. I will make more mistakes as a king, and I need someone brave and wise enough to stop me. But you must tell me. Will you be my inner voice? Will you honor me as my queen?" he asked.

"It would be my privilege," she stated clearly.

I let out a sigh while Aranya held him fiercely.

They made arrangements to have King Surya visit Aranya and Jay later, and he left with me.

He ordered a guard to bring the physician to his chambers, and we headed there.

Kapil met us halfway and accompanied us.

"My king, I have bad news," he said once we reached Jay's chamber. Worry lines appeared on his forehead.

Jay retorted, "Have you given me any good news lately? What is it?"

Kapil answered, "The quiver of arrows we found were dipped in poison. Someone used it to shoot a deer. The family who ate the meat have all had stomach ailments."

Jay asked, "Life-threatening?"

Kapil shook his head. "We don't know yet."

I stammered, "Is it p-possible Atul was shot with a poisoned arrow?" My heart thundered in my ears.

They both stared at me, and panic took root.

Jay said calmly, "Meera, it appears to be a weak poison. No one has died from it. Don't worry needlessly. We will ask the physician to check the arrows. He can prepare an antidote."

Still, anxiety gnawed at my stomach.

The physician arrived in a few moments.

"Shukla, the quiver of arrows we found earlier appeared to be poison-tipped," stated Jay.

The physician nodded. "Yes, my lord. A city guard brought them to me already, and I have one of my disciples checking it."

Jay said, "My brother-in-law was shot by an arrow. Could his arrow have come from the same quiver?"

Shukla rubbed his hands together slowly. "King Atul has not responded to my treatment. If his arrow was poisoned, that might explain it. Do not worry. Once I identify the poison, I will prepare an antidote for it."

"I don't want these suspicions about Atul getting out," Jay ordered.

Shukla dipped his head. "I am treating the family who ate the deer shot with one of these arrows. I will tell all my disciples the antidote is for them."

A few days later, Kantha arrived in Akash with my children.

She gasped when she saw me, "My queen!"

I took Amar from her arms and buried his face with kisses. He pulled my hair with his chubby fingers and babbled a word that sounded eerily like ma. "He is starting to talk," I exclaimed.

Kantha did not seem to hear me. She muttered, "I need to have a word with your maid, my lady. She has failed in taking care of you."

With everything that happened in the last few days, I had neglected to take care of myself. My maid was not at fault. It still felt good to hear Kantha's concern. She had mothered me since I was a young girl.

Nala asked, "How is Father, Mother?"

My boy of eight tried hard to keep fear at bay. Switching Amar to one arm, I pulled Nala closer to me and hugged him. He put his arms around my waist and buried his face in my stomach. I kissed his head and prayed to God Krishna to bless him with a long life.

"He is waiting to see you," I said, not answering his question.

"Where is Priya?" I asked.

"She went to see her cousins, my lady," replied Kantha.

I handed Amar to her and took Nala to see his father.

Atul sat on a chair, his clothes fitting him loosely. He had lost weight, and even his youth did not mask the toll of his illness.

Nala approached him unsteadily. "Seek his blessings," I whispered, and Nala bent to touch his father's feet. Atul patted his shoulder lightly and pointed to a space next to him. Nala dropped beside him, eyeing him with concern.

"How was your journey from Daya?"

"I rode on my horse most of the way. Uncle Rish said I'd a good seat. Priya and Rima would not listen to me and got mud on their clothes. Amar cried at night."

I smiled at his tale, and Atul ruffled his hair.

"Are you going to d-die, Father?" he stammered. I stood stunned, and Atul wrapped his arm around his shoulders.

"I am fighting it, Nala. But you and I need to be prepared for the possibility."

My heart nearly stopped on hearing his words. Atul glanced at me and continued, "If that happens, I want you to be brave and listen to your mother." He stroked his son's cheek and asked, "Can you do that?"

The boy nodded, eyes darting between his parents.

"Did Uncle Parth reach Daya?"

Nala inclined his head. "He came with Uncle Rish and stayed back in Daya."

I left the father and son alone and wandered to the garden. Yellow butterflies flitted from flower to flower, searching for nectar. Birds called out to each other, a gentle wind rustled the leaves, and voices of distant palace workers floated in. I sat down on a teak bench and closed my eyes.

A calmness settled over me, and I let my mind approach the possibility it wanted to avoid. Atul might die. Nala was too young to rule on his own. If Atul appointed Prince Parth as his regent, would he be loyal to his nephew? More importantly, would he be a strong voice for the Padi people? Prince Rudra already loomed large in Padi royal dynamics. His strength would increase. What advice should I give Atul in this matter?

Steps approached me, and I opened my eyes. Jay's guard Karan bowed to me.

"King Jay has urgent matters to discuss with you, my lady."

I accompanied him to the palace. Instead of taking me to Jay's chambers, he took me to Atul's.

He closed the door once I entered it.

Atul sat on his bed, and Jay and Shukla stood next to him.

Terror clutched my throat, and no sound came out.

The physician addressed Atul, "King Atul, the arrow shot at you was poisoned. Unfortunately, it is a poison I am not familiar with."

Jay said, "We are sending his disciples to our neighboring kingdoms to learn about it."

Atul gazed at me and said, "Death is coming for all of us. Today or tomorrow."

A sob escaped me.

He thanked Shukla and dismissed him.

"Meera," he called, and I shuffled towards him. He intertwined his fingers in mine and said, "I have many unfinished businesses to take care of. And I don't want to die here in Akash. If the end is near, I want to greet him gazing at the snow-clad mountains in Nanga. Let us leave after Jay's crowning."

My world spun around me.

22

Jay

Somu awoke me before the sun rose that morning.

Other fathers could witness greatness in their offspring during their lifetime. My journey began when my father's ended. It had been more than two moon months since I learned of my father's demise.

Somu had raised me from my cradle, and I asked him, "Somu, I am bound to make mistakes as a king. Will you speak your mind to me and tell me when I go astray?"

Setting out my clothes, he said, "My lord, it will be my honor to tell you the truth I see. In my experience, kind boys grow into kind men. You care about your people, and that is the main quality of a good king. And you are seeking advice. That is another great attribute."

He glanced at me and placed a hand on my shoulder. "Your mother would be proud of the man you have become."

"How about you, Somu?"

His eyes softened. "My lord, to serve you has been an honor. And my heart has been filled with pride since the day you took your first steps."

A lump formed in my throat. "I cannot do this once my head bears a crown. Bless me in place of my father."

I touched his feet, and he gathered me into his old arms. Arms that had comforted me many times as a boy.

Kapil entered. "They are waiting for you, my Majesty."

Somu handed me a dhoti washed in turmeric water. I wore it and draped a similar shawl around my shoulders.

They accompanied me to a room prepared specially for the occasion. A priest placed a rosewood pedestal inlaid with silver in the center of the room and guided me to it. I handed my shawl to Somu and sat down bare-chested.

Clay pots filled with water from all the rivers in Malla stood on the floor. As a few priests recited a hymn about each one, another poured the water over my head. The water scented with turmeric, sandalwood, or tulsi transported me back to my travels across my kingdom. The last pot held water from the Chambal river. As the cold water cascaded down my face, I imagined floating down the river. I'd built sandcastles on her shore and swam in her streams. Kapil, Vasu, and I had played for many hours along her bank. Her water cleared my remaining doubts.

Minister Kripa said, "My lord, you have been cleansed by the mighty rivers of Malla. You are reborn as our king. Please don your new clothes. The king's guards will escort you and Princess Aranya to the throne room."

The room emptied, leaving me alone with Somu and Muthu. They helped me drape my silk dhoti. More gold than ever adorned me in the form of armbands, necklaces, earrings, and other trinkets.

Aranya arrived wearing a red sari with golden threads weaved in it. I dismissed the servants and looked at her.

"Aranya, when you married me, I promised you would sit beside me as my queen one day. That day has arrived. In return, I ask you to speak your mind to me."

"I will keep my promise. Alone, you will hear all my views. And I will fight to get my way."

She stood on her toes and kissed me lightly.

"Among others, I will be your docile queen."

I grinned at her.

"Docile? Is this like the time you pretended to listen to me, only to ignore my wishes completely?"

"Completely? I only ignored your wishes half the time. As your queen, I will strive to do better. Get you to see my way instead."

"That is likelier than your submissiveness."

She smiled brightly.

A knock sounded on the door.

"Come in," I called, and Kapil peeked in.

"We are ready," I said and held out my hand.

Aranya grasped it, and we marched towards the throne room.

We stood at the threshold, and I scanned the room. Flaming torches mounted on the pillars and oil wicker brass lamps placed on the floor cast light and shadow around the room. The ornate gold throne that stood at the end drew my eyes. The throne my father and his father before had occupied beckoned me. The kings of the past carved into the pillars whispered to me to fight for Malla. Until my death.

I marched forward with Aranya beside me. Yellow and orange marigold flowers fell at our feet. Two musicians played the *Nadaswaram*, an auspicious wind instrument accompanied by percussion players using clay pots as their drums.

Priests chanted hymns in praise of Goddess Durga, a fierce warrior and preferred deity of soldiers. I scanned the crowds. Near the entrance stood prominent local families dressed in their finest silks. Many noblemen and elders assembled further inside. My father-in-law Mani Vindhya stood with his sons Darsh and Dayan. I spotted Rish standing beside them while Mano Biha directed his city guard leaders. My glance fell on an unexpected guest. Giri Thari bowed his head when he noticed me. He must have arrived in the early hours of this morning. Otherwise, he would have come to see me last night.

My stepmother sat near the front, and Sudha stood near her with my daughters. Atul and Meera were seated alongside them with their children.

Minister Kripa guided us to the thrones. Facing the crowd, I brought my hands together with my palms touching and bowed to the gathered.

As we took our seats, the music ascended to a crescendo and slowly dissipated.

A priest brought a silver tray holding the gold crown embedded with rubies. Mani Vindhya approached us as the priests invoked the blessings of the ancient kings of Malla. Vindhya chiefs had crowned the Malla kings for generations. At Minister Kripa's signal, he took the crown and placed it on my head.

Minister Kripa hailed, "God bless King Jay," and the audience echoed his words as yellow rice showered down on me. Cries of "Victory to Malla" followed.

A poet came forward to recite a song about me. Poems granted immortality to the man mentioned in them, even if folks forgot who wrote them.

He spoke of the son of King Vikram, whose sword glinted in the sun, as he fought a dozen men bravely. This warrior's feet danced on the forest floor and slew evil men to protect Malla. Instead of the glorious battle he depicted, I remembered smelling decaying rot, avoiding stepping on men's entrails spilled out on the floor, and sweat from fear dripping down my chin. The song continued with legendary blows I'd dealt my foes, one more far-fetched than the next. He finished with a portrait of the future of Malla under me, traders free to travel the king's road, boats sailing on the rivers, farmers with fat cows, and plenty of grains. Some of that I could achieve.

The massive crown on my head lightened the burden in my heart. As a king, my duty was to Malla and the welfare of her people. All else came second, including my own needs.

With clarity, I addressed the Malla leaders in the council room later that day.

"My father and forefathers ruled this land wisely, as protectors of the weak, defenders of the land, and renderers of justice. I strive to follow in their paths. There are many tasks ahead for me. Punish the traitors to the crown and select new generals for our Southern and Northern units. First and foremost is choosing virtuous and wise men to form my small council. Men who can guide me in my decisions. I will be seeking your input as I embark on this journey."

Aranya and I rode on an open chariot with Kayal and Heera on our laps through the streets of Akash. Under the late afternoon sky, people lined, on either side of the road, greeting us with flowers and yellow rice.

"Remember the last time we rode through the city like this?" I asked Aranya.

Gazing at the crowd, she answered, "It was on the day of our marriage."

I viewed the men, women, and children shouting my name. "Today is a marriage of sorts. It is my marriage to this land. Unlike you and Sudha, she demands my complete loyalty. Meeting her needs is going to come ahead of all else. My duty to her precedes my duty as a father and husband."

Aranya glared at me. "What do you want from me? I am a mother. And a daughter. I cannot forget that."

I said, "I am not a heartless monster. My duty to protect extends to you. It does not exclude you. Make your thoughts known to me. Don't go behind my back to act against my wishes."

"You told me this already. You have not forgiven my earlier transgression," she grumbled.

"Did you expect to regain my trust back instantly?" I snapped.

Kayal mumbled, "Don't be angry, Father."

Shocked at her perceptiveness, I pressed my cheek to hers. What had come over me? Why did I pick a fight with Aranya in front of our kids?

I reached out and squeezed my queen's hand, and she regarded me.

"Your father is not angry. Being king and queen is new to us. We are making sure we understand each other," she said.

The rest of the ride went smoothly. I pointed several monuments to Kayal and narrated the history behind them. We stopped at a few places and left the chariot to mingle with the city residents. I listened to older men extol the virtues of my father. Women worried about their soldier husbands. In the past decade, I'd strapped wings to my feet and flew near and far. Neither I nor my soldiers had stayed in Akash very long. Aranya spoke to them and pledged to keep me in Akash. I did not have a choice with a kingdom to rule.

In fading light, we reached the palace. A sliver of a moon appeared in the sky. I hoped the Malla kingdom mirrored the moon and would grow from the dark days of my father's death to a bright future. Heera had fallen asleep, and I helped carry her to her room. Letting the maids take care of the girls, I seized a few moments alone with Aranya.

"I am sorry about earlier, Jay. Today was a momentous day for you, and I spoiled it."

"You did nothing of that sort. It is an important day and made all the more special with you by my side," I said gently.

"Worries about you, Nakul, and my father have plagued my mind for months and..."

I interrupted her, "Don't worry alone. I can carry some of that burden for you."

She leaned her head on my chest, and I held her tightly. I'd been away from Akash too long and forgotten how to converse with my wife. I could not let our tussle continue. With many other uncertainties, this could not dominate my mind.

Feast and festivities continued into the night.

Past midnight, I went to my new chambers. The large formal room and the smaller sitting room remained nearly the same as before. I almost expected to see my father seated under his portrait in the sitting room. The young man staring at me from the painting appeared confident. He did not expect to ascend to the throne but had adapted to his duties and ruled wisely. Unlike him, I'd been groomed for this moment since my birth. Despite the lateness of the hour, my tiredness vanished. Pleasant anticipation filled me. My path would not be easy, but I was ready to walk in my father's footsteps. I squared my shoulders and peeked into the bedroom. It held my furnishings now.

Darsh, Giri, Kapil, and Rish arrived soon.

"Giri, did you find Karan Thari?" I asked.

Giri said, "I found my uncle in a Biha cell with Puri's help. He was raving mad and did not even recognize me." He paused with his lips drawn into a thin line.

"It took me several days of questioning to piece the story together. My uncle seemed convinced that King Atul was mounting an army to invade Malla. His Lieutenant got hurt a few months ago. With the king dead and my father, Chief Bhoj, sick, he had no one in authority to question him. He ordered his men to capture Atul and imprison him. Then his commands got strange. He wanted to execute King Atul for treason. Some members of his troop knew a general had no authority to kill King Atul and began to suspect his motives. They moved King Atul to a safer location that they kept hidden from him. Then, my uncle wanted to attack you, and the soldiers rebelled. Kapil arrived in time and asked them to maintain their charade for a while longer, but even without him, these soldiers would have left the northern command and joined you. Soon, my uncle's mental acuity deteriorated, and it looks like Chief Devan Biha ordered to keep him in the Biha cell."

Giri took a deep breath in, and many questions ran through my mind.

"How did his Lieutenant get hurt?" asked Kapil.

Giri shook his head. "I don't know the answer to that. Chief Devan might."

General Satya met with an accident in Saral. I worried about how easily someone had removed my Generals from the scene.

I mused, "Do you suspect he had something to do with the change in your uncle?"

He nodded. "All evidence points to Chief Devan working with King Nakul on this."

"Where is your uncle now?"

"I took him back to Thari, my Majesty. I asked our physician to care for him."

I rubbed my forehead. "I might need Karan to speak at Devan's trial."

This trial loomed large in my mind. I wanted to avoid the three pillars of Malla from finger-pointing and backstabbing each other. As a new ruler, I depended on their loyalty and support. How would I serve fair justice while remaining impartial?

Giri replied, "He was incoherent and rambling like a child when I left him. He will be of no use, my Majesty. I have brought some of the men under him, and Puri Biha was with me while I questioned my uncle. They can answer questions at the trial."

I observed the men around me.

"Rish, you have been quiet. What are your thoughts?"

"King Jay, from the facts I have gathered so far, King Nakul and General Devan conspired to take over Malla. They poisoned King Vikram. With you out of the kingdom, King Nakul plotted to incapacitate General Satya and General Karan, your southern and northern generals."

Following along, Kapil added, "General Satya got hurt in a horse accident. While our men were distracted, King Nakul moved his troops around to leave Saral by boat."

Eager to jump in, Darsh said, "With King Vikram dead, my father dispatched Dayan and me to Padi and Sunda. King Atul moved his troops to the Padi border to help fight off Nakul."

Giri stepped in. "If my uncle had joined King Atul, Chief Devan's plot would have unraveled. Somehow they convinced him that King Atul was the enemy."

How had Nakul accomplished that?

Rish blurted, "Poison! They poisoned King Vikram. Now we find out someone infected King Atul as well. They could have poisoned General Karan with a mind-altering herb."

Gasps escaped from the men.

Kapil muttered, "My Majesty, something urgent I need to take care of."

I wandered to the window, and my mind traced the path of the last few months.

Kapil called Dev and Karan and gave them instructions. "Check every food or drink King Jay consumes for poison. Talk to the cooks and his servants, Somu and Muthu as well." He dismissed them.

When he joined us, I ordered, "Find out who has been supplying these poisons. These are rare ones, and there are only a few sources for them."

He nodded. "I will talk to my father and activate our spy network to get this information."

That night, I laid on my bed, waiting for sleep to claim me. Through my large windows, I watched the moon peeking out of a cloud, traveling across the sky. Sounds from the tiny bells on a woman's anklets reached me, and I raised onto my elbows. Sudha stood outside with my guards. I waved the men away, and she approached me. The guards shut the door behind her as I stood up.

"Sudha, what are you doing here at this time of the night?" I asked.

"I thought you would come to see me tonight," she said.

"After all the celebrations, I'd other urgent matters to take care of."

My stepmother had been urging me to choose Sudha as my queen. While not as blatant, my father-in-law had been dropping subtler hints about it. I had disregarded their wishes.

"Sudha, while our kingdom is vast, there is only one throne beside the king . . ."

"I never had any interest in becoming the queen, my lord." She twined her fingers in front of her.

I stared at her as the color rose in her cheeks. "I want a small place in your heart," she whispered. *My heart?* Her father was the head of my wealthiest region, and I had married her for strategic reasons. Despite that, my feelings for her had grown over the decade, and she had tormented me in my dreams in Sunda.

I reached out to hold her hand and raised her knuckles to my lips. Kissing them, I said, "I believe you have already carved out a place in my heart."

She took a step closer and stammered, "I don't want to be mocked, my lord."

"Mocked?" I asked. "Who is mocking you?" I snarled. *Who would dare to mock her?*

"No one to my face. But they whisper behind my back. Calling me childless like my aunt," she said haltingly, and her pain pierced me. My treatment of my stepmother was not without blemish.

Pushing my guilt aside, I lifted her chin. "I have been a fool for not paying attention to what is happening in my castle. Let us put an end to any whispers. Organize a trip for just the two of us, and I will join you."

"To the temple?" she asked excitedly.

"If you wish," I answered. "As for the other matter of children, has it been . . ."

"Yes, one moon month, King Jay," she whispered and wrapped her arms around me. Grasping my neck, she pulled my head down to meet her warm lips. My want suppressed for too long surged like water bursting forth of a dam as I clasped her hips. The taste of her skin, the smell of her throat, the warm curve of her waist, and a thousand other details hailed down my senses.

23

Meera

Once I got Atul seated, I scanned the room. My eyes fell on Rish Vindhya, standing across the room and conversing with his cousin Mani. I averted my eyes quickly and went to chat with my stepmother. I'd been avoiding her since Jay had chosen Aranya as his queen.

Her austere white sari contrasted with the festive clothes of other attendees.

She whispered, "Sudha is bringing the girls to the ceremony. Not the role I wanted for her."

Her niece Sudha turned out to be a loyal wife and a great stepmother. Jay preferred a queen on equal footing with him and willing to speak her mind. A wise choice in my mind, but I did not want to admit that to my stepmother. Instead, I asked about her move to the queen mother's palace, a smaller residence adjacent to the king's. It had remained empty since my grandmother passed away.

"The palace was built for multiple widows of the king. It is large for just me," she said.

"King Atul," said Rish near me, and I tensed. What foolishness, I chided myself. I cannot avoid him forever. It would cause suspicion.

I made some remarks to my stepmother while my ears listened to the conversation between the two men.

"Thanks for bringing the children to Akash. Nala would have regretted missing the coronation of his uncle," Atul said. Rish muttered a response.

Eager to hear their discussion, I made my way back to Atul.

Rish lifted his eyes and acknowledged me with a simple bow.

My husband watched us, and he reflected, "Meera is mad at you. What did you do?" Atul knew me well. I was mad at myself more than at Rish. My emotions floated to the surface more often than in the past. I needed to rein them in.

Rish said smoothly, "I allowed you to be captured, my Majesty, and took her away from your side. She has good reasons to be angry."

Atul gazed at me and said, "Your duty was to protect her, and you did it well."

Our conversation was interrupted by priests starting their hymns, signaling the imminent arrival of Jay. Rish joined his family without a further glance at me. Atul started explaining the ceremony to Nala and Priya. All other thoughts vanished from my mind as Jay and Aranya arrived.

I watched him march through the hall, acknowledging people he knew, radiating strength that the audience could sense. As he came near us, his eyes swept through us quickly, and then his gaze remained on the throne.

Mani Vindhya stepped up to crown him, and the audience erupted in a chant of his name. As I observed my brother, a lightness filled my heart. Whatever the doubts of the past, he appeared ready for the arduous road ahead.

"Malla is in good hands," Atul whispered, and I agreed. Atul's health had improved over the last few days, and I allowed hope to steal into my heart.

At the feast after the coronation, I sat down beside Sudha. A servant placed an enormous banana leaf, the size of my arm, in front of me. Another heaped coconut rice, sesame rice, and tamarind rice on it.

Raw mango pickle, long beans stir fry, peanut and lentil stew, eggplant stuffed with spices, tender greens in a coconut sauce, and many other dishes made an appearance. The smell of the spices revolted my stomach. I steered clear of the rich food on my leaf and ate some yogurt rice with the mango pickle. The sour pickle with the cool yogurt calmed me.

Taking a bite of banana flower fritters, Sudha whispered, "Your brother looked elegant on the throne today." Her face shined with happiness, with no sign of resentment.

"He reminded me of my father," I said. Jay had the same determined look our father had when he would transform from an ordinary man to a king with just his eyes.

"You have not touched your food, my lady," she asked with concern.

"I am tired. That is all," I mumbled. Amar kept me up last night, and that took a toll on my body.

Many people wanted to talk to me that day, and I obliged. At the end of a long day, I settled next to Atul to watch a musical play in honor of Jay. The artists enacted his life, and I leaned against Atul's shoulder, fighting off sleep. He put his arm around me, allowing me to nestle against his shoulder, and whispered in my ears, "You know his story. Get some rest. I will wake you before it ends."

The next few days sped by in a blur. I met with many guests who had come to Akash for the coronation. The three girls, Kayal, Priya, and Rima, became inseparable and spent all day and night together. The youngest of them, Heera, could not keep up with the older girls and spent some time with Amar and me. I gathered them all one morning and taught them one of my mother's songs. Heera sat on my lap and joined us in singing the chorus.

On a clear day, Jay trained with Nala. I went to watch them as Nala showed his uncle all the moves he had learned. The pair stood facing each other in a secluded room on the upper floor of the palace. Sunlight flooded in through the large open windows, and a light breeze wafted in. Their feet moved synchronously on the stone floor while they held wooden swords. Jay held back, allowing his nephew to go on the offensive. After he pretended to lose to Nala a few times, he patted his shoulders.

"Train regularly, and you will be a better warrior than me," he said.

Nala beamed at his uncle and said, "Uncle Rish taught me some new moves. I have been practicing them daily."

"You are a good student then," Jay smiled at him.

Alone with me, Jay commented, "I will love to spend more time with Nala. I wish you were not leaving for Padi so soon."

"Atul wants to head back. He talks about unfinished business."

Jay observed me and asked, "His health?"

I exhaled slowly, "He is improving, and the wound is healing. The royal physician received some new herbs, and they appear to be effective."

Jay opened and closed his fist. "I will talk to the physician to send one of his assistants and his supply of herbs with you."

My heart pounded in my ears as I contemplated my decision. Rish was my safe harbor before. But now, all my foolish impulses surfaced around him, and I could not succumb to temptations. "Jay, I don't want Rish back in Padi," I muttered.

He regarded me and said, "Meera, the man cares about you. With Atul's ill health, you need someone on your side who is not part of the Padi royal clan."

I shook my head. "Jay, listen to me. He cannot come to Padi."

He sighed in frustration. "I will send one of Sudha's brothers in his place then. I don't want to leave you unprotected." He reached out and squeezed my hand, and I managed a weak smile.

"Meera, our Aunt Mohini has a daughter. Talk to Atul about strengthening ties with Malla and marrying Princess Mala to one of my future chiefs."

I regarded him and said, "Let me talk to Mala first. To know where her heart lies."

He stared at me incredulously. "Her heart? Meera, our hearts don't matter. Atul is going to decide marriage alliances based on what is best for Padi."

My hands trembled, and I clasped them tightly. "If a girl gets to marry only once, maybe her heart should matter a tiny grain."

His answer came slowly. "Very well. Talk to her."

A day later, Jay came to talk to Atul.

"King Atul, I need Rish for my mission to Saral. With your permission, I would like to send Dayan Vindhya to Padi," he stated.

Atul snarled, "Are you mad? You are sending a child in place of Rish. Even grown men cowered when Rish stared at them menacingly. I am ill, and if something happens to me, Meera and Nala need someone strong on their side."

Jay said calmly, "Dayan is a grown man, and he will come as an envoy of the Malla kingdom. Any harm that comes to Meera and her children will be met with a severe retribution."

Atul snapped, "I don't know what game you are playing, Jay. Rish knows the Padi clan, and they know him. Most importantly, he is loyal to Meera. Not to you or Malla but Meera. I want to talk to Rish myself."

Jay stood his ground. "I am the King of Malla, and you owe me your allegiance. Not the other way around. This matter is settled. I will send Dayan as my envoy."

Atul spoke slowly, "My brother, Parth, whispered a few things in my ears, and I dismissed them earlier. Maybe there is a grain of truth to them."

Nostrils flared, Jay muttered, "Parth is a drunk idiot, and if you trust him more than me, that does not bode well for your rule."

"He is my blood, and I do trust him," Atul sneered.

He spun around and asked, "Meera, you know Rish better than any of us. If something happens to me in Padi, who will you trust to help you?"

Both men eyed me as I struggled to keep my emotions under control. Rish had to stay behind for his safety and mine.

I groaned, "Atul, you are getting better. I want you to stop saying otherwise. I trust the two of you the most. So stop fighting when we need to worry about real enemies amongst us."

His eyes softened as he said, "You are right. Jay, you know your men the best. The stakes are high, so make sure Dayan is prepared."

Jay glanced at me briefly, and for a fleeting moment, I saw misgivings in his eyes about sending Dayan. Recovering quickly, Jay said, "Yes, I will."

A few days later, men packed and loaded our belongings and supplies onto carts.

An upset Nala came to me.

"Mother, I heard Uncle Rish is not coming back to Daya. Who will train me?"

Atul overheard the conversation and trudged in from the bedroom.

"There are many capable men in Padi. Your Uncle Parth can train you."

Fighting back his tears, Nala cried, "Uncle Parth mocks me when I do something wrong. Uncle Rish never did that."

I reached out to him, and he swatted my arm. "Nala, he is Jay's man, and your uncle needs him in Saral." All true, though I hid the full truth.

"I want Uncle Rish. I will go ask Uncle Jay to send him with us." He started to leave.

Atul said quietly, "Nala, you will do no such thing."

He halted and turned to gaze at his father.

"King Jay has to decide what is best for his people. Even if that means you lose your teacher."

The boy stood with trembling lips. I approached him and held out my arms. Slowly, he stepped forward and buried his face in my stomach. I bent down and kissed his head. My insides twisted, seeing him hurt because of me.

Later, I went to fetch Priya, and she ran and hugged my legs in tears.

"Why cannot Rima come with us?"

I brushed her hair with my fingers. "Her father is staying in Akash. You can come and visit them soon."

She flung herself on the floor and hit it with her tiny fists. "I want to stay here with her."

Before I could comfort her, Rish walked in with a wailing Rima in his arms.

"We came to say our farewell," he announced.

"Princess Priya," Rima screamed, and Priya ran to her.

"Uncle Rish, come back with us," she pleaded. Rima joined her chorus.

Rish shook his head. "King Jay wants me to go to Saral with him."

Rima asked, "Is it far?" He nodded. "Can I go with you?"

He shook his head. "I cannot take you with me. You will stay here with your Cousin Sudha and your grandmother."

Rima protested, "Grandmother only prays. She does not play." A smile appeared on his face.

She continued, "Can I go with Queen Meera? She tells great stories, and she sings better than Cousin Sudha."

Rish scrutinized me, and I nodded.

He hugged the small child to his chest. "Yes, you can go with Queen Meera."

The girls screamed in joy.

"I will write to you, and I will send for you when I return from Saral," he added.

"I cannot read, Father," she answered.

A whirlpool of emotions swept me as I said, "I will read his letters to you, and we can write back and tell him all the mischief you two are up to."

They giggled as I felt Rish's eyes on me. The grey clouds parted, and a tiny ray of the sun reached my eyes. I could keep a thread of connection to him through his letters. My treacherous heart refused to listen to reason.

He kissed her cheek and handed her to me. "I am leaving my heart with you," he whispered.

Our eyes met briefly, and I felt like I would burst into flames. My body protested the distance between us. My stomach coiled at the thought of not seeing Rish again, possibly forever. Suppressing my emotions, I took Rima and held her cheek against mine. *Farewell, my love.* Darkness cloaked me as he strode away without a backward glance.

24

Jay

Minister Kripa met me in the small council room.

"Minister, you served my father ably for many decades. My humble request is for you to continue to provide me advice and guidance."

He stroked his long grey beard and answered, "King Jay, it will be my honor. Your father listened to all of us in the small council. While the decisions are yours to make, I hope you take our views into account."

"Minister Kripa, I desire to surround myself with men who can not only support me but also tell me when I am wrong," I replied.

"Malla will prosper under such a king," he stated warmly.

"Minister, while I wish you will guide me for many years, there might come a time when I need—"

He interrupted me and said, "I have four disciples I have been grooming. Over the next few months, you and I can select one of them to replace me as Minister."

That settled, I moved on to the vital conversation.

"Minister Kripa, Devan Biha is accused of treason. I have to call witnesses to testify. Possibly the same people murdered my father and poisoned King Atul. Mani Vindhya and Giri Thari will want to speak at the trial. And Devan himself will state his case," I said.

Kripa said, "We have to be prepared for Devan to compare you unfavorably to King Nakul. We need witnesses to counter that."

I'd burnt my brother to ashes and usurped his throne already. I wanted to avoid slandering his name too.

I said, "That is indeed what I wanted to avoid. Smearing of my father's name and mine." *And my brother's.*

I added, "I want to serve justice. These deeds cannot go unpunished. But I cannot allow my liege lords to use this opportunity to paint each other negatively."

Kripa studied me and said, "My Majesty, this is your court. Now will be a good time to establish that. Talk to the men you are most worried about and draw the line they cannot cross. Devan himself is in a weak position to bargain. He will be worried about his sons and his daughter, Queen Riya. He will not want to antagonize his king."

That evening, Sudha and I set to the temple in an open chariot. She wore a strand of jasmine on her hair, and the buds burst open, filling the space between us with an intoxicating fragrance.

"My brother, Darsh, has been talking about you nonstop. It is always King Jay this or King Jay that," she said with a wide smile.

"He has proven himself as a trustworthy ally. We have to find him a suitable bride."

The chariot stopped in front of the black granite temple, and Sudha grabbed a basket of flowers for God Krishna.

"Do you need any help with it?" I asked, pointing to her basket.

"It weighs less than Heera, who I carry around often," she replied.

Temple goers stopped to gawk at us, and I greeted a few. She whispered, "I will see you inside," and vanished. I slowly made my way in, stopping to talk to other devotees.

An elderly woman grabbed my arm. As my guards rushed in, I gestured them to halt.

"What is it, ma?" I asked gently. She wore a worn but clean sari.

"Save the queen and her unborn son," she whispered urgently. "Protect her to save Malla," she pleaded, her fingers digging into my upper arm.

Queen? Unborn son? She must be mad. Neither of my wives was pregnant. I pried her fingers loose and stepped back. "I strive to protect all my people, ma," I stated and headed inside the temple.

In the main sanctum, God Krishna stood playing flute. The priest had covered his body with butter, one of the cowherd god's favorite foods. As the priest chanted a prayer, Sudha closed her eyes, her lips moving in earnest. Wisps of her hair had escaped her bun and touched the nape of her neck. In the light of oil lamps hung from the ceiling, her diamond chandelier earrings sparkled. A solitary diamond on her nose cast a web of light on her cheek. Suddenly, all others disappeared, and only her face remained in my sight. God Krishna, the lover of *gopikas*, his eternal consorts, would understand the images that ran through my mind. The priest waved a silver plate with lighted wick lamps in front of the deity. I started at the sound of the bells. He approached us and extended the platter to us. I cupped my hands over the flame to accept the blessing, and Sudha followed suit.

As we circled the courtyard, she stated, "You enjoy talking to people."

"Yes, something my father taught me. There is no better way to understand what is happening in the kingdom."

"Talking to strangers is not something I enjoy. Aranya is better at it," she said.

"You have been taking care of Kayal and Heera while she mourns her brother."

Her face lit up at the mention of the girls. "They call me mother, and there is no word for the feelings that well up in me."

Meera and I called our stepmother by the same term, a royal tradition. She remained distant during our childhood.

"That makes you more special than I'd imagined," I mused.

"Husbands should always think their wives special," she quipped.

I laughed, "Give me a list of all that husbands should do. I have time to practice."

Then I asked, "What did you pray for?"

"This prayer is not for my king's ears. He has done his part already. It is for God's," she said with a blush.

A few days later, I held court in the throne room. I carried a bronze scepter inset with turquoise, a reminder to be a just ruler. Mani Vindhya, Mano Biha, and Giri Thari represented their houses today. Biha brothers, Kapil and Puri, Rish Vindhya, and many other elders assembled in the audience.

Minister Kripa would run the proceedings. Dressed in a simple white cotton dhoti, he stood amidst his disciples.

Chief Guard Mano ordered, "Bring the prisoners in."

Devan and his son, Navin, shuffled in, their arms and legs tied in chains.

I'd served under Devan in my first battle in Saral. A tall man, he wore his battle scars proudly then. Today, he hunched forward, staring at the floor.

Minister Kripa announced his crimes, "Chief Devan Biha, you are accused of poisoning the king, consorting with King Nakul to bring the downfall of Malla and disloyalty to the crown of Malla. Do you deny any of these charges?"

Devan's voice cracked as he said, "My Majesty, King Nakul threatened to kill my daughter Riya if I did not aid him." Gasps went around the room on hearing this.

Devan continued, "I'd nothing to do with the poisoning of King Vikram. I would have passed a word to my brother, Mano—"

Mano erupted, "Don't call me your brother, you traitor."

I raised my scepter. "Let him speak, Chief Mano."

Devan sighed. "Mano is right. I have brought shame to the Biha house with my weakness. King Nakul, my son-in-law, initially asked my help to free his father. King Surya is a weak old man, and I saw no threat in him. I should not have attempted to release a prisoner without the king's orders, but I convinced myself this was not treasonous."

I leaned forward to listen to every word.

Devan wailed suddenly, "Please send men to check on my daughter and my grandson. Nakul said they would be killed if any harm came to him."

I'd already sent a messenger to Kathir Gomti and Hasan Vindhya when Nakul died. Kathir promised to safeguard Riya and my nephew Vasant. That boy was to be raised as my heir, and I wanted no harm to come to him. But I'd no interest in revealing this to Devan.

I stated coldly, "You are in no position to make any requests. Just answer the questions truthfully."

Devan glanced at his son, Navin, and whispered, "I promise to speak the truth."

Minister Kripa asked, "How did you aid King Nakul?"

Devan glanced at him and then continued staring at the ground. "One of my men is in the prison guard. He passed King Nakul's messages to his father."

I gazed at Mano, and he answered my unasked question, "I have dealt with him, my Majesty."

Minister Kripa continued, "Were you aware of King Nakul's scheme to poison our king?"

Devan looked up and cried, "No, not at all. I'd no hand in that. I would have stopped it if I'd any idea."

Mano wrinkled his nose and stated, "His men denied any knowledge as well, King Jay."

I clenched my fist. Aranya had played a role in this, not Devan. Though, she had no knowledge of Nakul's ploy to murder his birth father. I did not want to delve into this subject anymore, so I signaled to Kripa.

Kripa moved to another topic. "Why did you allow Nakul to invade Malla?"

Devan whimpered like a hurt dog. "He intimated that he would kill my daughter if I refused."

He then pleaded with me. "King Jay, I am not blameless. I betrayed my oath to you and this land. But it was done out of coercion. King Nakul even threatened my grandson's life."

Devan broke into a sob, and most men averted their eyes at the sight of a grown man crying.

I regarded him while turning things in my mind. How do I distinguish lies from the truth with Nakul dead? I detested the emergence of Nakul as a villain. I remembered our last conversation and his hatred. Could Devan's accusation be true? Frustration built inside me.

The sobs quieted down, and Devan wiped his nose with the back of his hand.

Kripa asked, "What did King Nakul ask you to do?"

In a broken voice, Devan replied, "He wanted a safe passage to Malla. My Majesty, he wanted to bring a large troop, and I told him I could only conceal a small number. I did that to make sure Malla men had the upper hand."

I pondered, "What caused you concern? Why did you take his threat of hurting your daughter Riya seriously?"

Devan flushed and mumbled, "Last time I visited Saral, Riya tried hard to hide her bruises from me."

Shocked, I stared at him. *Why would Nakul stoop so low to hit his wife?* The man I knew gave up his kingdom to protect his sister. What happened in the ensuing years to make him violent to another woman? Had Devan weaved this tale from his imagination?

Giri Thari shifted on his feet and asked, "What happened to General Karan Thari? What drove him mad?"

Devan lamented, "I don't know what happened. When I found him, he rambled about King Atul invading Malla. I threw him in Biha prison to keep him from hurting King Atul."

I inquired, "Why did you not release King Atul from his prison next?"

Devan rubbed his wrist. "Saral men would have killed him then. I ordered my best men to protect him."

I said, "Puri Biha, step forward." Kapil's younger brother moved to the front. As a little boy, he would follow Kapil and me around the palace and get us in trouble with his father. Taller and leaner now than his brother, he mostly lived in the Biha court.

"Tell us what you know about the fight between Atul and Malla men."

In a clear voice, he said, "King Jay, I was with my uncle, Devan, when a messenger said Karan Thari had captured King Atul. He appeared troubled and ordered his men to seize Karan Thari and protect King Atul."

I waved him back.

Kripa continued questioning Devan. "You fought against King Jay. Do you deny it?"

All color drained from Devan's face. He shook his head.

Kripa continued, "Were you hoping to install your grandson on the Malla throne?"

He shook his head vehemently. "I'd no such desire. I just wanted the boy to live. My Majesty, Biha men have served you loyally for many years. I betrayed my oath and honor. My son, Navin, and my brother, Mano, are blameless in this. Punish me. Not them."

It would be easy to behead both father and son and plant my loyal friend Kapil as the next chief of Biha. I'd questioned a few of his commanders before the trial. They denied Navin taking an active role in the conflict. Should a descendant be held responsible for his father's crimes?

I turned to Navin and asked, "Did you plot my downfall with your father?"

He shook his head. "Speak," I commanded.

"No, your Majesty. My father kept me in the dark."

"Why did you not advise him to uphold his oath?" I questioned.

He stumbled, "I obeyed my father's orders."

I prodded on, "Even when you knew they were wrong?"

He hung his head.

I looked at Puri again. He said, "Uncle Devan kept King Nakul away from us and did not share any details with us. Navin and I remained back when he left with King Nakul. We were both frustrated by the lack of news. When Kapil arrived, Navin helped us."

I observed the young man in front of me while Puri spoke. Navin tensed his shoulders and took in shallow breaths. I made a decision.

"Navin, do you pledge your life and loyalty to the Malla throne?"

He lifted his eyes and stammered, "Yes, your Majesty."

His father mumbled something, and the young man prostrated on the floor in front of me.

"Unshackle him," I ordered as he rose.

I gestured to Mano, and he handed Navin his sword.

He stepped forward and placed the sword at my feet and clasped his hands, and bowed his head.

I touched his head with my scepter. "I install you as the Chief of Biha."

Navin said, "Invoking Goddess Durga, I swear my life and fealty to you, my king. I swear to rule justly and protect the weak."

"Navin, your father's actions will cast a shadow on your rule as Biha Chief. You have to gain my trust and those of your people by your deeds. Till then, you will not join my small council or command my armies. And you will marry the girl I order you to."

He swallowed and nodded.

I held the scepter high. "Devan, you chose the path of a coward. Fear for one's life or that of a loved one is no reason to betray one's oath. I order death by beheading as your punishment."

Devan took a deep breath and gazed at me. "You showed mercy to my son, my king. I am grateful for that."

"Mano, allow him to say his farewell today and execute him at sunrise tomorrow."

As Kapil and I left the hall, I said, "Get ready to leave for Saral." I wanted to meet my nephew, Vasant. My heir to the throne. I also needed to unravel the mystery surrounding my brother's change. An uneasy feeling clogged my throat as I imagined facing his ghost.

25

Meera

I opened my eyes and parted the curtains. A cold wind grazed my face, and I wrapped my sari around my shoulders. The city of Daya came into view as the horses drew the chariot forward. Flowers bloomed in the courtyards of the stone buildings. Trees laden with tiny green apples greeted my eyes. Stores displayed colorful piles of fruits and vegetables. Street vendors hawked their wares to passersby. Spring had vanished while I was away. Summer would arrive soon.

Some children ran alongside our procession, trying to touch the horses. A guard chased them away playfully.

Soon the fort emerged. A long line of merchants waited to get into it. Guards held them up to allow the royal family to enter first. Atul had traveled by chariot for most of the way. He'd switched to a horse at the edge of the city. He now waved to the merchants as he rode in. The sight of him mounted and on the mend restored me.

Once inside and in my chambers, I collapsed on my bed without cleaning up. I shut my eyes when Kantha asked, "My lady, you have not eaten anything. Can I fetch you something?"

My stomach revolted at the thought of food. I shook my head and fell asleep.

I heard voices and opened my eyes a slit. "Meera," called Atul.

With effort, I sat up and looked at him. He wore clean clothes and looked concerned.

He sat by me and asked, "Are you unwell? Should I send for the physician? Kantha told me you had not eaten anything. And you are still wearing your sari from our journey."

I suppressed a yawn and answered, "I am just tired from the trip."

He stood up and said, "I came to see if you wanted to eat with me. I will ask Gambhir to join me instead. Get some rest."

I watched him leave the bed, wondering whether to go back to sleep or clean up first. Bright sunlight streamed into the room, and noises floated in through the open window.

I wiped my eyes and stretched my hands. I swung my feet down and stood up. My head spun, and my vision blurred. Clutching the poster, I shut my eyes. Slowly, the feeling subsided, and I took a deep breath in.

Kantha approached me with worry. "What is it, my lady?"

"I am just exhausted from the long journey. A warm bath and some sleep should cure me."

She ordered the maids to fill my tub, and I soaked in the citrus-scented water.

As I relaxed in the water, Kantha whispered, "My lady, I do not mean to pry, but when did you last get your flow?"

Startled, I sat up and tried to remember. Many things had happened in the last three moon months that I lost track of time. My heart raced as I mumbled, "It was when we received the news of my father's death."

Kantha's face brightened. She said, "That explains your tiredness. You must be carrying another prince or princess. I will ask the maid to bring some sweets to celebrate, my lady."

Her words did not reach my ears. I assessed my own body. My breasts felt heavy, and my hips fuller. I looked down to see blue veins covering my chest. With all the happenings, I'd not noticed the signs. I rubbed my stomach as I savored the thought of another child. *Another girl would be delightful.*

Something nagged my mind and wanted to disrupt the joy spreading

184 ~ ANNA BUSHI

through my limbs. When was the last time I'd been intimate with Atul? As I traveled backward through time to the point when Atul had gotten hurt, then captured, and my father's death, anxiety gripped my heart. It had been too long for myself and my husband.

An image of Rish and I floated into my vision. In a panic, I realized the baby would not be Atul's. I took a deep breath. I needed my wits about me.

Projecting a calmness I did not feel, I said, "Kantha, in about a moon month or so, I should feel the baby move. Until then, let us keep it among ourselves. I don't want to raise any false hopes."

Kantha nodded and whispered conspiratorially, "A baby princess would be good, my lady."

My days settled into a routine. Nala complained about his new trainer, who had replaced Rish. Priya and Rima took to dressing up baby Amar like a doll. Amar discovered climbing and climbed onto tables, shelves, and trunks. I had to ask the servants to move valuable sculptures out of his reach.

Outwardly, I performed my duties faithfully. Inside, I ran through options for my future and discarded them one by one. Unlike my other secrets, even my sari could not hide this for long. What would Atul's reaction be when I told him? Would he banish me, never to see my children again? Would he behead me publicly? Those results would be unlikely because then the secret had to come out. No, that would not be wise. The best option would be for me to die in childbirth and for him to mourn us publicly. Easy to arrange. The secret of my betrayal would remain hidden. Atul would marry another to preside over the kingdom with him. And he could avoid Jay's wrath.

I poked a hole in that plan as well. Before I could die at childbirth, news of my pregnancy had to be known and spread. That would put Atul in a dilemma to decide whether to denounce me or announce the child as his own. Better for me to meet with an accident before my body revealed my pregnancy.

I knew the penalty of infidelity in a queen. Yet, I'd followed my heart and breached Atul's trust. Guilt cut me into pieces.

Atul, Jay, Rish, and my father had trusted me and had expected me to act with wisdom. I'd failed them all. I'd failed my father and caused the death of his oldest son. I'd failed Jay by hiding the secret of his birth order from him. I'd failed Atul and Rish by being unworthy of their love. I did not deserve to live and cause more harm to those I love.

Would my death cause any affront to my children? It would cause more harm if my infidelity became known and provoked Atul's enemies to question their paternity. I could not allow that to happen. I could remedy my mistakes by my death.

A calmness settled over me when I'd decided what I should do.

I spent every waking moment with my children. I braided the girls' hair while teaching them songs from my childhood. Priya was the same age as Jay when our mother had died. *Would she even remember me?*

I held Amar on my chest as he fell asleep. He would forget me, and that filled me with a deep sadness.

I told Nala war stories of courageous men who'd fought for their land and the brave women who'd tended the fields in their absence. As I tucked his hair behind his ears, I leaned in to kiss his head. He would remember me, and I hoped he would keep my memory alive for his siblings.

Atul sat beside me one evening and regaled me with the stories of his day. I drank in the familiar shape of his lips, his nose, and his forehead as the setting sun cast his face in a golden light. He regarded me and asked, "Do you realize you are staring at me?"

"Just watching the light play with your face."

"You are glowing like a gentle wicker lamp," he said and leaned in to kiss me. Thinking this might be our last kiss, I returned it passionately with my fingers gripping his hair.

Gasping for breath, we pulled apart. Smiling sheepishly, he said, "I will be able to do more than just kiss you soon."

I told Atul I wanted to worship Lord Shiva at the hilltop temple.

"Do you want me to join you?"

"No, you rest. I will take my guards."

I dressed carefully in a sari in the color of rubies and wore matching jewels.

I tried to write a letter to Rish but gave up. Nothing I would say would lessen his pain.

As the daylight faded, I set out with Dayan and a few others. Instead of the Shiva in a dancer's pose, this temple housed a Shiva *linga* carved out of the hill.

Dayan stayed near the entrance, and I entered the inner sanctum.

The priest lit the lamps and performed *pooja*. I prayed for the welfare of my children and my land.

Then I walked around the yard, pretending to do my rotation around the shrine while searching for the back door. I spotted it and scanned my surroundings. On that moonless night, the temple lights flickered feebly. I remained alone in the darkness. Quickening my steps, I approached the door and opened it slowly. The door creaked, and I crept through it.

Behind the temple stood a small grove. After that, the hill ended with a steep drop to the ground. I planned to jump off the cliff. The darkness would prevent Dayan from finding me tonight. Scavengers might find my body before anyone else. In the morning, my sari would be visible from above. I tried not to picture my half-eaten remains as I made through the trees.

Suddenly, I heard voices and slowed down to figure out where they originated. An owl hooted and flew away, and my heart dropped to my stomach.

I did not want them to hamper my effort, so I hid behind a tree and looked in the direction of the sound. A man near me called out to someone. Another joined him and asked, "Do you have it?" His voice sounded familiar, but his face was covered, revealing only his eyes.

"Yes, my l——" started the first man, and the second man interrupted him, "Careful."

The first man asked, "Do you have the coins for me?"

Coins jingled in a pouch as the newcomer handed it over.

He opened the drawstring pouch and pulled out a coin that shone faintly.

"Gold coins," he said, pleased.

"You can examine them later. Hand the stuff over."

"It was difficult to get this stash. Malla spies are tracking down poison suppliers," he said and handed over something small.

The second man put it away and said, "Let me not leave a trace for them then."

In a swift motion, he plunged his dagger into the first man's chest and covered the victim's mouth with his other hand.

With a grunt, the wounded man collapsed. I stayed rooted to the ground, fear gripping me.

Pulling the dagger out, the newcomer wiped it in his shawl. Then, I heard a clink as he grabbed something from the dead man and strode away.

The word poison echoed in my head. Was this Atul's poisoner? Who did he intend to poison now?

Different images rotated in my thoughts. Forgetting my plan, I made my way back to the temple. *I needed to warn Atul.*

26

Jay

The hilly city of Lukla rose above us as we traveled south. Aranya rode alongside me and her face beamed at the sight of her home.

"Do you know we are missing the best mango season in Malla and going to Saral, where the season is at its tail end?" she grumbled.

We passed plenty of mango groves along the way laden with green mangoes. Vendors sold tiny raw mangoes in baskets. Soaked in saltwater with spices, they made excellent pickles. In a fortnight or two, the fruits would ripen to golden yellow. Biting into the juicy fruit caused a sensory delight like no other.

"We will find plenty of mango pickles and dried mango pulp in Saral. I am sure for the queen they could find a dozen or so late bloomers too," I teased her.

The heat surrounded us, and sweat dripped down my back. The kings of Saral built their city in the one place in Saral where you can escape the hot weather. That, combined with the ability to see for miles, made Lukla an ideal capital.

Our Southern command post was in the foothills bordering Saral. Soldiers stayed back to pitch tents in the fields while I rode through the village. I passed the training yard, weapons repair shop, stables, hospital to treat the wounded, dining hall, and kitchen to arrive in front of a mansion. Aranya, Kapil, Giri, Rish, and I dismounted as Hasan Vindhya greeted us.

"My king, I am sorry I missed your coronation," he said, bowing at his waist with his palms touching.

"Your presence here was more vital," I answered.

Rish touched his brother's feet, and they embraced warmly. The brothers followed in the footsteps of their father and trained in warfare, unlike my father-in-law Mani.

Aranya left us to refresh after the journey while Hasan escorted us to a room. An old table stood at the center with a map of Saral spread out on it.

"How is General Satya?"

"He will survive the fall, my Majesty. But his fighting days are behind him," answered Hasan.

With Karan and Satya incapacitated, I needed to appoint new generals for my northern and southern armies.

"What is the news from Saral?"

"Two factions have emerged, King Jay. Gomti house and King Surya's distant cousin Prince Alai are competing to become the regent for Prince Vasant. Whoever controls the boy now will solidify their influence over the kingdom."

I would need Aranya's help in wading into the royal dynamics.

"How is Queen Riya?"

"I sought her audience a few times, and she refused to see me, King Jay. Her focus remains on her son, and she has not indicated any preference to either of these factions."

I'd sentenced her father to death, so I expected a hostile reception. Her goal of protecting Vasant aligned with mine. How much influence did she wield in Saral? Depending on that, she might be receptive to hearing my views and accepting my support.

Later that day, I visited General Satya. He lay on a cot, and cloth wraps covered his body. As he tried to rise, I signaled for him to remain.

"I let you down, my Majesty," he apologized.

"You were a victim of a malicious plot," I answered kindly.

He looked at his fingers and said, "Enemies surround us. That is not new. I let my guard down when dealing with them."

"What do you know of your fall?" I inquired.

"My horse acted strangely that day and threw me off his back. I suspect someone tampered with his food."

"Poison?" I gasped.

"Not to kill him, but to alter his behavior. I have heard of herb concoctions that can cause an elephant to go mad. Useful to cause a stampede. Must have been something similar."

It all came back to poison, a weapon of a coward. Malla spies were working to trace the source for them. I hoped to find out who the culprits were soon.

I changed the topic and asked, "What is Queen Riya's influence in the court?"

Satya glanced at me and shook his head. "She has very little influence, my Majesty. I don't want to speak ill of the dead, but King Nakul mocked her in front of others. When a king disrespects his wife, others follow suit."

My jaws tightened, and I gritted my teeth. I found it hard to remain sympathetic to my brother. I fought with my wives privately. Taking a fight publicly and putting his wife down was undignified. I recalled fighting with Aranya on the day of my coronation in front of my children. Heat rose in my face. *My wife deserved better from her husband too.*

I guided my mind back to the present. "General, you have served Malla for many years. I would like you to join me in the capital at my small council after your recovery."

He sighed, "My wife will thank you. I guess the time has come for me to hand the reins to someone younger."

I smiled, "Your experience is still invaluable to me. What do you think of Giri Thari to replace you as General?"

Satya appeared pleased. "He is a good man. He served me well as my Lieutenant. He knows the Saral royal politics and has many local friends. He will be excellent."

He regarded me thoughtfully and asked, "Any trouble with Hasan?"

"None at all. I have something else in mind for him. Keep it quiet for now, General," I urged, and he nodded.

The next day, we set out to climb the hill on our horses. The forest canopy blocked out the sun, and climbers and vines hung from the trees. As the horses stepped on the plants growing on the ground, a strong fragrance filled the air.

"Cobra," Aranya shrieked, and I found a snake hanging off a tree.

The dangerous animal raised its head to strike, and Champak tossed it aside with his spear. I noticed with surprise that my guards had managed to flank me.

Kathir Gomti, Prince Alai, and others welcomed us at the entrance to the fort. After our initial greetings, I asked to see Queen Riya and Prince Vasant. Kathir escorted Aranya and me to Riya's chambers.

The mourning widow wore a simple sari in the color of rain clouds, and her forehead appeared devoid of the dot. The young boy hiding behind her legs drew my interest. With eyes too big for his face, he observed us intently.

Bringing my attention back to Riya, I addressed her. "I am sorry for the death of your father and Nakul. While I cannot change the past, I hope we can set aside our enmities and act as allies again."

Riya stared at me and opened and closed her mouth a few times.

Then, taking a deep breath, she said, "Help me protect my son, Jay."

Aranya went down on her knees and told the boy, "Vasant, I am your father's sister. Your aunt."

He looked up at his mother, and she nodded. He peeked at Aranya from behind her, and she held out her arms to him. He drew his neck in, hiding completely, and Aranya dropped her hands.

"I brought a gift for you," I said and showed him an ornate wooden box.

"What is in it?" he asked, speaking for the first time.

"Come and see for yourself," I said and held the box out.

Tentatively, he took a couple of steps and grabbed the box, and ran away. As we watched, he went under a table and opened the gift. Inside nestled a hand-carved wooden sword. He pulled it out eagerly and acted out some moves.

Sliding out from under the table, he ran to his mother and said in a rushed voice, "Look what Jay got me."

"Uncle Jay," his mother corrected him.

He glanced at me and asked, "Uncle Jay, do you know how to fight with a sword? My mother says I am too little. I don't think so."

I got down on my knees next to Aranya and said, "Your mother is right. You were too little until yesterday. But today and with me, you are big enough."

The boy squealed in delight and came closer. "Can you teach me now?"

"First, do you know what you should do when you see your uncle and aunt? You ask them for blessings."

"Why?" he asked curiously.

I glanced at Riya, and she explained, "Remember how you touched grandfather's feet? And remember how he blessed you to become strong?"

He answered, "I want to be strong."

Aranya and I stood, and he prostrated in front of us, and I said out loud, "Prince Vasant, I bless you to become the best sword fighter in Saral."

"Can we go fight now?"

Aranya replied, "Next, you hug your aunt and uncle."

He looked at his mother, unsure about it, and she inclined her head.

Aranya scooped him into her arms and pressed her cheeks against his. Tears glistened in her eyes as she remembered the brother she had lost. Slowly, she handed the child to me. Holding him in my arm, I ruffled his curly hair.

"Ready to fight?" I asked, and he screamed, "Yes."

I took him to a large hall, and my guards helped me move the furniture to the corner, clearing space in the middle.

I tied a sash around his waist and tucked his sword in. I showed him how to draw the weapon and brandish it. His interest in playing with the sword lasted a few moments.

After that, I whispered, "Let us hide and see if Uncle Kapil can find us."

"Is he my mother's brother?"

"He is her cousin." *And I was your father's brother.*

With the boy in tow, I hid behind pillars and crawled under tables. My guards made a game of searching for us noisily. Their antics caused him to giggle loudly, and I joined him in laughter.

Soon he grew tired and climbed on my lap and curled up like a kitten. My heart swelled at the sight of the child holding my finger as he slept.

I carried him gently to his mother and waited for her to join me in the sitting room.

After tucking him in, she came and stood by the window, her back to me.

"Riya, I need your help in understanding Nakul. Why did he decide to invade Malla? Why did he poison my father?" I thought to myself, *Why did he hate me?*

She spun to face me with fire in her eyes. "There is a nice walk along the top of the fort. Do you want to join me?"

Once at the top, we stopped to admire the view. Malla lay in front of us, and I could see the Chambal river glistening like diamonds.

"I never tire of this sight," she said.

We strolled on the narrow path with the wind whispering in our ears. Riya mumbled, "Because of me."

"You?" I gasped.

"And Queen Meera," she added.

"Meera?" I asked stupidly.

She glanced at me and said, "She filled my head with silly dreams of marrying you. Then like a rug sold off, she and others asked me to marry Nakul. As if one prince is the same as the other to a girl."

She laughed bitterly, and I regarded her, horrified. As a boy, many eligible girls wanted to marry me. I never paid them much attention till I met Aranya.

She continued, "He was nice to me, and I tried to forget you and make a life with him. I succeeded for a while."

She opened and closed her fist and walked in silence. "Then, one night, I uttered your name in bed."

"My n-name?" I stuttered in alarm.

She glanced at me with blazing eyes. "Nakul heard me and almost choked me to death," she said, touching her throat with her fingers. I now understood why he hated me. Remembering his eyes trying to burn a hole in me, I shuddered to think what he did to her.

"My life was ruined by a single word. He treated me like dirt and slept with other women openly."

My stomach tightened at her misery. I remembered something my sister had said to me. That a girl's heart mattered. No one had asked Riya about hers.

"Vasant?" I mumbled.

"Nakul came to my room drunk once and took me vengefully," she said with venom. "Out of that doom sprang a new beginning. Vasant is the only good thing to happen to me in this godforsaken kingdom."

27

Meera

Dayan approached me in the courtyard outside the temple, and I waited for him by the door.

When he arrived at arm's length, I whispered, "I heard a man scream outside and opened the door to peek. It is too dark to make out anything. Go and check it out."

"My lady, it was too dangerous for you to open the door," he chided me gently.

"I acted without thinking," I muttered. *Not today, but a few months ago.*

He gathered two other men, and they entered the grove with a flaming torch. My heart pounded as I stood under the stars watching the light disappear behind trees. Soon, I heard footsteps, and Dayan appeared with his sword drawn. He shut the door behind him and said, "My lady, we found a man stabbed to death. The guards are taking him to the court physician. I don't know if the murderer is still around, and I don't have enough men to search. My priority is your safety, Queen Meera. Allow me to escort you back to the palace."

Once we returned to the palace, Dayan and I went searching for Atul. We found him behind his desk in his sitting room, surrounded by books. Piles of them covered the desk, and spilled onto his floor, and made a trail to his other chambers. When he saw us, he cleared some space on a bench and guided me to it.

Dayan narrated the happenings of the night.

Atul scowled and questioned, "You left the queen alone in the court-yard?"

Dayan stammered, "I a-apologize for my mistake, King Atul. That will never happen again."

My stomach twisted into knots. I'd lost my chance to be alone. Still, Dayan was not at fault. "I desired to be alone, and Dayan merely fol-lowed my order," I said.

"Rish would not have left you alone," Atul whispered. On hearing Rish's name, I drifted in a tide of despair. I bit my lips to bring order to my emotions. Then Atul asked, "Do we know who the dead man is?"

Dayan shook his head. "His clothing does not appear to be from Padi."

Atul dismissed him and said to me, "I will ask General Gambhir to investigate."

I whispered, "Atul, I heard him hand a vial of venom to the man who killed him. Someone poisoned you and my father. I am worried about a new target for this blight."

Atul took my hand and murmured, "Meera, what were you thinking, putting yourself in danger like that?"

I could not tell him the real reason I was out in the grove that night.

"Atul, I should have called for help immediately," I said to appease him.

His finger stroked my cheek, and he mumbled, "I don't want any harm to come to you."

I took his hand in mine and held it against my chest.

"What if someone attempts to poison you or Nala?" I asked him.

He said, "We are taking necessary precautions now. Jay and I talked before we left Akash. All our food is checked twice and guarded closely. It will be difficult for someone to poison us."

I sighed in relief. His kindness made it difficult for me to say what

I'd in mind. But it had to be done. I could not hide my condition for long, so I put my trust in his mercy and plowed ahead.

Drawing in a deep breath, I said lightly, "There is something else."

"What?" he asked, regarding me.

"I am pregnant," I revealed.

Like a lightning strike, joy erupted on his face, and he pulled me into a hug. Releasing me, he cradled my stomach.

"How far? Four months?" he asked. Without waiting for my response, he leaned in to kiss me. "It will be lovely to have another girl," he whispered.

Temptations arose in me to pretend the child was his. No, that would not do. I cared for Atul and cherished him. I could not lie to him. Also, this child had no place in the Padi royal succession. To pretend otherwise would be a betrayal of my duty as queen.

"Three months," I said, with my heart in my throat, blocking my breath.

"Three?" I could see the wheels turning in his head.

"You were mourning your father's death, and then I got captured and then injured."

His face darkened, and I steeled myself.

"Didn't you get your flow after our last time together?" he hissed.

He clasped my hand tightly, his nails driving into my skin. "Who is it?" he growled against my ears, and a tremor ran through my legs.

Suddenly, awareness sprung in his eyes.

"Rish," he whispered and let go of me. Hurt and pain filled his eyes, and my heart dropped to the floor. I hated that I'd hurt him this way.

"I knew he worshipped you. But I trusted you, Meera. I loved you with my entire being." His voice shook at his words, and a knife twisted in my chest.

"Forgive me, Atul. I was stupid—foolish. I will do anything to make up for this." My heart broke into pieces, and my breath came in shallow gasps. I did love him, and I wished I'd not wounded him.

His nostrils flared, and he said, "Were you mocking me behind my

198 - ANNA BUSHI

back? Laughing at my gullibility? While you carried on with him in my castle?"

His words brought forth anger I'd held at bay. I slapped him hard, and the sound of my palm hitting his cheek shook me awake.

Covering my mouth, I cried, "I have carried my duties to you faithfully all these years. Then, in a moment of weakness and panic, I made a terrible mistake." Tears stung my eyes to call what happened with Rish a mistake.

The spark died in his eyes as he ordered, "Leave."

28

Jay

Sleep eluded me as I thought about what Riya had revealed to me. Her battle scars ran deeper than mine. My stomach clenched at what she had endured at my brother's hand. Would her life have been better as my wife? Not as my third one.

I knew why Meera proposed the match. She had groomed Riya to be a queen. When I brought Aranya home, she had assumed Riya's future would be secure as Queen of Saral. Her good intentions did not account for human nature.

In matters of heart, as the crown prince, I could plan, plot, and act independently. Even Meera did not have the same luxury. What had Riya suffered all these years?

Footsteps approached me, and I tossed my thin blanket and sat upright.

Kapil materialized and said hurriedly, "A room has caught fire, my Majesty. We need to get to safety."

I could smell something burning. I got ready quickly and went with him.

"Is Aranya safe?"

"Guards are escorting her."

"Riya and Vasant?"

He paused and said quietly, "The smoke is coming from her chambers."

"What?" I asked, color draining from my face.

He urged me forward as he said, "My cousin has shut herself in her chambers and started a fire."

I placed my hand on his shoulder and ordered, "Take me there."

"We have men..."

"Kapil," I demanded.

He let out a sigh and called out, "Dev, Karan, and Veer."

"At the ready," Karan said, and we broke into a run.

The smell of smoke grew stronger as we entered the hall leading to the queen's chambers. A small crowd had gathered outside. I spotted Kathir Gomti and Prince Alai among them.

"What is going on?" I asked as I came to a stop.

"Queen Riya is inside with Prince Vasant."

"What are you waiting for? Why haven't you broken open the door yet?"

"The queen has ordered us to leave and——"

I commanded my men, "Break it open."

An ax appeared in Karan's hand, and he swung it with precise force on the latch. As it splintered, Kapil and Dev shouldered the door and forced it open.

Riya stood in the middle of her bedroom with Vasant in her arms. The boy whimpered at the commotion. Her curtains blazed, filling the room with smoke.

As I stepped into her sitting room, she warned, "Jay, stay there. If you move, I will jump out the window."

The smoke and fire shrouded her in mystery.

She threatened my heir, and I had no tolerance for it. I ordered in a cold-clipped tone, "Shoot her leg."

Prince Alai exclaimed, "She is our queen and is holding our prince."

I ignored him as Dev notched his arrow and released it. It grazed her right thigh, and she screamed in pain. He loosened another, this time scraping her left leg.

One of her bedposts fell on the ground in a shower of sparks, and the jute rug on the floor caught on fire. Roaring flames soared in the air creating a wall between us.

"Those were warning shots. If you move, the next arrow will be for your throat," I growled and walked forward with Kapil.

"Cousin Kapil," she pleaded. "Let me go."

Her voice grated my ears, and I steeled myself. I had to save Vasant, and then I would deal with this idiot.

"Riya," said Kapil tenderly. "Whatever it is, I can help you. You don't have to choose this."

"Help?" she wailed. "Where were you all these years when I was treated like a slave?" She threw her words at him.

We kept her engaged as Veer crept along the walls surreptitiously and then crawled along the floor. The smoke hid his passage, and then suddenly, he grabbed her shoulders from behind.

Riya struggled and kicked him, while Prince Alai shouted without moving from his spot. "That is our queen."

I ran to Riya and snatched Vasant from her hands, and stepped back out of her reach. The fire blistered the skin on my arm. Vasant howled at his mother. Veer let her go, and she collapsed on the floor.

"Riya," I said softly. "I know I did not help you all these years. But the future need not be a mirror of your past."

She gazed at me and said, "It will be no different. Vasant and I will continue to be pawns in your games."

"I will protect him," I promised.

She jerked upright and ran towards the window, leaping through the blaze. Her sari caught on fire.

"Stop her," I shouted, and Kapil ran towards her. Another post nearly fell on him, and he darted around it.

"Keep your promise," she whispered with a backward glance and then plunged into the night.

I stood rooted in shock. I'd failed to save Riya. I'd assumed she would abandon her wish to perish once I took her son away. Instead, she had abandoned the boy. He sobbed in my arms, bringing my senses back.

Giri arrived at the scene. He and Kathir directed men to put out the fire. Those two friends were a force to reckon with on the battlefield. This small fire would be vanquished by them in no time.

Kapil whispered in my ears, "This way, King Jay." I glanced at him and followed him outside.

"I am sorry," I murmured.

"You are not at fault here, Jay," he whispered back.

"I am not blameless. Send a message to Riya's brother, Navin."

As we made our way back to my chambers, Aranya burst forth.

"Is it true?" she asked, breathing hard. I nodded and handed the child to her.

She cradled him and said, "We will raise him."

That was what Meera wanted me to do. My sister had asked me to foster him in Akash. And pass the crown, his by birthright, to him.

Aranya fell in step with us and muttered, "He can marry Heera when he grows older."

No, I thought. *That would not be appropriate. Nakul and I were brothers.*

"Aranya, not now. Let the children grow up without us tying their futures," I chided her. I had to reveal the truth to her one day. But not now, while I needed her to raise him as her nephew. The boy had no blood tie to her. I worried that she would become aloof from the boy if I revealed that fact. My own cold relationship with my stepmother colored my view. Vasant cried himself to sleep. Leaving him in Aranya's care, I strode out of her room.

Earth bid a teary farewell to the night as heavy mist hung in the air.

"Find Rish," I ordered a guard and awaited him at the top of the fort.

The first rays of light peaked out of the cloud as he arrived covered in sweat.

"You started early today," I stated.

"After I helped douse the fire, I decided to train below in the yard, my Majesty."

We drew our swords and circled each other.

"I should have done more to save Riya." I shared my thought with him.

"You could not have anticipated her actions," he stated. I did not reveal what Riya had told me. I knew her state of mind and had done nothing to prevent this.

I directed my anger into my combat and lunged at him. He parried my attack.

"My brother, Hasan, is writing to his wife," he said. Hasan married Gita Biha, Riya's aunt.

We fought wordlessly for a while.

"I served a better queen," he mused. Would Meera abandon her children and take her own life? She had a spine of iron and had taught me to persist. She would choose death only when all hope perished. Fear gripped my heart, and I shook my head to clear the dark clouds.

He thrust his sword at me, and I retreated. Our feet glided along the cold floor as the birds left their nests.

Slowly, I forgot about all else, and only his blade stayed in my vision. It sparkled like a diamond and came at me swiftly. We danced as the metals clanged. Fighting with him demanded my complete attention. One stray thought, and he would beat me.

"King Jay, Uncle Rish," Kapil called us as our blades slid along each other. Rish stepped back and bowed.

Sweat dripped down my back as I turned to Kapil.

"They are waiting for you in the council room."

Muthu helped me dress in my royal finery.

I went to see Aranya next. My nephew ran to me and held my knees.

"Are we playing again?"

"Soon," I smiled at him.

A maid took him away.

"Aranya, tell me about Prince Alai," I asked.

"He is a coward," she said scornfully. "Never left his castle while Nakul and I traveled in rags, hiding from the Malla army."

She glanced at me and added, "My father was partly to blame for that."

I held her hand and rubbed her wrist. "Circle of violence that I'd hoped to break with our marriage."

She leaned on my shoulders and said, "We still have work to do. We will raise the boy to forge peace in Magadha."

"What do you think of Kathir Gomti?"

"Didn't he fight with you in Sunda? Nakul's mother hailed from the Gomti house."

Looking up, she added, "Your mother, too."

The same mother gave birth to us, I thought.

"They helped us throughout the war. I would trust Kathir more than Alai. He is your cousin, so there are blood ties."

I nodded and revealed my plan to her. She listened and suggested some changes. With her help, I tied the loose ends and headed to the council room.

29

Meera

I waited for the guards to come and imprison me. Throw me in the dungeon. Banish me from the kingdom. Behead me. My imagination ran wild in meting out punishment.

Instead, Atul ignored me.

I stayed away from him and carried myself as before on the outside. My insides, however, burned like a volcano spewing fire.

His place remained empty at mealtimes with the children.

One day, Nala said, "Mother, do you remember how Uncle Parth acts strangely sometimes?"

"Hmm," I said absently.

"Father acted like that this afternoon," he muttered.

Color faded from my face as I gazed at him. Atul had started drinking? I wanted him to punish me, not himself.

"Your father is taking some medicines to help him heal. That might cause such behavior sometimes," I mollified him.

How would I find out? I wished Rish had been here. I trusted him to be discreet and could have asked him to find out.

Dayan would consider it strange that I did not know details about my husband. Gambhir would think such a question unusual too. I trusted Kantha, but she had already suspected something with the lack of pregnancy announcement from the king. I did not want to feed her suspicion.

Then an idea presented itself. A dance troop arrived in town and planned to perform before the crown tomorrow. Ordinarily, I loved attending these events. The music would transport me to another world, away from my worries. With the rift between us, I'd intended to plead ill health and skip the event. Atul would be there, and my attendance would give me a chance to observe him in person. I decided to attend.

I wore a sari in the color of a lotus and stood in front of the mirror. The sari pleats hid my tiny bump. It would not last long but would be sufficient for now.

My Aunt Mohini and her daughter, Mala, accompanied me to the hall. My aunt wore a beautiful silk sari in the color of corals, and she had worn her grey-lined hair in a bun. Mala wore a sari in the color of the amaranth flower, embroidered with golden flowers along the border. She had braided her top part, leaving the rest free, creating a beautiful cascade of her long hair.

"Cousin Meera, I draped the sari the way you taught me," she said and spun around to show me.

"You look like one of the beautifully sculpted statues that adorn our temple," I said.

"How was Jay's coronation?" asked my aunt. "I wish I'd attended it. I'd witnessed your father's," she mused.

"He did look like the younger version of my father." He resembled how my father looked when my mother was still alive. Vibrant and full of life. I described the festivities to them as we entered the hall.

I greeted other attendees as we made our way to the front. Woolen rugs were placed on the floor in the royal section adjacent to the stage. I sat on one depicting a peacock. My aunt and Mala sat behind me.

I twirled my sari end, waiting for Atul. He arrived with Parth and stopped to talk with members of the court. I regarded him carefully, and he appeared steady on his feet.

When he saw me seated, his eyebrows raised for a brief moment. He smiled and greeted the royal members sitting around me and took his place beside me.

I waited for the music to start and the dancers to appear on stage. As the musicians invoked God Nataraj to witness their performance, I leaned towards Atul. Tiny lines appeared on his previously smooth forehead.

I wanted to tell him I loved him. That I rued injuring him.

Instead, I accused him. "Our son witnessed you drunk."

Atul's nostrils flared as he said, "*Our* son?"

Anger surged in my body as the implication of his words sank in. That boy looked like his father. I listened to the music for a few moments, waiting for it to dissipate.

"Are you drinking, Atul?" I whispered.

"Do you blame me?" he asked, gazing at me.

My lips trembled as our eyes met. I glanced down and mumbled, "Where do we go from here?"

He did not answer me for a long time. As the song ended, the dancers bowed to us, and he threw a pouch of coins at them.

"Everywhere I turn, I only see walls enclosing me," he answered as the singer began another song.

"I can disappear," I whispered to the rhythm of drums.

"Do you think the thought has not occurred to me?" he asked quietly.

My breath caught in my throat, and I opened my mouth to gulp some air.

"I have heard you sing this song to Priya," he murmured. I listened to the song about snow melting in spring and the land donning a dress of green after being washed off winter thoughts.

"Memories that just hurt me now," he added bitterly.

Why did I come? I could not leave now. That would cause gossip that we both could ill afford. My foolish act had caused this mayhem, and I needed to put things right.

"I will do anything to take your pain away," I whispered.

"Don't make promises you cannot keep," he warned me.

When the dance ended, I went to greet the performers. Afterward,

I searched for Atul. He had disappeared from the hall, and I made my way back slowly. Atul had ruled the land wisely. My actions could not be responsible for him forgetting his duties.

A few days later, General Gambhir came to see me.

"My lady, may I request your presence in the small council?"

"Small Council? Is Atul asking me to come?"

Color crept up his face, and he looked at the ground.

"His majesty appears indisposed, and the council is divided about moving to Nanga, our summer capital."

"Indisposed? What is going on?"

"My lady, when I went to visit him earlier, he appeared intoxicated," he mumbled.

I drew a sharp breath.

"King Atul had asked me to consult you in his absence before, and we need to make a decision soon. All arrangements are made, and a group of people typically start the journey to Nanga to get the place ready for the king."

"And?" I asked.

"Prince Parth and Prince Rudra want to halt the preparations. Minister Drona and I want to send the first group to Nanga."

"I will come. Give me a few minutes."

With my maid's help, I put my hair up in a bun and wore a crown with a sapphire studded peacock. Matching earrings and necklace adorned me, and I made my way to the small council with Dayan.

Atul loved Nanga, and the change of scenery would be good for him. The mountain air might heal our wounds.

"Queen Meera," Parth smirked at me.

Did Atul reveal anything to his brother? I dismissed the thought quickly. He wouldn't have.

"Welcome to the council, Queen Meera," Gambhir greeted me.

"How can I help?" I asked.

Minister Drona answered, "My lady, since spring, we have been planning our move to Nanga. Men have cleared our roads, stocked our supplies, and cleaned the rooms. Now the first set of royal staff with Chief

Guard Desh will make their way to be followed by the rest of us in a fortnight."

"My brother is recovering from his wound, and I suggest we skip the ritual this year," said Parth.

"I agree," said Uncle Rudra.

I glanced at Gambhir, and he said, "My lady, until a fortnight ago, the king approved of our plans and wanted to go to Nanga for the summer. Unless he directs otherwise, I recommend we stick to his plans."

The situation turned out harder than I'd imagined. I could not openly come out against Atul's brother and uncle, not when Atul himself remained ambivalent about me.

I needed time, so I said, "Allow me to talk to the king to ascertain his views."

It gave me a chance to check up on him, so I went to his chambers next. His guards allowed me in. I took that as a good sign that they did not forbid my entry.

His orderly pile of books in the formal sitting room appeared disturbed. A few had spilled onto the floor. The dining room had a large portrait of us painted after his coronation. I strode past it into his bedroom.

The drawn curtains kept the room in darkness. I opened one of them, and light spilled onto Atul's repose body on his bed. He rested on his stomach, naked to his waist, with a cloth wrapping his wound. If his furniture could speak, they would scream at me to leave. *I'd caused enough damage.*

Quieting the voices, I approached him tentatively. "Atul," I called.

When he remained motionless, I sat on the bed and touched his hand. His hot skin shocked me.

"Atul," I called again, touching his neck and chest. The heat from his body caused my alarm to rise.

I ran outside and ordered his guards to fetch his servants and the royal physician.

His servant came first.

"Your king is ill. Why didn't you fetch the physician?" I snarled.

"Ill?" he asked. "Prince Parth said he was working off——" he stammered.

The physician arrived and inspected him.

"Is it his wound?"

"That appears to be healing well, my lady," he answered.

He ordered his assistants to mix some herbs and handed a cup to me.

"Please feed him this and have the servants wash his body in cold water. I will check on him soon."

With the servant's help, I leaned Atul on my chest. I sent him to fetch some water while I spooned Atul the medicine.

He stirred and opened his eyes. "Meera," he whispered.

"It is me," I said, my voice cracking.

He closed his eyes and murmured, "I was dreaming about you." A knot formed in my stomach. "I am always dreaming about you."

I wiped his mouth with my sari and laid him back. His breathing steadied into a quiet rhythm.

The servant arrived with the water, and I asked him to fetch some gruel. Slowly, I dipped a clean cotton cloth in the water and wiped Atul's forehead. As I traced the familiar contours of his chest, I remembered our good life together.

After I fed him some gruel, I stayed beside him the whole day.

Kantha brought me some food.

"I am not hungry," I protested.

"You have to eat for the little one," she urged.

That night, I slept beside Atul with Amar between us. I studied their faces. While Nala looked like his father, this one had inherited both our features. I wondered about the child growing inside me. Who would she look like? I drifted off to sleep, dreaming of a hand pouring venom down my throat.

I woke up to "Oy" and sat upright. The first rays of sun peeked into the room. Atul rubbed his eyes and peered at me and then Amar. Amar had shifted to rest with his feet on his father's chest. He must have kicked him awake.

Atul flinched as I touched his forehead. Warm still but not burning hot as before. I dropped my hand.

"Atul, is your food still checked for poison?" I asked.

He raised his eyebrows and said, "Not that again. No one is trying to hurt me."

Apart from me, his eyes seemed to convey. I had given him plenty of reasons to be mad at me. Yet, I struggled with his fury. Before I could reply, our son burst in.

"Mother, Father," Nala exclaimed as he ran into the room. "Do you remember what day is today?"

"It is my birthday," Nala continued without waiting for us to answer the question he posed and climbed on the bed.

I pulled the boy into a tight embrace. "I told the cook to make all your favorite dishes today."

"I am nine," he said, bursting with pride. "Can I start fighting with a real sword?"

"Yes," laughed Atul and punched his arm.

He stood up and swayed slightly on his feet. I reached an arm out and then dropped it as he steadied himself.

"Come," he called out to Nala. "I have a surprise for you in the stables."

"What is it?" Nala asked, jumping off the bed.

"Patience will be rewarded," he said and tousled his son's hair.

They took a few steps, and then Atul clutched his chest and collapsed on the floor.

"Atul," I wailed and ran to him.

30

Jay

I watched as Aranya helped Vasant get ready.

"I have to sit on a chair?" he asked while allowing her to apply coconut oil to his hair.

"Yes, it is a beautiful golden throne. My father and your father sat on it," she said. Her face shone with her fierce love for the boy. *Would she still love him if I had told her the truth about Nakul?*

He pouted and looked at his feet.

"I don't like it. It is big."

"I liked hiding under the throne," I said, grinning at him. The throne never scared me as a child, but I was terrified of the duties that came with it.

He glanced up, his eyes bright.

"Can I hide under it?"

Aranya finished dressing him, and I held out my hand. He ran to me and clasped my index finger.

"Not today. If you sit quietly, when I ask you to, I will play with you. What game do you want to play?"

"Horsey," he screamed.

"I will take you on a horse ride," I agreed.

We arrived in the throne room, and the golden throne stood on a raised platform with three steps leading up to it. The ornate chair had legs carved in the shape of fish, with its open mouth holding up the seat. It had been more than a month since my own coronation. Instead of the throngs then, a small group had gathered in the chamber now.

Seeing others, Vasant hid behind Aranya's legs. *What bad memories did he hold?*

Gesturing at Aranya to keep walking, I said, "We have to get some sugarcane."

He peeked at me, "Sugarcane?"

"For the horse," I whispered.

I got on one knee and addressed him, "Your Majesty."

That elicited a giggle from him.

"Do you see the fishes on the throne?" I asked.

He squinted at it and nodded.

"I want you to walk by yourself and count the fishes on it. Do you know how to count?"

He held up his fingers and whispered, "One, two, three."

"Good. Hold them up to show me how many fishes. And then sit on the throne. Can you do it?"

He gazed up at Aranya, and she bent to kiss his forehead. "I will be right here waiting."

He took his first tentative steps.

Nadaswaram notes floated in the air, and a priest chanted a hymn in praise of Lord Muruga.

"Poor child. He cried for his mother last night," Aranya muttered in my ears. I let my fingertips touch hers.

"He will forget her soon. And only remember his Aunt Aranya." I had. Meera's stories about my mother had long supplanted my actual memories of her.

He looked back at us. Aranya nodded at him encouragingly. He climbed the three steps and walked around the throne, counting the fishes. With a smile extending from ear to ear, he held up four fingers.

My lips curled up, and I motioned him to sit. He climbed onto the throne.

My uncle, Kandan Gomti, stepped forward. My mother's brother placed the royal crown symbolically on Vasant's head and put it back on the tray. He took the smaller crown designed for the young king and crowned him.

"Long Live King Vasant," I chanted, and others joined me. Vasant removed the crown and held it in his fingers, examining the sparkling gems in wonder.

"Go with your aunt. I will come and get you soon," I told him.

Aranya scooped up the boy.

I led the men to the small council room.

Kathir stood with his father, Kandan. My uncle wore his curly grey streaked hair short while his son wore his charcoal hair long. The differences ended there, and father and son resembled each other in looks and height.

"Kathir, I appoint you as regent to the king. He is under my protection and will continue to be until he comes of age." I'd made this wish known to them in private.

"Cousin Jay, I hope to serve him and Saral well," he said solemnly.

"With the passing of his mother and father, Aranya and I will foster him in Akash," I announced.

Prince Alai cleared his throat. "He is a Saral king, and growing up in Malla will not teach him our ways. Allow me to foster my cousin."

I shook my head. "Aranya is his closest living relative, and she is a Saral princess. She will ensure he is trained in Saral ways."

I gazed at my men. "I have appointed Giri Thari as my southern commander. His role will not be confined to protecting Malla's borders. He will be helping you keep peace in Saral." I affirmed my trust in Giri Thari with this appointment. He had proved his worth many times in the last few months. As the next Thari chief, I needed his loyalty.

Kathir welcomed this news with a pat on Giri's shoulders. "I have fought with General Giri in Sunda. His bravery and compassion earned him praise among his soldiers."

Giri acknowledged him with a bow.

Kanban said, "King Jay, Saral is in turmoil with the news of King Nakul's death. I heard you went on a pilgrimage in Malla to introduce yourself to her people. I propose you and the queen travel through Saral with our young king to calm our people."

We had discussed these matters yesterday. Alone, he had addressed me as son and asked me to visit my mother's hometown Kadal. Strange longing had filled my heart, and I'd accepted.

"Uncle, it is a great idea. Aranya wanted to tour some sites in Saral too. Let me consult with her and pick a few places for us to visit. Then we can start making the arrangements."

I looked at Hasan and Rish. "Join me on my horse ride with the king."

I gathered Vasant, and we walked to the stables. A stableboy came to aid us.

"Choose a horse, your Majesty," I said.

"I cannot see them, Uncle Jay," he complained.

I lifted him onto my shoulders, and he pointed to a big white stallion.

"That one," he exclaimed.

"Is he trained?" I asked.

"He is, King Jay. He is not the gentlest horse, but he is sharp," replied the stableboy.

He saddled the horse and brought him out. I held Vasant in my arm and handed the piece of sugarcane to him.

"Go ahead and feed him," I said, and he held the cube out. The horse tossed it around in his mouth.

"Ooh, he licked me," said Vasant and wiped his hand on his dhoti.

I placed my nephew on the saddle and climbed behind him.

Rish, Hasan, and Kapil joined us. "Of course, you had to pick the biggest stallion for your ride," Kapil teased me as we started on a trot. His brown mare snorted as she fell in step.

"My nephew is a natural at being king. This horse drew him without my guidance."

"Vasant, hold these reins," I said and guided his arms.

He grabbed them tightly and moved his arm up and down. The smart animal moved with the tiniest of pressure from my legs, so I let the boy play with the reins.

"Hasan, you managed the southern troops admirably in Satya's absence. I need similar help in the north. Go home to your family first and spend time with them. Then, head to our northern command post and take charge. After matters are settled there, check on your brother-in-law Karan Thari. Provide what help your sister, Asya, needs. I am still holding out hope that he may recover." Meera had asked me to take care of Asya and her girls.

"When I am back in Akash, I would like to talk to your nieces." To give them a say in their future. *What if Tanisi revealed she'd pined for me as well?* I pushed that thought away. I'd no interest in taking another wife. If she pined for me, she would stay a maid.

He inclined his head, "I will leave shortly, my Majesty."

I glanced at his brother, Rish. "Giri and Kathir have work to do here in Lukla. Accompany me on my tour of Saral."

In a few days, we left Lukla and headed south. Aranya wore a sari in the color of vermillion, and she blazed like a beacon. The king sat on her lap in the chariot while I rode beside them.

We stayed in each place for a few days. Villagers arrived from the surrounding villages to get a glimpse of their new king. In the evening, I shared meals with the elders and merchants, listening to their concerns and promising to take action where needed.

One day, Aranya and I went in search of a small temple nestled among trees. The sandstone façade came into view in the morning sun. We halted under a tree with its branches spilling into the temple courtyard.

I grinned at my queen, remembering her climbing onto the tree and jumping down the other side.

"I can still do it," she challenged me with a smirk.

"Oh, I believe you."

A family of monkeys peeked at us from the tree branches.

We entered the courtyard, and a sparkling temple met our sight. Fine sand crunched under our feet in the yard, and I spotted no sign of cobwebs. A young priest welcomed us and performed *pooja* for us. The serene face of Muruga looked upon us, clothed in silks and silver jewelry.

"Back then, we were a fleeing couple in rags, and the lord wore similar clothing. Now, his attire matches ours," she whispered in my ears.

As we walked around the yard, Dev muttered, "Is this where you hid, King Jay?"

"Yes. Imagine the place in ruins. With my injuries, I would not have survived a night without Aranya." He had rescued us and took us to safety. "We would have perished if you had not found us." He flushed at my words.

A brave monkey followed us and stretched out his hand. Aranya placed a banana in it, and he scampered away. We watched him scurry among the trees disappearing from our view.

On our journey south, jackfruit trees lined the roads. Giant green fruits clung to the tree trunk like ugly lumps. In the heat, the strong sweet aroma of the fruit permeated the air around us. That morning, I'd eaten the delicious fruit soaked in honey. The boiled seeds made their way into our stew last night. Paddy fields glistened with the young plants on either side.

Freckles covered the bridge of Vasant's face. At our rest that evening, Aranya gave him coconut water.

He took a sip and made a face.

"I don't like it."

"It will keep you cool," she argued.

He came running to me.

"I don't like it, Uncle Jay," he whined.

"You know the rules, Vasant. We listen to Aunt Aranya."

The next day, I'd asked for an elephant to transport us to Kadal. Vasant's fingers dug into my legs as we approached the animal. I carried him in my arms. Even a baby king must hide his fright.

I stroked the trunk of the elephant and fed him a banana.

"You can touch him if you want," I whispered, and my nephew shook his head.

I signaled, and the elephant went down on his knees. I climbed up with Vasant.

As we moved forward, the boy relaxed and started pointing out the various sights to me.

Fields and hills gave way to the sea on our left. The water shimmered in the morning sun. He stared at it, mesmerized.

"Have you been to the seashore before?" I asked.

"What is that?" he replied.

"It is endless water with a sandy beach. Look, there is a lighthouse." A cylindrical tower carved out of rocks stood on the sandy beach, warning sailors.

The elephant swayed side to side while walking, and the gentle motion rocked him to sleep. Soon, he leaned on my chest and fell asleep. I wrapped my arm around him to support his head.

The city of Kadal came into view, and castles and temples rose above the water. The granite structures glinted in the sun's reflection. A pyramidal temple capped with an octagonal peak stood in prominence. Beside it stood a rectangular castle with a row of eight pillars in front. Carved elephants welcomed visitors to the palace.

People lined both sides of the broad street as our procession made its way to the castle. Uncle Kanban waited on the steps with a row of women holding oil lamps.

I slid down the back of the elephant, and the motion woke up Vasant. I waited for Aranya to disembark from the chariot and join us.

The royal herald announced my arrival, "King Jay, the ruler of the great kingdom of Malla, brave as a tiger, queller of pirates and vanguard of seas; son of the noble and just King Vikram, conqueror of Saral; grandson of esteemed King Karan, keeper of the peace in Malla; great-grandson of the warrior King Jay, ruler of the three worlds."

A young woman waved a plate of turmeric water around us to ward off evil, and my uncle greeted us.

"Welcome home, son of Saral."

On a private tour, he showed me a portrait of my mother as a young girl. My breath caught in my throat as I gazed at her. The girl in the picture looked at me with my eyes. My uncle noticed it and said, "She did leave a lot of her in you."

We walked to the sea that evening. Aranya and Vasant chased the waves, her hair glinting in the bright sun and her sun-kissed cheeks glowing. Vasant screamed as the warm water lapped his feet, and Aranya leaped the waves with him. I wanted to hold that joyous image of Aranya in my head, the unfiltered happiness animating her face. My uncle cleared his throat, and I strolled with him on the wet sand, away from others.

"I was younger than my sister, Kayal, so I did not understand all that I saw at twelve. I have had decades since to think about things and arrive at a conclusion. Is Nakul her son?" he asked.

His question shocked me. Why did I not think there might be others who might have guessed what happened? I stammered, "Uncle—"

"No need to reply, Son. I have kept my thoughts to myself, and they will perish with me. You have chosen to foster the boy. I will, however, advise you on one thing. I understand you have no heirs now. But you are young, and one of your wives will beget you a son soon. Sometimes, better to let the past die. Otherwise, two kingdoms will be in turmoil."

I reflected on what he said as I swallowed. I'd just crowned Vasant as King of Saral. That would be in jeopardy if folks suspected his father's birth. A son of mine would have a better claim to the Saral throne through Aranya. The Malla crown resting on my head belonged to Vasant.

"Being an advisor is easy. I don't have to make the decisions," my uncle muttered, and I said, "My duty is to Malla and Magadha. When the time comes, I hope I can remember that."

After the feast, I sat at a desk reading the messages from Akash.

Rish and Kapil entered with a nondescript man of medium build and height.

I regarded them, and Rish said, "A messenger from our spy chief."

"King Jay, we found who has been inquiring about poison. Sarp, Prince Parth's right-hand man."

31

Meera

A breeze floated in, caressing my skin gently, like the touch of a lover. That word conjured an image of a man with a broad smile, and I banished it. I'd no time for pity or impossible dreams.

Atul moaned from his bed, and I rushed to his side. I adjusted his blanket as his chest rose and fell with each ragged breath. He had not regained consciousness since his fall yesterday.

Kantha brought Priya and Rima over. And a bowl of broken wheat porridge cooked with jaggery and topped with ghee roasted cashews for me. The delicate scent of *elaichi* rose in the air along with the stream. As I ate, the girls wrote their alphabets on rice spread on plates. For each alphabet, we took turns telling a short story or singing a song that started with that letter. While my songs did portray a tale, the girls delighted in describing an animal doing a random action. More ridiculous the act, louder their laughter: monkeys with long tails flew in the air; tigers rowed boats clutching the oars in their sharp claws; snakes wore crowns and curled up on thrones. Their imagination lightened my dark mood.

"Queen Meera," Atul's servant called me, and I sent the girls to play and went into the sitting room. His guard commander and his servant waited for me.

"Did you question the cook?" I asked the servant.

"I did, my lady. No one touched the king's food apart from the cook and me," he replied.

"Did anyone visit him? Anyone who might have brought food?"

His guard shook his head. "Only you, Prince Parth, General Gambhir, Prince Nala, and his servants have visited him."

These were his family and loyal friends. "Be extra cautious," I warned them. I stared at a web of deceit, and I needed to untangle it without getting snared in it.

After they left, I let my shoulders slump. My back hurt, and I longed for a hot bath. I dreaded leaving Atul alone for more than a few moments. I entered the bedroom and sank into a chair.

My mind traversed through Atul's journey. Someone shot him with a poison arrow in Akash, and they tried to finish the work they started here. Who would benefit from his death? General Gambhir's fortunes would diminish with another ruler. Would Prince Rudra hurt his own nephew?

General Gambhir! What did he tell me yesterday? He believed Atul was intoxicated. Atul's servant thought the same and had allowed him to rest, assuming it would wear off. He mentioned Prince Parth had told him his brother needed to sleep off the liquor. Two people had named Parth in connection with Atul. I remembered Parth's arrival that night in Akash and the chaos that ensued after. Fear gripped my throat with its cold fingers, and I struggled to breathe. Likely Atul had asked his brother for his hidden stash. Had Parth poisoned his brother's drink?

I dragged myself up straight. Anger rose in me like a flock of birds rising. No time to panic. I'd a kingdom to save. I quelled my temper. First, I needed to send a message to Jay. I sat at Atul's desk and penned a letter. After the usual greetings, I wrote, "I am unable to sing today." I finished the letter with other mundane details and called Dayan.

"Send this to Jay with utmost urgency," I said.

After he left, I pondered what came next. Should I call a meeting of the council and question Parth? No, I could not do it without evidence. What if I was mistaken? An accusation of this nature would be devastating to make. How would I collect evidence? Slowly, I considered one idea after another and rejected it.

Dejected, I sat next to Atul and held his hand.

"Forgive my transgression, Atul. I cherished you as a wife and bore your children. Then my past led me astray from a path I'd set." My voice choked with emotions.

I rested my head on Atul's shoulder, listening to his breathing. "I loved him first," I whispered in his ears. "Before I met you." Tears streamed from my face to land on Atul's chest. I'd sacrificed my love and traded it for duty.

"I thought our marriage vows sufficient to keep my feelings at bay. I was wrong. And weak." *And in love with two good men who had been kind and generous to me.* I'd lost them both.

"I never meant to hurt you or mislead you." A shudder passed through me. "I love you. Come back to me," I whispered.

My mind cleared slowly, like waves subsiding on a pool. If Parth was poisoning his brother, I needed allies to protect Atul and Nala. My Aunt Mohini would be a powerful ally on my side. General Gambhir, Atul's friend, would be another.

Nala strode in from his lessons. Seeing his father collapse had shaken the boy.

"How is he?" he muttered, his eyes twitching. He bounced from one leg to another, swaying on his feet, and I said gently, "Stand still for a moment, Son."

He stopped fidgeting and gazed at me.

"If something happens to me, I want you to stay with your father. Make sure only his trusted guards and servants serve him food."

"What is going to happen to you?" he stammered.

"Nothing. It is just a precaution," I said and squeezed his hand. "You can trust General Gambhir, Kantha, and your Uncle Jay."

"And Uncle Rish?" he asked.

"Yes, you can trust Uncle Rish," I mumbled. "And remember you are the prince of this land and your father's heir," I whispered as I bent to kiss his head.

After he left, I slumped on my chair. Tiredness took over me, and I slowly drifted off to sleep. "I trusted you, Meera," Atul cried, and I screamed, "I did not mean to betray you."

"Queen Meera," a voice called, and I roused myself. The royal physician cleared his throat, and I sat up straight.

"How is he?" I asked, and then my glance fell on Prince Parth and Prince Rudra behind him. A warning note tried to penetrate my drowsiness.

The physician went to inspect him and turned to Prince Parth.

"He has been poisoned, my lord. I have given him an antidote. Hopefully, he will respond to it and recover soon," he said, avoiding my eyes.

Fear reached its cold tendril out to grasp me.

Parth dismissed him. My sleepy head awoke sluggishly, like wet burning wood.

I took a deep breath and raised to my feet.

"What is going on, Parth?" I asked, keeping tremors out of my voice.

He moved languidly to his brother's side and glanced at him.

Then he spun around to scan the room. I followed his eyes, and Chief Guard Desh emerged from the shadows. I'd not noticed him earlier. The urge to flee took hold, and I folded my arms.

"You tell us, Queen Meera. When you took him to Malla to aid Jay, Malla men captured my brother and kept him imprisoned. You went missing for days with Rish while your brother paraded around on elephants."

I stared at him while anger bubbled in my stomach. "Saral men and their allies captured Atul, and I barely escaped their clutches," I said coldly, hiding my rage.

He smirked and said, "Then, in the presence of Jay and you, my brother was shot with a poison-tipped arrow, and you kept me from visiting him. I fought to see him and threatened to turn Malla to ashes if any harm came to my king."

Fear took root in my mind and spread its branches into my blood.

He gestured around the room dramatically. "I fought for my brother and shed my blood in his name. And in my castle, he is being harmed. I won't allow it."

I stood tall and stated, "I am your queen. Careful what you accuse me of."

He bared his teeth like a snake showing its fangs. "He fought with you, and he told me he wanted to set you aside. And marry another woman for his queen. Before he could announce his decision, he was poisoned. Poison is a woman's weapon."

I was taken aback by the accusation in his voice. He'd plotted to kill Atul. I could not endure him to see me weak. I laughed while my mind spun furiously. "King Atul and I did fight. Like many husbands and wives. That is the only truth you have uttered, Parth. The rest are lies conjured by a treacherous mind."

I called his guard, "Did the king order you to forbid me from entering his chambers?"

His eyes darted around the room. "No, my lady," he said.

Parth asked, "Has my brother visited the queen's chambers recently?"

"No, my lord," he answered. A triumphant smile flashed on Parth's face. He would do whatever to grab his brother's crown. Including killing him and blaming me for it. For a brief unguarded moment, his thirst for power flared in his eyes. Despair and fury swirled in my mind.

Dayan arrived and muscled his way in.

"What is going on here?" he shouted.

Parth and Rudra exchanged glances, and Uncle Rudra spoke for the first time. "Queen Meera's recent actions are suspicious. With the king's life threatened, the small council has decided to keep her confined to her chambers till we can ascertain what happened."

I felt like a hammer dropped on my bones, shattering them to pieces.

Dayan looked at us, confused.

Chief Guard Desh ordered, "Take the queen to her chambers and make sure she does not leave it."

Two men came forward. Dayan cried, "Wait, she is under my protection."

Desh said, "No harm will come to her. You can continue guarding her. My men will join you."

They escorted me to my chambers and shut the door behind me. Alone in my room, my world came crumbling around me as I heard the latch being bolted.

32

Jay

I stared incredulously at Rish, with my mouth hanging open. Before the numerous insects flying around decided to take refuge in my mouth, I shut it.

I hauled myself up and asked, "Sarp? Isn't he dead? Is he a ghost now?"

Kapil jumped in. "I did find him with his throat slit. But before he died, he inquired about poisons and purchased a few kinds."

I rubbed my eyes. "Do one of you want to finish the story, or do you want me to drag it out of you one question at a time?"

Kapil rolled his eyes, a subtle action, easy to miss, only noticed by a lifelong friend.

Rish answered, "These poisons are rare and expensive. Sarp is not wealthy, and he has no personal enemies to murder deceitfully. The obvious assumption is Sarp was buying the poison for someone else. One who had money and enemies to dispense. Sarp worked for Prince Parth and might have purchased them on his behalf. King Nakul might have infiltrated Prince Parth's circle of friends and used Sarp as well."

I strode to the window and stared at the twinkling stars in the sky. A half-moon hung above the city, bathing it in soft mellow light. Nakul had murdered our father. Slowly a pattern emerged in my head. What I saw shook me.

I turned around and paced the floor. "We know four people who were poisoned: my father, Karan Thari, General Satya, and King Atul. Nakul benefitted from all their injuries and the one death. But before we could question him, he was killed by Prince Parth."

I clenched my hand. What a fool I'd been. I gazed at Kapil, and his lips folded into a thin line. He had reached the same conclusion.

Rish stated it aloud, "It was Parth who plotted with Nakul then. Not General Devan Biha."

"Yes, an alliance between them makes sense in light of what we know. Parth would have helped Nakul capture Malla. In turn, Nakul would have helped him overthrow Atul," I said.

Kapil added quietly, "When we disrupted his plans, Parth worried he would be exposed. So he killed an unarmed Nakul."

Rish remarked, "And murdered Sarp to throw us off his tail."

Kapil blurted, "My Majesty, remember he tried to stab you with a dagger in Sunda? We dismissed it then as the actions of a drunk." I recalled it vividly. Kapil emerged out of the air and had kicked his arm with force and caused him to drop the weapon. He saved my life and thwarted Parth's attempt. Was it all an act? Pretending to be drunk, so he could say and do things that would not be examined closely?

"Someone shot Atul with an arrow that night. After Parth had stabbed Nakul. Could it have been Parth's man?" I asked.

"Sarp!" exclaimed Rish. I nodded, and we exchanged glances.

A coldness spread in my body despite the heat. We did not have proof for any of it.

"King Atul might still be in danger," Rish whispered. "And Queen Meera."

"Kapil, leave us alone," I commanded. He regarded us and left.

I pushed Rish against the wall roughly and clasped his throat.

"What happened between you and my sister?" I snarled.

His eyes viewed me calmly, and he choked out, "It is not my secret to reveal."

"I am your king," I said as a threat and order.

"I swore to protect Queen Meera with my life," he answered.

I took my dagger out and pressed the sharp edge against the soft skin on his throat. "I can have men cut you up into pieces."

His eyes twinkled, and I dropped the act.

"Did I pass your test, my Majesty?" he smirked.

"You proved your loyalty to Meera," I said.

"I know the queen well." A boyish flush crept up his face as he said that. He continued, "She trusts you the most in the world. You don't need me to tell you anything."

Meera had guarded her secrets closely and kept one from me for a decade. No anger clawed its way through my skin. I trusted her despite that.

"I am reversing my earlier decision. Go to Padi immediately. Take some reliable men with you. I will send a message to Hasan to head to the border straight away. I underestimated Parth, and he has proven to be a sly adversary."

He rubbed his throat and asked, "How do I convince King Atul that his brother tried to kill him?"

"King Atul has faith in you," I said, and Rish turned crimson at those words. "He wanted you back in Padi. He vehemently protested my decision to keep you with me. A wiser man than I. Still, I will pen a letter for you to take."

Rish muttered, "He is a bigger man than I. In my first fortnight in Padi, I'd issued him a warning. I told him you had ordered me to destroy him if he hurt Queen Meera."

"Useful threat. It kept Meera safe," I said.

Rish mumbled, "He would never hurt her." His hands raked his hair as he sighed. I'd no desire to become entangled in this web.

I sat down and dipped a peacock feather in ink and wrote, "Sending Rish with an urgent message for Queen Meera and King Atul." I put my name down and wrapped the palm leaf with my seal.

I handed it to him, and he grabbed it and asked, "What should King Atul do? He cannot execute his brother. Kinslaying is frowned upon."

I scowled at his question. What would *I* do? Keeping my father-in-law in a dungeon for a decade did not help. Parth might foster a shadow confrontation from his cells. Noblemen unhappy with Atul's rule might rally to his side and sow seeds of discontent. How then to punish him for his deeds? I abhorred all the hurt I caused Nakul. And we never grew up as brothers. Atul and Parth grew up together.

"Banish him from Magadha. Alone. His wife and family will remain in Padi," I replied.

"Potential hostages," Rish said.

"If a man stooped to kill his brother, I am not sure he would care for the lives of others. But, yes, his family will be wearing invisible manacles around their necks."

He remained quiet for some time. Then, he said, "King Jay, your sister sent me away. I will be disobeying her order if I return." Of all the things I'd asked him to do, going against Meera's wishes appeared to be the line he hesitated to cross.

I regarded him and stated, "She made a mistake, Rish. You are a Malla subject, and I am ordering you to go back. Tell her I gave you no choice."

She and I'd committed many errors. Some had grown to storms brewing at our threshold.

He seemed unconvinced, and I said, "If all is well in Padi, meet King Atul privately and pass this message to him. If Parth has made his moves, then you know what to do."

"Burn the city down if he harmed her," he said, his head rising and eyes flaring.

"Rish, revenge leaves you dissatisfied. And we have no evidence for any of this. Parth is a formidable opponent. Don't underestimate him," I cautioned.

"Apologies, my Majesty. My goal is to prevent any harm befalling King Atul, Queen Meera, and their children, but I cannot bear the thought of harm coming to them."

I imagined Parth approaching Meera or her children with a dagger, and my throat constricted. I'd left her unprotected. "Warn him that I will hunt him to the edges of the world and delight in feeding him to the wolves," I stormed.

"If he has crossed that line, I don't plan on leaving anything left for you to hunt." His eyes glinted as he grasped the hilt of his sword.

"I will take your leave, my Majesty," he said and departed.

33

Meera

I reclined on my bed. Tiredness swept me. Every bone in me ached. I wanted to rest. But sleep proved elusive. How had I fallen so easily into Parth's trap? Now, Atul's life remained in danger. I'd become helpless and useless. Hope fled me.

As the night wore on, sleep sneaked upon me, and I drifted into her arms. Rish caressed my neck. "I am leaving my heart with you."

"No," I shrieked. "You left me a child."

Atul asked, "Do you trust me, Meera?"

"I do," I screamed.

"What is going to happen to me, Mother?" Nala asked.

I came out of darkness to light, like a butterfly breaking out of its cocoon.

Nala, Priya, and Amar. Parth might harm my children. I would not let him win. The fight was not over.

My room stayed quiet, lacking the usual bustle of maids and kids. I rose and washed my face. I fixed my sari and hair and paced the room to collect my options.

I heard voices outside and stopped.

"I am bringing the queen her food," Kantha said. A guard answered, "Give it to us. We will take it to her. We are not letting anyone in."

"Are you also going to clean her room and wash her hair? She is the queen. I have been her maid since she was a child. What are you afraid of? That I will sweep you away with my broom?" I imagined Kantha with her hands on her hips as she said this.

Another voice joined her. "Let her in. I want to see my niece too. Don't worry. I am not hiding a dagger in my sari." Aunt Mohini!

There were commotions and whispers, and the door opened. Kantha entered with a covered basket, and Aunt Mohini followed her heels.

"Meera!" "My queen!" They both exclaimed simultaneously as the door closed behind them.

"I brought you some bread stuffed with spicy lentils," said Kantha. She opened her basket and handed a steaming plate to me with two thickly rolled bread with yogurt dipping sauce and a grated mango pickle.

My stomach growled at the sight of the food. I did not realize how hungry I was till I tore a piece of the bread and put it in my mouth. I'd not eaten since yesterday morning. I relished the ghee spread bread with the sour mango pickle, and the tangy yogurt cooled the heat.

Letting me eat, Aunt Mohini sat beside me and said, "I told Rudra he had gone mad to keep you confined. To even believe you would harm Atul is atrocious."

I handed my empty plate to Kantha and gulped the saffron milk next. My hunger sated, I turned to them.

"Don't worry about me. Please make sure Uncle Rudra guards Atul with trusted men. He was poisoned once, and we need to prevent another attempt." I needed everyone to be on the lookout so Parth would not dare another attempt.

My aunt nodded. "I will talk to the king's guards on my way."

I swallowed. "How is Atul?" If Parth wanted to usurp power, Atul, Nala, and Amar all stood in his way.

"No change," she said and reached out and squeezed my hand.

"Kantha," I called, and she stopped arranging my things and approached me.

"Is the Malla physician's apprentice still here?"

"Yes, my lady. I was talking to the boy just a few days ago. He is from my village."

"Take him to the royal physician. He helped mix herbs in Malla, and he can aid him."

My aunt looked at me and said, "Meera, if Parth is accusing you of poisoning Atul, is it good for you to send someone to the physician? Parth will accuse you of meddling in Atul's treatment."

I refused to play this game in Parth's terrain. I wanted to send the apprentice to our royal physician as a warning. That someone watched his actions. Someone with ties to Jay and me. If Parth tempted him to misdiagnose or slow Atul's treatment, an extra set of eyes would cure him of that malady. I did not want to disclose all this to my aunt. While she cared for me, her loyalties ultimately lay with her husband.

Keeping my face neutral, I said, "You are right, Aunt Mohini. We don't want to give fodder to wagging tongues. But I want Atul to get better, and the Malla royal physician trained his apprentices well."

I glanced at Kantha. "Talk to the boy discreetly and plant the idea in his head to offer to help. Don't utter my name in his presence."

Kantha said, "I will take him some honey cakes when I visit." Kantha effused warmth and safety, and people let their guards down in her presence. And I wanted my aunt to mention this conversation to Uncle Rudra. I hoped it would deter any foul play they planned with our physician.

My aunt left with a promise to visit again.

"Kantha, I long to see Amar and——" Voices outside stopped me.

"I am here to see my mother," said young Nala, his voice carrying over.

"My lord, we were ordered not to let anyone in."

"On whose orders?" he demanded, and a smile formed on my lips.

"Prince Parth."

"I am the firstborn son of King Atul and your future king. You can stop me only on the king's order," he stated calmly. The guards stammered. I imagined Nala standing tall and looking at each guard into their eyes. No one would want to go against their future king.

"Open the door," he ordered, and I could hear the door being unlocked.

Nala entered with Amar in his hands and Priya and Rima on his heels. I stood up, and the girls ran to hug my knees.

Amar leaped into my arms, and I covered his face with kisses. I bent to kiss Priya and Rima.

My eyes shone when I gazed at Nala. I pulled him into a tight embrace and kissed his forehead.

"Have you eaten?" I asked.

"Yes, Mother," Nala answered.

I gestured at Kantha to close the door. The guards had left it open, no doubt unsure how to act with their prince in the room.

I sat on the rug with Amar in my lap. Priya and Rima wandered off to play with some dolls.

Nala settled next to me.

"Should I dismiss these guards from outside your room?" he asked, his forehead furrowed. I reached and rubbed the spot between his brows. I did not want him to shoulder the burden of this kingdom. Not yet. Not for many years.

"No, let them be for now." Parth had his eyes trained on me. I wanted it to remain there and away from my children. It was one thing for Nala to want to see his mother. That would not raise any suspicion. It was another for him to take command.

"Did you see your father?" He nodded and did not say anything else.

I played with Amar, giving Nala time to reveal more about Atul's condition. Three jute baskets stacked one inside another kept Amar's attention. He walked around them first. I said, "Open." He repeated the word, and opened each one, and squealed in delight to find a tiny sandalwood carved elephant in the last basket.

"He did not open his eyes when I called him. I even tried to pry open his eyelids," Nala said after a long pause.

My stomach twisted into a knot. "Was he breathing?"

He nodded vigorously.

I let out a sigh of relief. "Go about your day as usual. Learn and train. Just check on your father as well a few times. Come to me if there are any changes in his health."

Leaving Amar with me, Kantha left with the others.

The day passed like a raindrop sliding down an iron pillar, moving slowly.

Saras came to see me the next morning.

The guards let the Chief Guard's wife in.

Her plump face shone, and her thick dark hair braided down her back swayed side to side as she ambled in with her baby.

"My lady, I came as soon as I found out. Desh said King Atul was poisoned. Who would poison the kind and generous king? Then Desh said Prince Parth accused you of hurting the king. That made no sense to me. Why would she hurt him, I asked? King Atul has treated you well. They quarreled, he told me. You and I quarrel thirty times between sunrise and sundown, I told him. I sparred with him about you, my lady. I told him he was wrong. He got angry and left," she rambled on without pausing for breath.

Her husband, Desh, commanded the king's guards. I hoped he had remained loyal to Atul.

"Saras, you are a brave woman to fight for me. While many things don't make sense, one thing is clear. King Atul is in danger. Please ask Chief Guard Desh to protect him." My eyes beseeched her.

"My lady, Desh is loyal to his king," she said. "He will stand guard himself to safeguard him."

I thanked her, and we continued talking about domestic matters.

My mind traveled many paths, saying the necessary words to keep the conversation flowing. Saras did not expect many responses from me as she told me all about her life as a new mother. I could sense why Desh married her. She provided a refuge for him from the royal machinations of his day.

The child in her arms whimpered, and she cradled him.

"How is he doing?" I asked.

She gazed at him as if the world revolved around the child and said, "He is the sweetest baby, my lady. I followed your suggestions, and my milk started flowing."

"Let me hold him," I asked, and she swaddled the baby in a cotton blanket and handed him to me.

I cooed at him, holding him close to my face. Rocking him gently, I said, "He has his father's nose and your eyes, Saras." The baby in my arms reminded me of the child growing in me. Soon, I would no longer be able to hide the bump. Atul had not claimed the child yet. Others would wonder why. Instead of vague accusations, Parth would have a crime to pin on me. I felt like a bright bug caught in a spider web, each move tangling me. The eight-legged insect with bulging eyes stared at me, ready to devour me.

Nala approached me that evening, looking troubled. I gestured for him to sit next to me. He chewed his lips while I waited for him to tell me what weighed on his mind.

"Uncle Parth asked me to share his midday meal with me, Mother," he said, his eyes troubled. Anger surged in me like a fire that was fed new wood. I needed to protect my child.

I kept it from showing in my voice. "Did you go, Son?"

He nodded. "My uncle asked me about my weapons training. He wanted to come and watch me tomorrow."

My child gazed at me with the eyes of his father and said, "Uncle Parth said my father might not survive for much longer, and when that happens, he would help me rule." His voice broke, and I wanted to bury him in my arms and protect him from the world. I kept my feelings in check to allow him to continue.

Nala took a breath and inched closer to me. "He wanted to know why Father fought with you. I told him I did not know." I swallowed the lump in my throat, my eyes never leaving his face.

"When you told me who to trust, his name was absent from the list, Mother," he stated. I regarded my child with pride and shock. Young he might be, but Atul had groomed him to rule.

I pulled him onto my lap, and he allowed me to cuddle him. I felt his tremors, his fear of the unknown. His heart beat rapidly against mine. A feeling of helplessness washed over me. My child. I wanted to prevent him from becoming a pawn in the royal games. I held him tightly for a moment longer, and then I released him. Pushing his hair behind his ears, I whispered, "There are folks among us who wish us ill. As the heir to the king, you are vulnerable. I need you to lie low and not call any attention to yourself." I wanted to strangle Parth for baiting my son with his words.

"Can you do that?" I asked.

He wiped a tear gathered at the edge of my eye and nodded.

"I remember Father's last words to me. He asked me to listen to you."

34

Jay

A cool breeze blew in through the open windows, bringing along the smell of the forests around us. Vasant slept beside Aranya, his tiny fingers clutching her sari. He cried out for his mother last night. I watched as Aranya comforted him tenderly and calmed his demons. I'd lost my mother at a similar age. My stepmother never rose to the occasion, and the role of consoling me fell to Meera, a child herself.

Worries about my sister plagued me. I regretted not sending Rish with her and leaving her vulnerable to Parth's schemes.

Like the blush of a girl on seeing her lover, the light from the sun painted the sky. I put my worries aside and rose with the birds leaving their nests and began my day.

I met with Giri, and we pored over the Saral map spread on an old teak table. With the king living in Akash with us, I wanted to make sure we protected his land. Tracing seaports and rivers, we discussed where to station men to defend Saral.

As he rolled the map, I asked, "Did you meet your family, Giri?" He had been with me since Sunda.

He smiled ruefully. "Briefly, King Jay. When I took Uncle Karan home."

"Don't become a stranger to them. Let us find you a Lieutenant. After you set up everything here, come visit me in Akash to give me a briefing and then go spend some time with them."

He bowed his head to accept my offer.

On the way back to my chambers, Kapil said, "He is a King's man, your Majesty. His time is yours, and his family understands that."

A cold hand touched my skin at his words. I glanced at Kapil. "How about you?"

He shrugged. "I told my wife before our wedding. That I was pledged to another, and my prince commanded my life. She has arranged her life around that."

My throat constricted, and I'd no words to express my gratitude for the sacrifice of my men and their families.

"I honor your sacrifices," I began feebly, and he interrupted me.

"You make the biggest sacrifice of all, King Jay. We place our trust in you and follow your commands. That is easy to do when you believe in a man. You bear the burden of agonizing over your choices and making the right decisions. And you have spent as much time away from your family as the rest of us."

My mind floated like a feather and sunk like a rock at the same time.

"I don't make the right decisions many times," I confessed. I sat on a throne that, by law, belonged to my nephew.

He flashed a smile. "No man can, Jay," he whispered. "That is why I consider it my duty to knock you off your pedestal." I punched his arm playfully.

I spent the next few days closeted with Kathir and Giri arranging all matters. Food went cold, and our plates returned to the kitchen as full as they arrived, as we read scrolls and debated for hours. Disputes of all nature required my attention. Border settlements between regions, claims to water and land, and trade disputes. I asked Kathir to start with diplomacy to find a mutually agreeable solution and resort to force only when all else failed.

"Take Giri along on these talks. His sword can speak if they stalled."

Kathir inspected Giri critically, and he stood to strike a pose with his sword held high over his head.

Kathir smirked, "I have to remind folks his bite is sharper than his bark."

Kathir and Giri had many questions that needed answering, and sometimes we covered the same ground again. I left them both instructions to send me frequent messages.

The day dawned crisply, and we descended the Lukla hills. A wispy cloud hung over the forests, and its shadow kept us cool. Morning dew dripped from the leaves onto the ground, creating a mist around us and kept the summer heat from descending on us. Birds sang merrily, and their sounds filled the dense forest. Frogs croaked while they filled their bellies with swarming insects.

Aranya and Vasant rode in front of me on a brown mare. She believed him to be her beloved brother's son and accepted him into our lives. What would she do when I revealed the truth to her? That she had no blood ties to him.

I worried about his welcome in Akash. A Saral teacher and his servants joined us on this journey, and I had to train him to assume his kingship when he came of age. Saral would have to accept him as their king after a childhood spent in Akash. How could I groom him for the Malla throne? Making him my heir would cause a rift in the kingdom. He had no known Malla blood ties unless I divulged the secret.

The next few days, we traveled through fields laden with young grains. Summer fruits ripened on the trees, ready for harvest. Heaps of small purple and green eggplants fought for prominence among beans, bitter gourds, and squashes.

The river flowed to a trickle in some places. We mostly avoided villages facing mild droughts, not wanting to add to their burdens. Many had appealed for help to dig new wells. I'd asked Mani Vindhya to send them money from the royal coffers.

We arrived in Akash during the wedding season. Mango leaves strung on the thresholds fluttered in the wind, and bees buzzed around the two banana trees flanking the entrance to homes. As our procession made its way into the city, ordinary folk stopped momentarily to peer at us. The pomp of the king's guard revealed who was returning to the city, and people halted their activities to get a glimpse of me. I galloped past them on my black stallion, waving and acknowledging the greetings.

The fort doors swung open, and the herald announced my entry. I dismounted in front of the king's palace and handed the reins to the stable hands. As Aranya's chariot arrived, she passed Vasant to me. The boy stared in wonder at the bustling city. A temple elephant made its way down a street, swaying side to side, its bells tolling its passage. Four-wheel bullock carts loaded with vegetables and fruits passed by us. Holding him in one hand, I stretched my other to Aranya. Grasping it, she alighted from the vehicle. Sudha stood on the steps with a plate filled with turmeric water. Beside her stood Kayal and Heera, staring at Vasant. I ascended the steps with Aranya and Vasant. As Sudha waved the plate around us to drive off evil spirits, the girls threw flowers at us.

After our initial greetings, Kayal pointed to the boy and asked, "Is he our cousin?"

I nodded and placed him on the ground. "Yes, this is Vasant. Vasant, these are your cousins, Kayal and Heera." He kept his gaze on the floor and peeked at them shyly. "Treat him as your brother," I told Kayal.

I scooped Heera in my arms and walked forward. Kayal extended her hand to Vasant, and he looked at Aranya. She smiled at him and said, "Go with her."

I'd been gone for nearly two months, and many things demanded my attention. I spent most of my day with my small council and reached my chambers as the sun sunk.

"A letter from Queen Meera arrived just a day or two ago," said Somu as he handed me a letter. I opened and skimmed through it quickly. "Unable to sing!" Those words caught my eyes, and I slowed down and reread the note carefully. Most of the substance was about the children, and only these words departed from it. She was in trouble.

"Kapil," I called, and Karan appeared. "Find out if Rish sent any messages."

Kapil arrived with his father shortly. Mano said, "Rish passed through Akash about ten days ago. He is probably in Padi and a day or two from Daya. He promised to dispatch a messenger as soon as he arrived there."

He paused and stared at me. His brows furrowed, and his lips drew into a thin line. My stomach plunged, and I waited for him to share the news with me, like anticipating the bitter taste of medicine in my tongue.

"We heard rumors from Daya that King Atul has fallen ill, and Prince Parth has confined Queen Meera on suspicion of poisoning him."

I gripped my hilt tightly and clenched my jaws. How dare he? Dread clawed my skin. I was too far to defend my sister. Several images flashed through my mind: My father gasping his last breath; my brother, Nakul, clutching a spear protruding from his body; Nakul's late wife, Riya, jumping out of her window. I failed miserably to save them. I could not lose Meera too.

"Rumors?" I hissed. "I sent Dayan to protect her. Did he send any messages?"

"None that reached us yet," Mano answered.

"Where is Hasan?" I asked.

"He headed north a few days after Rish."

Anger boiled in my head and threatened to spill over. I paced the floor, only vaguely noticing Mano leaving. Kapil stayed with me.

After a while, Kapil spoke up.

"Jay, Parth is playing a dangerous game. He knows you have the superior army and can destroy him on a battlefield. So why hold Queen Meera captive?"

I swallowed. Parth wanted to cast Meera in a suspicious light and turn people against her. If he turned Atul against her, my army could only protect her physically. They could not shield her honor from gossip.

"He knows I will send an emissary," I said, and my skin crawled. Meera forbade Rish from seeing her. Now, he will arrive to rescue her. And fall into Parth's trap linking them.

Kapil stated loudly, "He is setting a trap for us, and like flies crawling towards honey, we are wriggling towards our bait."

I gasped. "I need to warn Rish."

"It is too late," he said starkly.

35

Meera

The next few days stretched like a frayed rope used to draw water from a well.

The door opened, and Kantha entered. The guards shut it behind her, and I could hear the latch locking us in.

She deposited the basket she carried and approached me flustered.

"My lady, I was in the supplies room off the kitchen, getting a few things for you. The door was open a palm's length, and I heard your name. I froze in place. Parth's man was in the kitchen, gossiping with another servant."

I sat up straight, bracing myself. Kantha paused and wrung her hands.

"What did you hear?" Subtle ears could sense the shaking in my voice.

She whispered, "I dread to even utter these words. They did not see me and assumed they were alone. He said you ran off with Rish, leaving Atul to be captured."

Parth had hauled the same insults at me earlier.

She stammered, "He said King Atul found out about your dallies with Rish and wanted to set you aside. And you poisoned the king to halt that."

Her hands covered her mouth as I absorbed this. Parth wanted to soil my honor, and he found a tale with some truth in it.

"Curse that man," she exclaimed vehemently.

Very clever. Atul might set me aside when he regained consciousness. He had been slipping in and out of it. If he failed to recover, no one would come to defend my honor. And Parth would be the puppeteer pulling Nala's strings. As my son's face drifted in my memory, a voice urged me to fight. For him and the kingdom.

Mala came to see me the next day.

"Cousin Meera, my father forbade me to visit you. Otherwise, I would have come earlier."

She had parted her hair in the center and braided it on both sides. Her sari in the color of a pomegranate showed off her delicate curves.

"I cannot condone disobedience of one's parents," I muttered. I could not alienate her father, Prince Rudra, any further.

She rambled nervously, "I told my mother I was visiting you. My lady, I was talking to General Gambhir in the gardens yesterday." My ears perked up at Gambhir's name.

She continued, not noticing my reaction. "The general said his hands are tied. My father and cousin Parth had cast your actions in a suspicious light. While he trusted you, he had no proof to counter them. While you are suffering, Parth is throwing a banquet."

All the threads from her conversation tangled up in my head, and I picked one strand.

"Banquet?" I asked.

"Yes, my lady. He has invited all the nobles to Daya. He is celebrating his victory in Sunda."

To show them he ran the kingdom and to gather their support. Nothing I could do to stop it.

I unraveled another thread. "Mala, strolling the gardens with a man like Gambhir will cause tongues to wag. What is the story here?" I asked gently.

She blushed and mumbled, "A few months ago, my cat climbed up a tree, and he helped bring her down."

"Has he said or done anything to indicate an interest in you?"

"He looks at me like I am a flower that might wilt just by viewing. Otherwise, he has been distant," Mala grumbled.

I needed Gambhir on my side in this battle with Parth. Though a childhood friend of Atul, he had made no moves to protest my confinement. He, however, had a reason for his lack of exertion on my behalf. Unlike his peers, he had no royal family connections. So he could ill afford to antagonize Parth. These reasonings tore through my mind as I framed my response.

"He is an honorable man. Watch your step, Mala. When the king recovers, I can put a word in for you. But our lives belong to the king, and he decides what to do with them. I don't want you to get hurt."

"King Atul recovering is my only hope then. Otherwise, my father will never agree to the match, and cousin Parth will not go against his wishes," she said softly.

The next afternoon, while I chased Amar around my room, Nala burst in.

"Father is having a seizure," he cried and grabbed my arm. Before I could comprehend his words, he pulled me forward. I picked up Amar and went with him. The guards parted, letting us through. I briefly noticed Dayan, and he came to life on seeing me.

"Queen Meera!" he exclaimed and followed us.

"Nala, tell me what you saw," I urged.

"I visited Father after my training and narrated all the moves to him. I do this every morning, even if he does not hear them," his words caught in his throat. Brushing tears that threatened to spill, he said, "Father opened his eyes today and called my name. As I approached him, he trembled all over, and his mouth twisted, and his eyes rolled back, and his hands jerked." A slight tremor passed through him, and I squeezed his hands.

"I called for his servants, and while they took care of him, I came to fetch you."

We arrived in Atul's chambers, and no one stopped us from approaching his bed. His physician bent over him, and he straightened as we entered.

"How is my father?" Nala took the lead.

"Alive," said Atul weakly.

"Father," he squealed and ran to him. A sob escaped me, and I leaned against the wall.

"What is going on here?" Parth asked, striding in.

The physician's eyes darted between the king and his brother, and he remained quiet.

Nala touched his father like he was a fragile dry leaf that would disintegrate and said, "You had a seizure, and I did not know what to do. So I ran to get Mother. Uncle Parth kept her locked in her room."

"Locked?" Atul asked quietly.

Nala nodded.

"Help me up, Son," he said, and Nala aided him to sit up.

Atul's eyes found me with tears streaming down my cheeks. He scanned the room and ordered, "Fetch Desh and Gambhir," and a servant left to get them.

"Care to explain what is going on?" he asked Parth.

"Brother, you fell ill, and all evidence pointed to Meera having a hand in it. Till I could confirm it, I'd her confined to her room."

"It is Queen Meera," Atul hissed. "I was poisoned, and you suspected my wife?" *Did Atul remember my warnings about poison?*

Parth's nostrils flared as he snarled, "She has made a habit of injuring my brothers. Though you vehemently denied it, I always suspected she murdered our brother, Amar, in cold blood. Or maybe it is easy for you to pretend rather than face the truth."

"Amar invited his death by his wicked deeds. I hold Meera without a blemish on this. Stop repeating this accusation or else face my wrath." Atul defended me against the allegation about his brother, Amar, a past buried deep. One I'd no interest in digging up.

"She and Jay appeared to be plotting to take the kingdom. How do you know Jay was not behind the order to capture you?" Parth shouted.

"Jay was under attack by Nakul, and he needed our help, you fool," Atul growled.

"You are the fool to let your wife carry on with her guard. While you were captured, they sauntered around Padi—"

"You dare insult me?" questioned Atul, but a cough racked his chest, ruining his menacing tone. I grabbed a cup of water and ran to him. Handing his brother to Nala, I supported Atul's head and brought the cup to his mouth. He touched my hand lightly as he took a sip. His skin was dry, and he appeared exhausted. His eyes sought mine, and a fountain of emotions poured out of them. Anger, yes. And jealousy. Also, something tender that gave me hope. A tiny seed sprouted in my heart as I laid him down and stepped back.

Desh and Gambhir entered the room, and Atul watched them, his eyes tracking their motion.

As they came closer, he said, "Gambhir and Desh, you allowed my queen to be held captive."

Desh swallowed and stared at the ground. Gambhir flushed and muttered something incoherent.

Atul regarded his men and stated quietly, "My queen represents my reign in my absence. She is also carrying our child. Announce this at court. Light lamps around the palace." His eyes found mine, and my breath caught in my throat. He had claimed the child as his own. I felt faint with emotion.

Fear and a more sinister reaction flitted through Parth's face, but he swiftly arranged it neutrally. Men scurried about to carry out the king's orders. I gazed at Atul, and he had closed his eyes, breathing shallowly, as if exertion had worn him out.

I sat beside him for the next few days. I wiped his face with warm water, wishing to erase his disease and the ill feelings between us. I asked his servant to shave his face and trim his hair. All these did not hide his illness. His skin remained warm, and a battle still raged in his body. His muscles had wasted from lack of use. As I fed him gruel and boiled water infused with dry herbs, my stomach twisted into knots.

Parth continued his banquets, and rode around the city, and trained in the yard. Compared to a child or a sick man, he moved like a monarch.

My mind wanted to scream and hide when I thought about the possibility of Atul dying. I gritted my teeth and took a deep breath. Nala needed a regent to rule till he came of age. As a woman, Atul could not choose me. I would become the queen mother. Prince Parth, son and brother to kings, would be a favorite for that role.

Parth had shown his ambitions. He stooped to poisoning his own blood and slaying his kin. He had easily pulled the court elders to his side when he confined me. My children's lives would be in danger in Parth's court. What weapons did I have to thwart him? King Jay, the answer came to me. I needed my brother's help to protect my kingdom and its heirs.

I wrote to Jay about my child. I'd worried myself for weeks about the pending birth, and Atul had solved my problems with just a few words. He had claimed the child. Now the rest was on my shoulders. I invited Jay to come and visit me. I hoped he rode in with an army.

Greetings poured from the court, wishing us well. Priya wanted to touch my stomach and feel the baby move. She wished for a sister, and I did too.

One day, as I left the room, Atul whispered, "The mountains call to me. Take me to Nanga." I rushed to his side, my breath coming rapidly. He stayed still. Did I imagine him speak? I waited by his side for a few more moments. I'd asked Jay to send his physician Shukla to Padi. The treatment here did not improve the patient, and my mind swung from hope to despair with each of his labored breaths.

I summoned General Gambhir and Minister Drona to my chambers. Kantha helped me put my hair up in a bun, and I wore my crown as a man heading to battle wears his armor.

"King Atul wants to leave for Nanga," I told them. "With his health, mountain travel will be hard, so we have to make the necessary arrangements."

"We will arrange for him to travel by palanquin, my lady. A team of men can take turns carrying the litter," offered Drona and I nodded. Four men can easily carry him on their shoulders.

We planned all the details for food, rest, and roads to take. I said, "If some royal families choose to remain, that is fine." It might be welcome to leave Parth and Rudra behind, though I would miss my aunt. As they stood to depart, I said, "General Gambhir, do stay. I have another matter to discuss with you."

He remained standing, waiting for the minister to exit. Then he said, "My lady, I apologize for allowing you to be confined. I am the king's man, and I forgot my vows."

I regarded him and said, "Your path to resist might have led to bloodshed. Sometimes, allowing events to take place is our best course." Clearing my throat, I asked him, "Is there a woman in your life, General?"

My question surprised him, and he opened and shut his mouth a few times. Pushing his hair back, he said, "My duty to the king leaves me little time for anything else."

"What do you think of Princess Mala?" I asked, and the question flustered him.

Wiping his brows with his shawl, he stammered, "I honor her as I do other women. Any other notion is beyond my station." Gambhir grew in a poor family and came to join the Padi guards. A young Atul had used him as his sparring partner. As a second son, Atul's friendships went unscrutinized, and his bond with Gambhir grew.

"For your service, the king might not be opposed to such a union," I suggested, and his lips curled up. He bowed to me wordlessly and took leave.

Frantic preparations took place the next few days for our departure to Nanga. Refusing to cede the court to Parth, I oversaw the activities during the day. I spoke to the stablemaster and his hands about mules for the journey. I talked to the cook about food to pack. At night, I dressed up and attended the banquets. I moved among the guests and asked after their family.

A delegation from our coastal regions sought an audience. I convened the court and sat on the queen's throne to listen to their stories. The larger king's throne remained empty save for Atul's crown.

One of the village elders stepped forward. "My lady, the additional levies on our villages is a burden many cannot afford. It will result in starving children and families or no seed grains set aside for the next crop."

I wore a silk sari in the color of a peacock feather, and a gold crown rested on my head. Torches illuminated marble and granite statues that adorned the hall and the rich woolen rugs on the floor. These outward signs of royalty trapped me. What opulence when children might starve. Additional levies? How much of the administrative actions did I miss at Atul's bedside? I had to plead ignorance and ask my council what levies we imposed.

I turned to Minister Drona. "What new levies did we impose?" I asked.

Minister Drona said, "My lady, the council imposed new levies a month ago because the crown's funds are low."

Parth had done this while he had me confined. I wound my sari and gathered my thoughts.

"When did our coffer deplete?"

Parth smirked, "We have been waging too many wars. King Atul sent me to Sunda with our troops. We needed coins to pay their salaries, uniforms, food, and weapons. Before I returned, another expedition to Malla had begun and hemorrhaged our gold. And now, despite my admonishing to remain in Daya, we are heading to Nanga. How do we pay for all these? Do you believe money grows on trees? Or do you want the crown to renege on its promises?"

His barbs with a grain of truth twisted a knife in my throat. He was right, though. We had incurred costs with these forays, but Atul had previously maintained plenty of reserves.

"What happened to our reserve funds? King Atul had set aside coins every year to pay for a drought or severe winter storm or an attack."

Parth answered again. "What we don't spend on warfare goes to fine silk and gold on our women." A tremor ran through me. Parth, with his desire for feasts, drinks, and women, accused me of spending the crown money. Anger unfurled in me, and I almost lashed out at him. *Careful*, a voice cautioned me. I'd underestimated him many times.

I asked a few more questions, ignoring the taunts from Parth.

I addressed the gathering, "Elders, Padi's prosperity lies in the hands of its farmers, artists, and merchants. I will ask my council to suspend the new levies till I understand what our reserves and revenues are."

A murmur went through the group.

Uncle Rudra spoke calmly. "My lady, with a baby in your arms and King Atul to take care of, you don't have the time for these matters. We do not need our queen to exert herself."

A stillness crept into the room. All eyes focused on me, and I shifted in my chair. I'd neglected all the king's duties and created a hole for others to fill. Parth would use it to turn the folks against Atul and Nala. I could not allow it.

I smiled and said boldly, "My lord, many of our women farm and weave with a suckling baby at their breasts. They will expect no less from their queen."

We discussed the matter some more, and we reached an agreement. Folks dispersed to share meals.

The next few days, I pored over our expenses with the small council. I delayed the purchase of new horses and halted many renovations of the city beyond repair. I ordered simpler meals to be cooked in the royal kitchen and reduced the royal allowances.

If Parth seethed internally, he kept it well hidden. He appeared courteous and deferred to me publicly.

Soon, an unexpected visitor arrived in the capital. Dayan Vindhya knocked on my door one early morning. Upon entry, he said, "My lady, Hasan Vindhya is here and is seeking to meet with you."

Hasan? I heard Jay had given him temporary command of the Malla Northern army.

I summoned a guard. "Gather the small council," I ordered.

After he left, I asked Dayan to bring Hasan there.

I waited in the council room with the Padi elders. When Hasan arrived, he stood framed on the tall wooden threshold, and my breath caught in my chest. He looked like his brother, Rish, in height and stature. As he came closer and bowed, I noticed the differences. Older, the hair around his temple had grey streaked with black. A beard hid his chin and jaw, and his eyes lacked the sparkle in Rish's.

He addressed me, "My lady, my felicitations to you and King Atul on the pending royal birth. King Jay has appointed me interim commander of the Malla northern unit. As is tradition, I come as King Jay's emissary and offer my services to the Padi king."

His eyes scanned the room, and a smile played on his lips. His arm rested lightly on the hilt of his sword, and his alert stance conveyed his life as a soldier. Hasan was not a man who idled his time.

"Did you bring many men with you? Padi can extend her courtesies to all of them. We can see that they are fed and kept warm."

He gazed at Parth and said, "I traveled with a small group of soldiers to come here swiftly. We will appreciate your offer of shelter and food. A few hundred men are following me with their own supplies. I only need permission for them to camp in your meadows."

Malla army at my beck and call to act as a deterrent to Parth's efforts. I saw his jaw tightening.

Later, Hasan and I retired to the quiet of my chambers.

"My lady," he whispered, seated across from me, "my brother, Rish, accompanied me to Padi."

My heart pounded on hearing his words.

"He refused to enter the city, but I can tell he is worried about you. I have King Jay's orders to help you in any way I can."

"Your presence here is all the help I need for now."

"My nephew Dayan is like a puppy. He wants to follow you and be petted. I apologize he did not protect you from the machinations here," Hasan said, stroking his beard.

"Don't be mad at him. I'd asked for restraint," I said, letting out a deep breath.

"My lady, I don't know what Rish did to displease you. He would be a better guard than Dayan, and he would not be cowered as easily. And I can tell he is sick with concern for your safety."

My heart rattled against my ribs. Hasan knew Rish too well. I could not afford for him to guess the reason for his departure from my side. No ready answer came to my mind, and I chose a coward's way out.

"Rish Vindhya has fought many battles for Padi and sacrificed much. The decision to bring him back lies with King Atul," I said softly. He regarded me intensely and pursued this no more.

He leaned forward and said in a low voice only I could hear, "My lady, we have word from our spies that Sarp bought poisons. Presumably for his master Prince Parth. If he so boldly imprisoned you while the king lives, he will not hesitate when . . ." he paused. Then he added sheepishly, "I apologize, my lady. I got carried away. The danger to you is real."

I gazed at him and said, "I suspected as much." While I had arrived at the same conclusion about Parth, my body tensed at his elaborate deception.

"My lady, King Jay will want a firsthand account of King Atul's health from me. Please grant me an audience with him."

In the time before twilight, I took Hasan to Atul's room. Atul's breathing sounded shallow, and behind his closed lids, his eyes moved frantically. I sat beside him and held his hand. My touch calmed him, and I lightly rubbed his forehead. He opened his eyes suddenly and startled me.

"Meera," he moaned, and I whispered, "I am by your side."

His eyes drooped to close, and I added, "We have a visitor."

He opened his eyes with an effort, and I felt guilty, causing him this pain. He found Hasan and said, "Rish, you are back."

Choking on my emotions, I remained wordless.

Hasan said lightly, "I am his brother, Hasan."

Atul said, "Summon Rish. Ask him to join me."

The talking tired him, and I fetched some hot water with honey and herbs in it. He sipped a few mouthfuls and then fell back to sleep.

Hasan eyed me questioningly. I'd brought this on myself. Having told Hasan that Atul was responsible for the decision to fetch Rish, I could not disobey a direct command from Atul, nor could he. I inclined my head imperceptibly, feeling like a boat tossed in a wild storm.

36

Jay

Vasant played with brightly painted wooden horses lying on his stomach. I stood watching him arrange the horses in neat lines, imitating our journey from Lukla.

"Vasant, would you like to go train with me?" I asked.

He gazed up and got onto his knees. "Fight with a sword?" His eyes shone with interest. I nodded, and he rose.

"Can I come too, Father?" Kayal asked. She sat across him on the rug, practicing her lettering. Her hair plaited into two braids tumbled below her shoulders. Aranya had learned to use a dagger. I shuddered to think of my daughter on the run like her mother.

"Yes, join us," I said reluctantly, looking at her eager face.

At the training yard, boys trained with swords and spears, and we stood to watch them for a few moments. I offered words of encouragement and instructions to some of the new recruits. Then I found a quiet corner.

"Dev, find a bow and arrow for Kayal," I ordered. Her eyes widened at my words.

I handed a sword to Vasant and practiced a few moves with him.

Soon, the four-year-old lost interest and wandered to watch the older boys.

"I will keep an eye on him," said one of my guards.

Dev brought a miniature bow and a quiver of arrows. Facing Kayal in front of a scarecrow, I taught her how to hold the bow. She notched the tiny arrow and let it fly, and it landed just a few feet from her. Color rose in her cheeks as she sensed all the eyes on her.

"Your first attempt was better than mine," I said, and her shoulders relaxed. She listened carefully, and by the time she shot the last arrow in the quiver, it landed just a foot from the scarecrow.

My face broke into a wide grin, and I bent to kiss her head. "In a month, you will be making holes in the target." A matching grin lit her face. *In a month? Did I just promise she could train again? And why not?* Swords and spears require strength she might never gain. Bow and arrow require skill and patience. At only seven years old, she unexpectedly had plenty of both. Why couldn't we train more women as archers? I decided to talk to Chief Guard Mano about it.

A message arrived from Meera shortly. She mentioned her pregnancy and asked me to send our royal physician to Daya. I noticed what she failed to write. No word of Atul's health or her confinement. She must worry about someone intercepting her messages. And she did not trust her physician. I grew impatient for messengers from Rish or Hasan.

"Muthu, summon Shukla," I ordered as I read my other letters.

When the physician arrived, I said, "Send your best healers to Daya. King Atul's health has not improved, and Queen Meera is concerned."

Shukla asked, "Healers who have dealt with poison?"

I nodded. "And can stay quiet."

"I have two that are trustworthy. I can send them with my collection of herbs and potions."

"Make swift arrangements for them to leave," I said, and he departed.

Aranya found me later that day. I looked up from a map I pored over.

She approached the table and peeked at it from my elbow.

I answered her unasked question. "We had little to no rain in some areas. I am dispatching my men to measure water levels and report to me."

"How will that help the farmers?" she asked, following my finger as I traced the areas.

"It will help me decide what aid to provide. We will ask some farmers to plant drought-tolerant crops rather than rice. If fewer of them plant rice, we will have to release grains from our granary storage."

I took her hand, and guided her to a bench, and dropped down beside her.

"Kayal told me about her morning archery lessons," she plowed directly into the conversation. Her aged pearl earrings glowed like the moon on a dark sky.

"I came to teach Vasant, and she proved to be a better learner. Do you have any objections to the girls learning archery?"

She shook her head slowly. "Nakul taught me how to use a dagger. It came in handy when I was on the run." She still retained her image of her brother from her past. Untainted by his descent into madness recently. I had no intention of disturbing her view.

"Change comes slowly. I intend to talk to Mano about training more girls. To defend their homes and themselves."

Her hand, held in mine, trembled. "I killed a man once. With the dagger. In self-defense. His blood covered me, and his life ebbed away slowly while he called out to his loved ones."

I traced the back of her palm with my thumb. Killing another was never glorious as depicted in epics. I'd killed many mere boys whose only crime was serving the wrong king. My wise father once told me not to keep count. Still, the mind repulsed against what the body did. I had toiled to avoid shedding Malla blood. That was why I'd asked Kapil to concoct the elaborate ruse in the battle against Nakul. To save lives.

She changed subjects. "You asked the girls to treat Vasant as their brother." She did not miss much.

"We are raising them——" I began, and she interrupted me.

"Jay, Queen Meera has two sons. Will you want to marry your daughters to one of them?"

"Aranya," I protested, and she continued, "Is it wrong for me to further the tie with my brother's son?"

"You know the burden of the crown. Why draw our children earlier into a web that will last all their lives? Sacrifices they need to make can wait," I argued. I would have to reveal the truth to her someday. Nakul and I were brothers. Our kids could not marry any more than siblings could.

"You are still mad at Nakul for invading Malla, and you are taking it out on his son," she whispered heatedly, her nostrils flaring and lips drawing into a thin line.

"The boy is not even five. I am not having this conversation now," I said, anger rising in me. I tried to imagine what my actions looked like to her.

She pulled her hand away from me and rose. "I am a foreigner in this land, and I don't want him to feel the same way." Her voice trembled with emotions. She fled the room, and I did not stop her.

That night Nakul entered my dreams, vowing to kill me. As I ran towards him, he transformed into Aranya. Tears poured from her eyes, and she held a small body in her arms. Her wails pierced my heart, and I approached her with dread. Before I could see the face of the child clutched to her heart, a voice called out, and I emerged into wakefulness.

Muthu opened my curtains, and the weak morning sun entered my room like a shy maid. After my council meeting, I stayed to speak with Mano.

"Did you hear about Kayal's archery lessons?"

He grinned. "I heard the princess's skills put many boys to shame."

"Uncle Mano, I wondered if we could teach more girls the use of weapons."

His smile slowly disappeared as he listened.

"Archery is an obvious one. Fighting with a dagger can help in close quarters."

"My Majesty, are you planning to add them as soldiers to our army? We cannot take them to battles. A woman captured in a war will be defaced or worse, and our soldiers will have to worry about their safety," he argued.

"No, I don't want them with me on foreign land fighting our enemies. I want them to be able to defend their homes. When I go on my campaigns to defeat pirates off our coasts or to help an ally defeat invaders, I take able-bodied men with me. We leave women to defend their homes with old men with stooped backs and beardless boys. Shouldn't they be able to guard our watchtowers and defend their lands and homes?"

He watched me with curious eyes, and I met his gaze.

"Let us start small. See if we can find a dozen girls to train with Kayal," I commanded. He kept any misgivings to himself and left to carry out my order. While he had served my father for many years, I had occupied the throne only for three months. It had been five months since my father's demise. While I hoped my father would approve my decisions, this was my reign, and the burden to rule rested solely on my shoulders. *I will make you proud, Father.*

One cloudy day, on my way to the training yard, Kapil stopped me.

"Messenger from Hasan," he muttered, and I marched to my chambers.

A young man with his long hair pulled back entered shortly after me.

He immediately launched into his tale. "General Hasan met with Queen Meera. She is well." I did not realize I'd held my breath till I exhaled slowly.

"He had a brief audience with King Atul, who ordered him to return with Commander Rish. General Hasan left his brother in the Padi court with a dozen men and another 100 outside the city. Commander Rish has resumed his guard duties for Queen Meera. General Hasan is on his way to the border post," he recited.

"Rish is back in King Atul's court?" I asked, making sure I heard him correctly. The man dipped his head. Meera did not want him there, and

Rish had resisted my urgings to go back to her. For him to return, he must have perceived a great danger to her. I felt better with him at her side. Especially with her carrying a child.

"How is King Atul?"

"General Hasan said his health was poor."

"You have traveled long. Get some rest today. I will send you back tomorrow with a message."

After he left, I walked to the training yard with Kapil.

"Healers have left for Padi?" I asked, and Kapil inclined his head in assent. Nothing more for me to do right now.

I went to visit my stepmother. The rooms that belonged to my grandmother once had been redecorated to Queen Mother Charu's taste. Her paintings of Vindhya women adorned the walls of her sitting room. My eyes found her seated on a carved wooden chair polished to a gleam with oil. She wore a sari in the color of ash, and her hair had more gray than black. I sought her blessings and settled on a chair opposite her.

After the initial inquiries of my visit to Saral, she asked, "How is the boy doing?"

"Vasant is adapting to Akash, Mother," I replied.

She sighed. "It cannot be easy on him having lost both parents in quick succession. What caused Riya's plunge to her death?" she asked, curious.

"Sorrow and despair," I shrugged. "She lost her husband and father." *Cruelty by one who should have protected her*, I thought, but kept it to myself.

"Jay, I heard you and Aranya are thinking of fostering him?" she asked, leaning forward.

"Yes, Mother. The boy is grieving, and so is Aranya. She is his closest relative."

She shook her head. "The boy's grandmother, Princess Lata, is still alive. Listen to me. You have no heir now, but one of your wives will beget you a son soon. When that happens, it will set up a rivalry between the boys. Keep him here for a few months. Then send him to Biha to his grandmother. That is best for all."

I took a deep breath. Princess Lata was my father's cousin, and she had married General Devan Biha. I sensed the wisdom in my step-mother's words. But she mistook my objective. I wanted to make him my heir. The throne rightfully belonged to his father and him.

"Wise words, Mother. Aranya will not agree to part with him now. In time, that might change."

She clasped her hands and said softly, "Your father never bedded me after you were born. He feared a rival tiger cub. You don't have a cub yet, so the danger from that boy is far greater. Send him away soon." She could not keep the bitterness out of her voice. My father had hurt her deeply.

On a dark night, the stars twinkled in the sky like diamonds spilled on a woman's hair. No moon rose to vie with them. I entered Sudha's chambers and found her combing her hair. I took the silver comb from her and gently ran it through her trusses. I'd married her with no love in my heart, only thinking of building a bridge to her Vindhya house. In the years since she had become my refuge from palace intrigue and royal games. A bond had grown between us, stronger than I'd expected.

I looked at her face in the mirror. A lantern on the table cast a golden light on her and her eyes danced. She rose slowly and took my arms. She guided one to her stomach and whispered against my chest, "I am carrying your child, my lord." My heart soared and then plunged. She had lost them before. I cupped her face and leaned in to touch her brow with mine.

"I have a good feeling about this," she murmured, and my lips brushed hers lightly.

37

Meera

Atul slipped between wakefulness and sleep as his servant, and I bathed him in warm water. He stirred under my ministrations but did not arouse. We dressed him warmly and placed him back on his bed.

As I stood conversing with the servant, a guard entered.

"Commander Rish and General Gambhir are here to see the king, my queen," he said. My heart pounded like drums. Not trusting to speak, I gestured for him to bring them in.

I settled beside Atul, my back to the visitors. I heard approaching footsteps, and my ears could catch Rish's measured stride.

"Queen Meera," Gambhir greeted me.

"My queen," Rish followed.

I tilted my head in acknowledgment.

"Commander Rish just arrived, my lady. He wanted to pay his respects to the king. We can come later."

Atul stirred and opened his eyes slowly.

"Water," he whispered, and I held a mug of warm milk with honey and herbs to his lips. He took a few sips and glanced at the visitors.

"Rish, you came," he muttered, and Rish approached his bedside.

"A dog for . . ." Atul mumbled, and Rish bent his ears to his mouth.

When Atul closed his eyes, he straightened and said, "King Atul wants me to visit the stables."

Puzzled, I glanced at him. His smoldering eyes glimpsed mine briefly, and he marched out.

Later, I worked with Priya and Rima on their lettering while Nala ran into the room.

"Mother, look at Father's gift to me. It is a puppy. Uncle Rish is here, and he took me to the stables to pick one from the litter."

A warm brown furry pup nestled in his arms and yelped in excitement. The girls ran to the puppy, and Nala let them scratch his ears. Another footstep followed, and Rima jumped.

"Father," she threw herself into his extended arms, and Rish scooped her into a tight hug.

Commotion reigned for a time, with running paws and feet. At my gesture, Kantha took the children away, leaving Rish and me alone.

Neither of us spoke for a few moments, and then he asked, "Did my brother tell you about Parth?"

I nodded, swallowing down the emotions that surged in me. "I heard two men trade poison in the grove behind the temple. After the poison and some coins changed hands, one killed the other. I suspected something then. Hasan's words confirmed it."

Rish moved closer to me. "Behind the temple? You heard two men in the daylight?"

"At night," I whispered.

"They did not see you?" He asked too many questions.

"I was hiding behind a tree," I mumbled, and I realized how ridiculous I sounded.

He stayed quiet. Then, he asked, "Why were you hiding?"

I remembered my despair and my decision to plunge to my death. I wanted to unburden my worries to him and let him comfort me. With an effort, I controlled my tremors and wound my sari in my fingers.

Rish inhaled sharply. "Meera," he gasped. "Promise you will come to me before deciding anything rash."

I gazed at him. "I can make no such promises, Rish."

He stared at me with pressed lips, and I could sense his rising anger. His fingers combed through his hair, messing it.

"Does King Atul know about his brother?"

I shook my head. "He has barely any awareness, and I do not want to burden him."

He stepped close for me to feel his breath. "I am not leaving your side again," he hissed. A threat or a blessing, only time would tell.

So many things remained unsaid between us when Rish departed.

I didn't see him again for days, though I longed for a glimpse. I chided myself for my wishes. Two physicians arrived from Shukla, and they wanted to try a banana stem wrap with turmeric to draw out the poison from Atul's body. They set to work with our royal physician, and I stayed with Atul.

"The king is too weak to travel, my lady. Please allow him time to heal," one of them said. I pushed our departure to Nanga on the advice of these men.

Slowly, I sensed a change in Atul. His appetite increased, and color returned to his skin. He remained awake for longer periods.

During one such time, he summoned Nala and the small council.

"Send for Rish too," he murmured to his guard.

I helped dress him, and the servants carried him to his chair in the sitting room. Soon, men assembled, and Atul regarded us.

"I have come close to dying many times this year, and Meera has pulled me back from the brink each time." He looked at me, and tears brimmed my eyes.

"While I am alive, I have two urgent matters to take care of. I install my son Nala as the crown prince of Padi," he stated, and Nala stared at his father. He spoke to him, "Your mother will take care of the formal ceremony, Son."

Atul took a pause, and I could sense his strength ebbing away. He took a breath to steady himself.

Addressing us, Atul continued softly. "If I fail to escape death's ropes, Nala needs a regent to help him govern Padi. I would appoint

Meera for that role if I could," he said, glancing at me again. All eyes darted between us.

Atul scanned the room, and his gaze rested on Rish, standing in the back of the room. "Instead, I appoint Rish Vindhya as the regent for Nala. I order Rish to continue to seek the small council's advice in governing."

A murmur went around the room, and I stood shocked.

Rish stepped forward as others parted for him.

He laid his sword at Nala's feet and swore another oath that bound him to my family. "I pledge to be faithful to Prince Nala and govern to maintain his safety and honor and the welfare of the people."

As he rose, Atul waved to dismiss the gathered. Nala, Rish, and I remained.

"Nala," he called, and the boy approached him tentatively. Atul pulled him onto his lap, and Nala looked as if he worried he would break his father. "Sit still, Son. I can bear your weight for a few moments."

"I wish for time to spend with you, your sister, and your brother. My wish may yet come true. But I cannot delay telling you a few things. The most important thing I can tell you is a king should be ready to sacrifice everything for the welfare of his kingdom." Atul glanced at me briefly, and I understood what his actions today meant. He had appointed Rish for the welfare of Padi. Not because he forgave me. A knot twisted in my stomach.

"Rish will help you govern this kingdom well. Always listen to your mother. Even when you grow taller than her."

Nala leaned his cheek against his father's, and Atul kissed his head. "Now go runoff," he said.

Alone with Rish and I, Atul gazed at his fingers. "Rish, are you still bound to Meera by your oath?"

"Yes, your Majesty," Rish answered, surprised by the question. He watched us both puzzled.

"Good," answered Atul. "Obey her commands. I cannot set her on the throne. I am doing it through you," he said and gestured to his servants to carry him.

Summer ended, and Atul's health deteriorated.

"The poison is shutting his organs one by one," muttered a physician. One of them stayed with Atul regularly. I spent days and nights with him, with gloom as my constant companion. Worries plagued me during the day and nightmares my night. Rish came every day to report the day's events and to ask about my views on various subjects. The baby grew in me, and I could sense her move at night when I rested. While I cared for Atul, Kantha took care of me. She brought me food, forced me to take baths, and coerced me to take naps. I felt disconnected from the living around me.

"Sing for me," Atul whispered one day. I'd just crawled into bed. I dragged myself up slowly and adjusted the pillows for my back. I reached out to hold his hand, and he gazed at me with a tenderness that melted my insides. I sang a song about a girl who had lost her love to the sea. Giant waves took him away to the lands deep in the ocean, and the girl wished she could swim underwater to find him.

His breath deepened, and I kissed his dry lips softly.

Days faded into one another. Outside, the leaves turned into the color of sunset. My gentle husband and father of my children had lost his flesh and youth. The disease aged him decades: his hair had lost its luster, and his skin clung to his bones. Atul never spoke again. Slowly, his body stopped working, and death embraced him with its cold hands one crisp autumn morning.

38

Jay

I arrived in Daya as trees shed their leaves. Grains were harvested, and bundles of hay stood on the fields. I'd ridden for a dozen days, from sunrise to sunset, taking only brief respites in between. Kapil rode with me silently, sensing my need for solitude.

Rish met me at the steps to the palace. "Take me to Meera," I ordered.

As the door to her chambers opened, she looked up from her bench. She wore a widow's white sari. As I gazed at her bare forehead, my throat tightened. No jewels graced her neck or ears. She greeted me with sunken cheeks and dark shadows under her eyes. I'd seen corpses on a battlefield with more life than her.

As I stepped in, the door shut behind me, leaving us alone.

"Meera," I uttered and rushed to her side. Dropping down on the bench, I pulled her tightly into my arms.

"Jay," she whispered and leaned her head on my neck. "How could he die and leave me to handle everything?" she cried. Tears streamed down her cheeks, and then sobs rocked her chest. What started as a trickle gathered into a storm, and she wept in my arms. I held her, my cheek pressed against hers, and let her cry.

Slowly, her tears halted, and she sat straight, wiping her eyes and nose.

"You look terrible," I commented, and she laughed madly.

Suddenly, I noticed her swollen stomach.

"How is the baby?" I asked, and she stared at her nails.

After a pause, she said, "She is fine. I can sense her moving inside me." We remained quiet for a few moments, each mourning the deaths of the past year. Father had died eight months ago, Nakul had followed him a month after, and Atul four weeks ago. So many kingly deaths in such a short time.

"He wanted to die in Nanga, looking at the mountains. He died here in Daya instead." A deep yearning filled her voice.

"Death claims us on his time, Meera."

She glanced at me with her haunted eyes. "We fought before Atul got sick. I hurt him deeply, and I never got to apologize. He died before he forgave me," she said. All life had seeped out of her.

"Meera, he appointed Rish as the regent. That was his way of forgiving you." I took her hand. Hers felt cold, and I covered it with mine to warm it.

Another long pause followed. "Atul did it for the kingdom." It looked like she wanted to add more, but she did not.

"Meera, you are a warrior's daughter, wife, and sister. When you sent us to battle, you knew we might never return. This illness was his battle, and you tended to his needs. He knew you were beside him. His hurt probably dissolved in your care. He lost his battle. Let him go. Let your guilt go. You have a kingdom to rule. And a son to teach."

She regarded me, and some life came into her eyes. "When Mother died, I took care of you. Now, you are bearing the responsibility to care for me and all of Magadha."

She reached and pushed some hair from my forehead. My words caught in my throat.

"Meera, with a grieving father and a stepmother buried in self-pity, I would have been a boat headed to rocky shores. Crashing into pieces.

You were the lighthouse that guided me to safe harbor. I don't know how you managed to learn so much when you were a child yourself."

"It is easier for a child to observe and learn, Jay. As adults, we don't notice them under our feet." She gazed at the floor.

I reflected on her words. In less than a year, all three kingdoms had a new ruler. Two of them still children. The duty to safeguard Magadha rested on my shoulders while Vasant and Nala grew.

Not just mine. My sister would share my burden.

"Nala needs you more than I ever needed you. Be there for him."

She lifted her eyes and said, "Self-doubts plague me, Jay. I've made mistakes. Many of them." Her voice shook.

"No more than Atul or me. Or Nakul. Our father's mistakes still haunt us. I fought with Aranya, and now we have an uneasy truce. Like two jungle cats, a single word can set us off. Then we are at each other's throats. Even love does not make it easy to forgive another." I opened up to her.

"She is your queen. Treat her well, Jay," she admonished me. My lips curled up.

"Atul trusted you. He handed the reins to you, Meera. He moved past your mistake."

We sat quietly for some time, my arm around her shoulder.

My stomach grumbled. "Have you eaten, Jay?" she asked.

I shook my head. "Not broken my fast yet."

She called her maids, and soon two plates of warm food arrived. We sat at the table recalling stories from our childhood. Kantha hovered over us, loading our plates again. I smiled at her.

"I am glad you came so quickly, Prince Jay," she said. She corrected herself quickly, "King Jay."

"I can stay a prince for you, Kantha."

She grinned and heaped more rice onto my plate.

On a cloudy day, the Padi elders crowned Nala as a priest sang a hymn in praise of Lord Rama, the embodiment of kingly duty. Meera wore a jasmine color sari and tiny pearl earrings. A sign of her starting to live again. I spent my mornings with the boy. In the training yard, on long rides, walking around the palace gardens. He had a boyish view of ruling. One I outgrew only recently. I mostly told him stories of how past kings ruled.

"Meera," I called one afternoon. She sat cross-legged on the floor, playing with Amar.

"Hmm."

"Parth cannot go unpunished for his acts."

She looked at me. "What do you propose?"

I told her my thoughts, and she disagreed with some of them. After some discussion, we settled on a path.

Rish summoned Parth to the small council room, and the man's anger became apparent on his face as he entered.

"How dare you low——"

"Parth," I interrupted him.

He spun around. Kapil shut the door and stood beside it.

"I know you poisoned your brother and king," I said.

His eyes twitched. "You have no proof of it. I can convince Padi nobles that you murdered Atul like you murdered my other brother, Amar."

"Say a word like that, and you will die of a thousand cuts," I said coldly. He stared at me. He knew I needed no proof to murder him and throw his body to hungry jackals.

"Rish can preside over a king's court and mete out justice," I offered.

He swallowed. "Or, we send you on an expedition. A boat, supplies, and a couple of men. You will be banished, never to return."

"My f-family?" he stammered.

"Stays here under the king's protection."

Rage flitted through his face. "If anything happens to them . . ."

"You are in no position to issue threats," I warned him. Like a cornered animal, his eyes darted between us. He swallowed several times while the three of us stood glaring at him, our fingers grasped around the hilt of our swords. I commanded an army more powerful than any he could muster. His chest caved, and his shoulders slumped.

My men escorted him out of the city the next day.

"Kill him in a year or so and make it look like an accident," I ordered Kapil. I could not let this danger against my nephew persist.

Rish and I rode our horses to a small forest outside the city. At a clearing, I jumped off my mare, and he followed. My guards remained out of earshot.

"Meera is a widow. There will be no husband to claim another child of hers," I plowed directly.

Shocked, Rish stood still.

"I need you wedded before I depart for Akash."

"There is no room in my life for another woman," he muttered.

"Do you think this is a game?" I snarled.

"Game? I wish it were. For years, I'd been content to watch her happy. And now, I return to see a shell of the woman I loved. Clinging to despair, wading through the gloom, and refusing my help. Did you know she pondered taking her own life?" His face contorted to reflect his anger and pain.

It was my turn to be shocked. "Suicide?" I struggled to get the word out. An image of Riya leaping out of the window surged into my mind.

He nodded. "Meera's trip to the temple and eavesdropping on men trading poisons only makes sense if she wanted to run away or more likely meet her death."

He knew her better than me.

"Rish, I wish we lived in a time where my sister could marry you. That is impossible. She is a widow of King Atul and must remain so all her life. No hint of a rumor can taint her. You need to marry again," I urged.

"And ruin an innocent girl's life," he barked.

"Offer a girl a leash at life. Mani found a bride for you. Daughter of a merchant, she lost her ability to hear and speak as a child. Her father despaired he would never see her married. He has many other daughters to wed, so he cannot offer much in dowry."

Rish stayed quiet for many moments. "Well, she cannot hear me moan another woman's name in my bed," he sighed.

I flinched at his words. Cold and ruthless I might be, though not a monster.

"I will marry her," he sounded resigned.

"Good, father and daughter arrived yesterday." Aversion filled my stomach at my deed. I'd no other choices. No one could ever find out about my sister and Rish.

I presided over their simple wedding. The plain bride glowed beside her brooding groom. Later at the wedding feast, I watched him sign with his hands to his new wife. She smiled and signed back. He may not love her, but he would take care of her.

Winter arrived in Daya, and with it, the rains. Rish, Kapil, and I stood around a circular table covered with ink and scratches. Kantha rushed in and declared, "It's a boy."

39

Meera

Kantha sighed in relief when the baby started nursing. I checked his tiny fingers and toes. All in order. His wrinkled face resembled a newborn. That would change as he grew. Rish's tall frame and long hair swam into my head. I could not raise this child here, where swirling rumors might compare the child to the man. I made a decision that cut my heart into pieces.

Jay made preparations to depart Daya. He had spent days with his nephew, grooming him, while I mired in doubts and pity.

I approached him in his chambers, the first time I'd left mine since Nala's crowning. I wore a sari in the color of snow with tiny golden stars woven into it. Bangles clanged on my arms, and I paused to hear them. *Atul loved that sound.* Grief, ever-present, prickled my skin.

Kapil and Jay stood together, deep in conversation, when the guard announced me. I remembered the two as boys, running around with their wooden swords. The trace of the boys had remained only in their eyes and the curl of their lips. The two men exhibited a fierceness that could send a dagger down an enemy's chest even without them raising their swords.

They looked up, and warmth spread in Jay's eyes.

"Queen Meera," Kapil bowed and left us.

"You are looking well, Meera," Jay said.

"Kapil has served you well," I remarked.

Jay became pensive. "I have become reckless in battles, trusting my guards to protect me. Kapil has deflected many a blade headed to my throat. I owe him my life."

I remembered Rish guarding me when we escaped. "I wish I'd learned to wield a weapon," I said, and he watched me strangely.

"Why?"

"I was useless and helpless when we fled Saral men. I tired easily and could not even kill a snake that threatened Rish's life," I rambled.

"Kayal is learning to use a bow," he said.

I looked at him, surprised. "I'd planned to ask Rish to train Priya," I said.

"Change is coming," he said. We both stayed quiet, swimming in our thoughts. Slowly, I steered the conversation.

"Jay, you are fostering a Saral royal in your court. Allow me to present a Padi baby to you as well," I said the words with dread. If the boy grew to be like his father, he would be safer in Malla. Without Rish around, less of a chance for someone to stumble upon their likeness.

"You are asking me to foster your newborn child?" Jay asked. I saw his mind making the connections.

"Yes. In the past, younger sons were sent to be fostered in other kingdoms to develop a kinship," I replied. Waves of despair pounded my heart, and I struggled to keep tears away.

"Do you have a name for him yet?"

"Atul," I said. A name to protect his identity and thank the man who had claimed him as his son.

"Wise choice," Jay agreed. "I will care for him like my own," he affirmed, understanding my decision and my desperation.

"Delay your travel by a few days till I wean him off and find him a wet nurse," I said.

Jay stepped closer and grasped my elbow.

"Meera, did you contemplate taking your own life?" His voice low and barely a whisper. I glanced at him, and he tensed at the truth in the circles under my eyes.

"Riya took her life," he cried. "I failed to save her. I cannot bear—I need you, Meera. Your boy needs you. Don't . . ." he stuttered.

"Jay, I am not a coward. I only decided on . . ." I paused and exhaled. "Atul and I fought, and I thought it best for Padi and Nala."

"No," he denied vehemently. "Don't choose death."

"Don't you choose death when you head to battle?" I asked angrily.

"That is different. That is fighting for my kingdom." His voice calmer, he searched my eyes for a promise I could not give.

"This was my battle for the kingdom, Jay. Atul saved me by claiming my child. If he hadn't, I had no other choice."

He tightened his grip on my arm. "There are always other ways. Our mother found one with Nakul."

Our mother did find a way. To society, she had remained an unmarried maiden when she became pregnant with Nakul. She had hidden her pregnancy and passed the baby off as her cousin's son. She had chosen life.

"Come to me when there is a problem. We will find a way together." His plea twisted my stomach. I swallowed and nodded. He released me and ran his fingers through his hair.

"No more secrets from me, Meera. And no leaving me to rule Magadha alone."

A grim determination swept through me at his words. No more burying my head when faced with problems. I decided to meet them like a soldier at war. "You can count on my wisdom for years to come," I promised.

He smiled crookedly. "We are both competing for the most foolish acts performed."

I joined his laughter. "We can be witless together."

I started making arrangements to send baby Atul with my brother.

Rish came to my chambers one evening. He had not spoken to me since Atul's death.

"King Jay told me he is taking Prince Atul to Akash. Is it true?" he asked. I nodded without meeting his eyes.

"Can I hold the child, my lady?" he asked quietly. My heart thudded like thunderclaps. I'd never revealed the truth about this baby to anyone except Atul. But Rish must have guessed it. Just like Jay. I moved to the crib and wrapped him in blankets, and handed him to his father. One who could never claim him as his own.

He supported the baby's head in his elbow and gazed at his face. A rainbow of emotions washed his own. He gently kissed his forehead and placed him back in his wooden crib.

"Rish," I began, and he interrupted me.

"The less said, the better, my lady." The knot in my stomach grew as he departed.

"Meera," Atul's voice shook me out of my slumber, and I surfaced, gasping my way into wakefulness.

"Atul," I called, sitting up on my bed. I reached over to his side, and my hand came up with emptiness. *Gone*, screamed my mind. *Forever*. I stood and stumbled to the crib. Empty. I'd left the baby with his wet nurse. Grief tossed and turned me like a fish caught in a current. Loneliness stretched for eternity in my future. No man to hold me in his arms, kiss my neck, or whisper my name. I collapsed against the bedpost and hugged my knees to my chest. Sobs rocked my body.

A knock sounded on the door, and I gazed through my haziness. "Mother," called my daughter. I wiped my eyes and nose with my sari end and stood up. With faltering steps, I reached the door and opened it.

Priya rushed into my arms. "I could not sleep," she mumbled, pressing her cheek into my thighs. I waved the guards off and shut the door. Picking her up, I cradled her against my breasts. She brought me to the present, letting my worries fade. I walked to the bedroom. We plopped on the bed, and she curled up against me. I rubbed her back, singing a song about a star twinkling in the sky. Sleep claimed both of us.

A few days later, I wore a sari in the color of the winter sky. Sapphires graced my neck, a present from Atul. General Gambhir and Prince Rudra attended me in my chambers.

"Uncle Rudra, General Gambhir sought Mala's hands in marriage. I have sanctioned the union. He seeks your blessings."

Misgivings resided in my mind about General Gambhir. He never came to my aid during my confinement. I put that aside to focus on the rebuilding of Padi.

A simple wedding celebrated their union.

Jay gave me word that Parth had sailed the seas. I set that thought aside as well.

One evening, I sat on Atul's rug with the baby in my arms, Amar on my lap, and Priya and Nala next to each other. Scrolls still spilled from the table onto the floor and benches. I'd asked his servants to leave everything as it was.

"Bring the book of poetry that your father liked to read," I told Nala, and he brought it back.

"Read us a poem, Son," I asked, and he obliged. His voice cracked as he read the words slowly. Tears dripped down my chin as I listened to the poem of a boy and his father traveling on a road while I rocked the baby. Priya leaned on her brother and put her arms around him as she listened to his words. The poem celebrated just a walk through a forest road, with the father viewing things with the wondrous eyes of his son. *Atul, you are not gone from us. We will read the books you had loved to read and find you in their words.*

A winter morning dawned with a hint of a promise for spring. I dressed baby Atul warmly for the travel and handed him to the wet nurse. A woman who had given birth to a still-born. Childless, she and her husband agreed to accompany Jay to Akash with Atul. An older maid who had raised many children went with them.

I applied *tilak* to Jay's forehead as he bid his farewell. He would rule Magadha wisely. With my help. He touched my feet and pulled himself up.

"Jay, our father wanted you to rule Malla. Even though he knew his oldest son still lived. He crowned you his heir. You are the rightful ruler of Magadha. After your reign, you can decide to pass it on to another worthy of the title."

"You and I are entrusted with ruling Magadha, Meera. I will be sending as many messages seeking your advice as providing them," he said, his eyes crinkled.

"Our guilt will protect Magadha," I answered.

"And our nagging doubts," he agreed.

I hugged him tightly. "Farewell, my brother."

I watched the procession from my balcony as the chariots, carts, and horses left the palace. Rish stood beside me as my sari in the color of new spring leaves fluttered in the wind. The hole in me grew larger as I watched them depart with my child. Tears flowed down my cheeks and dripped down my chin.

Rish whispered, "He will be safer with King Jay."

I peeked at him through my misty eyes. What should I do about the man who stood beside me? My one constant in a world of turbulence. Atul had entrusted the Padi rule to us and tied our fates together. Had he done this to punish me? To see if I'd the strength to do what was right? *No, Atul had never treated me with cruelty.* He had faith in us to protect Padi.

"Do you remember calling me your sun, Rish?" I asked.

"Yes, my lady. An eclipse almost ruined my life," he said.

I gazed at him. His eyes traced my face, more intimate than any touch with his hands.

"You are my moon. On a dark night, when despair and hopelessness fill my heart, you rise to shine my path," I said, my voice breaking.

Our eyes spoke poetry more poignant than words could express. With Atul gone, a chasm had opened in me, never to be filled. Still, a tiny glow floated in my heart, thankful for Rish's presence beside me.

A thorn pricked my bosom as I remembered his marriage to another. Wise move by Jay to protect me from my own foolishness.

"Treat your bride well," I urged him, and his look pierced my innermost self.

"I will, my lady. A simple smile and a kind touch brighten her day.

She does not ask for more than I can give. And she is good to Rima." My heart ached at losing Atul and being many miles away from Rish despite our proximity. I was more lost to him than before.

"Meera," he sighed as he wrapped me with his eyes. "She does not haunt my dreams and my waking hours like you do. The moon waxes and wanes. But my heart is more yours than when we met as a young girl and boy," he whispered, in a voice only I could hear.

"I am a king's widow and the king's mother. Even our shadows cannot touch." Why did it hurt so much to utter these words?

"My lady, I don't care about the physical distance between us. It is the barrier of mind I want to get past. Allow me to share your burdens and lighten your load."

Rish had already claimed a place in my heart. And he had stood beside me all these years while I'd ruled as another man's wife. Atul had wanted him to share my burdens. Rish had never overstepped his boundaries. It was my weakness that worried me. His eyes swept my face tenderly. I drew strength from him and nodded as his tenderness spread to my limbs and overflowed my heart.

He pushed on, "I have been losing my mind since I learned about your decision to take your own life. Promise me you will seek me before you choose death. Not all battles are fought on a battleground. You don't have to fight them alone. I am bound to you by my sword, life, and love. Send me to fight yours." His eyes blazed while he waited for my answer.

Rish had not failed me once in the years I'd come to love him. Atul had left me a blessing as his parting gift. A sign of his forgiveness of my folly. He had bequeathed me Rish's companionship, so I was not alone. Gratitude surged through my blood.

"I already chose you as my champion all those years ago," I whispered, my heart taking wings. Rish showered me with a smile that cocooned me with its warmth.

"Mother, Uncle Rish, there is a messenger from General Hasan," Nala shouted as he entered my chambers.

Rish asked, "Shall we meet him in the council room, my queen?"

Both gazed at me, waiting for my answer. Atul had wanted me to rule Padi till our son came of age. He had chosen Rish as the regent, the one man bound to me by love and loyalty, to help me. To honor Atul, I needed to respect his wishes.

I inclined my head. "I will join you shortly," I said and watched the young king leave with the man I'd trusted to keep us safe. I dipped a cloth in the water basin, wiping my tears, and along with it my guilt. I sat down in front of the mirror and placed the wingspread peacock crown on my head. A gift from my grandmother, a Padi princess. Atul had forgiven me. The harder part was up to me, to forgive myself. I took a deep breath and relaxed my shoulders. Slowly, I emerged from my room as the Queen of Padi.

The End

Epilogue

I paced my room, impatient for news. Kapil stood in the corner and watched me with amusement.

Aranya strode in, light sweat glistening her forehead.

"It's a boy," she said, with her eyes sparkling.

Warmth spread in me like light sweeping a dark room.

I marched with her to Sudha's chambers.

Servants hurried to light lamps all over the palace.

I entered Sudha's chamber alone and found her nursing our child. She glanced at me, and pride and happiness mingled in her face, covering her exhaustion. I bent down to kiss her forehead and sat beside her to watch my son.

"Your son and heir, my lord," she handed a sleeping child to me. A sudden pang hit me at her words, but they vanished as I regarded the baby in my arms. A strange elation filled my heart as I'd never experienced before.

Bells rang all over Akash to welcome the birth of Prince Vikram.

Book Three

This historical saga concludes with book three.

Meera and Jay face their biggest test yet. Love of their children pitted against their duty.

Want to know when I release a new book? Sign up for my new release notification at https://annabushi.com/contact-me/

Acknowledgements

This fictional tale is set some thousand years ago in the Land of Magadha. This land is a figment of my imagination and is a loose composite of several medieval Indian kingdoms and cultures.

As a modern woman, I find solace in writing about medieval characters. While the royal court struggles are distant from my daily life, the emotions that incite them into action still resonate with me. The human heart in conflict is what I like to explore in my stories. This tale is about the mistakes we make as adults and facing the consequences. I hope this story tugged your heart as much as it did mine.

When I published Heir to Malla, I knew I wanted to time jump a few years for the next book. When this book starts, Meera, Jay, and the land of Magadha had a few years of peace and prosperity. That, of course, changes by the end of the first chapter. Our protagonists have grown into adults, and they face daunting challenges. I enjoyed writing from both Jay and Meera's points of view. This allowed me to compare and contrast the siblings. Their power and place in society differ, and this story gave me several opportunities to explore those differences.

I used *Thirukkural*, an ancient Tamil language text consisting of 1,330 short couplets, as a guide to the ethics and morality of rulers. This universal book covers wide-ranging topics, including justice, rule of law, king's council, among others. These verses served as a basis for some of the ethics and laws in my book. Of course, in fiction (and reality), not all kings were just rulers.

The norms and cultures during this period are vastly different from today's world. In crafting an emotionally engaging story, my characters engage in acts that might be frowned upon in today's society but were common practice then. Polygamy is one such act. Noblemen engaged in polygamy during this time. I strived to write without judgment and from the perspectives of characters who accept that and other such practices and what struggles it posed for them.

While writing is a solitary journey, I have many people to thank for this book. I am indebted to my friend, Priya Nagarajan. Other friends who helped me with my series also deserve a special mention, especially Mary Logue, Smita Bhattacharya, Ellora Mishra, JR Jean, and Harshita Nanda.

Thanks to Christa Yelich-Koth for helping refine this book and the beautiful cover art.

R.J. Van Wart took my back of the napkin scribbling and transformed it into the Map of Magadha.

On the personal side, thanks to my parents for nourishing my love for reading. I thank my husband and my daughters for their endless support. To my brother, cousins, and extended family, thanks for believing in me.

Many friends supported my journey, and I would like to thank them all. I am thinking of Melina, Devina, Devi, Uma, Smita, Neesa, Brian, Sushma, Suchi, Leena, Meera, and many others. Your support has meant a lot to me.

To all my dear readers, I thank you from the bottom of my heart.

About the Author

The stories I read growing up inspired me to write. I am interested in medieval India and within that society, examining the human heart in conflict. I like to place my female characters in difficult situations and see how they learn to survive with no actual power. And watch my male characters fall in love while fighting for king and land. I love exploring the struggle between love and duty.

I live in California with my family. Visit me at annabushi.com to learn about upcoming books.

Reviews are priceless to authors like me. Your reviews would introduce my book to other readers. ank you for supporting me by posting a review.

Follow me:
@anna.bushi.book on instagram
@annabushibook on twitter

www.ingramcontent.com/pod-product-compliance
Lightning Source LLC
Chambersburg PA
CBHW050227110726
47898CB00007B/2057